Published by Hesperus Press Limited
28 Mortimer Street, London w1w 7rd
www.hesperuspress.com

Love Insurance first published 1914
First published by Hesperus Press 2014

Typeset by Sarah Newitt
Printed and bound in Italy by Grafica Veneta

isbn: 978-1-84391-525-6

Love Insurance

Earl Derr Biggers

Chapter I
A Sporting Proposition

Outside a gilt-lettered door on the seventeenth floor of a New York office building, a tall young man in a fur-lined coat stood shivering.

Why did he shiver in that coat? He shivered because he was fussed, poor chap. Because he was rattled, from the soles of his custom-made boots to the apex of his Piccadilly hat. A painful, palpitating spectacle, he stood.

Meanwhile, on the other side of the door, the business of the American branch of that famous marine insurance firm, Lloyds, of London – usually termed in magazine articles 'The Greatest Gambling Institution in the World' – went on oblivious to the shiverer who approached.

The shiverer, with a nervous movement, shifted his walking stick to his left hand, and laid his right on the doorknob. Though he is not at his best, let us take a look at him. Tall, as has been noted, perfectly garbed after London's taste, mild and blue as to eye, blond as to hair. A handsome, if somewhat weak face. Very distinguished – even aristocratic – in appearance. Perhaps – the thrill for us democrats here! – of the nobility. And at this moment sadly in need of a generous dose of that courage that abounds – see any book of familiar quotations – on the playing fields of Eton.

Utterly destitute of the Eton or any other brand, he pushed open the door. The click of two dozen American typewriters smote upon his hearing. An office boy of the dominant New York race demanded in loud indiscreet tones his business there.

'My business,' said the tall young man weakly, 'is with Lloyds, of London.'

The boy wandered off down that stenographer-bordered lane. In a moment he was back.

'Mr Thacker'll see you,' he announced.

He followed the boy, did the tall young man. His courage began to return. Why not? One of his ancestors, graduate of those playing fields, had fought at Waterloo.

Mr Thacker sat in plump and genial prosperity before a polished flat-top desk. Opposite him, at a desk equally polished, sat an even more polished young American of capable bearing.

For an embarrassed moment the tall youth in fur stood looking from one to the other. Then Mr Thacker spoke: 'You have business with Lloyds?'

The tall young man blushed.

'I – I hope to have – yes.' There was in his speech that faint suggestion of a lisp that marks many of the well-born of his race. Perhaps it is the golden spoon in their mouths interfering a bit with their diction.

'What can we do for you?' Mr Thacker was cold and matter-of-fact, like a card index. Steadily through each week he grew more businesslike and this was Saturday morning.

The visitor performed a shaky but remarkable juggling feat with his walking stick.

'I – well – I –' he stammered.

Oh, come, come, thought Mr Thacker impatiently.

'Well,' said the tall young man desperately, 'perhaps it would be best for me to make myself known at once. I am Allan, Lord Harrowby, son and heir of James Nelson Harrowby, Earl of Raybrook. And I – I have come here –'

The younger of the Americans spoke, in more kindly fashion: 'You have a proposition to make to Lloyds?'

'Exactly,' said Lord Harrowby, and sank with a sigh of relief into a chair, as though that concluded his portion of the entertainment.

'Let's hear it,' boomed the relentless Thacker.

Lord Harrowby writhed in his chair.

'I am sure you will pardon me,' he said, 'if I preface my – er – proposition with the statement that it is utterly – fantastic. And if I add also that it should be known to the fewest possible number.'

Mr Thacker waved his hand across the gleaming surfaces of two desks.

'This is my assistant manager, Mr Richard Minot,' he announced. 'Mr Minot, you must know, is in on all the secrets of the firm. Now, let's have it.'

'I am right, am I not,' his lordship continued, 'in the assumption that Lloyds frequently takes rather unusual risks?'

'Lloyds,' answered Mr Thacker, 'is chiefly concerned with the fortunes of those who go down to – and sometimes down into – the sea in ships. However, there are a number of non-marine underwriters connected with Lloyds, and these men have been known to risk their money on pretty giddy chances. It's all done in the name of Lloyds, though the firm is not financially responsible.'

Lord Harrowby got quickly to his feet.

'Then it would be better,' he said, relieved, 'for me to take my proposition to one of these non-marine underwriters.'

Mr Thacker frowned. Curiosity agitated his bosom.

'You'd have to go to London to do that,' he remarked. 'Better give us an inkling of what's on your mind.'

His lordship tapped uneasily at the base of Mr Thacker's desk with his stick.

'If you will pardon me – I'd rather not,' he said.

'Oh, very well,' sighed Mr Thacker.

'How about Owen Jephson?' asked Mr Minot suddenly.

Overjoyed, Mr Thacker started up.

'By gad – I forgot about Jephson. Sails at one o'clock, doesn't he?' He turned to Lord Harrowby. 'The very man – and in New York, too. Jephson would insure T. Roosevelt against another cup of coffee.'

'Am I to understand,' asked Harrowby, 'that Jephson is the man for me to see?'

'Exactly,' beamed Mr Thacker. 'I'll have him here in fifteen minutes. Richard, will you please call up his hotel?' And as Mr Minot reached for the telephone, Mr Thacker added pleadingly: 'Of course, I don't know the nature of your proposition –'

'No,' agreed Lord Harrowby politely.

Discouraged, Mr Thacker gave up.

'However, Jephson seems to have a gambling streak in him that odd risks appeal to,' he went on. 'Of course, he's scientific. All Lloyds' risks are scientifically investigated. But – occasionally – well, Jephson insured Sir Christopher Conway, K.C.B., against the arrival of twins in his family. Perhaps you recall the litigation that resulted when triplets put in their appearance?'

'I'm sorry to say I do not,' said Lord Harrowby.

Mr Minot set down the telephone. 'Owen Jephson is on his way here in a taxi,' he announced.

'Good old Jephson,' mused Mr Thacker, reminiscent. 'Why, some of the man's risks are famous. Take that shopkeeper in the Strand – every day at noon the shadow of Nelson's Monument in Trafalgar Square falls across his door.

'Twenty years ago he got to worrying for fear the statue would fall some day and smash his shop. And every year since he has taken out a policy with Jephson, insuring him against that dreadful contingency.'

'I seem to have heard of that,' admitted Harrowby, with the ghost of a smile.

'You must have. Only recently Jephson wrote a policy for the Dowager Duchess of Tremayne, insuring her against the unhappy event of a rainstorm spoiling the garden party she is shortly to give at her Italian villa. I understand a small fortune is involved. Then there is Courtney Giles, leading man at the West End Road Theater. He fears obesity. Jephson has insured him. Should he become too plump for Romeo roles, Lloyds – or rather Jephson – will owe him a large sum of money.'

'I am encouraged to hope,' remarked Lord Harrowby, 'that Mr Jephson will listen to my proposition.'

'No doubt he will,' replied Mr Thacker. 'I can't say definitely. Now, if I knew the nature –'

But when Mr Jephson walked into the office fifteen minutes later Mr Thacker was still lamentably ignorant of the nature of his titled visitor's business. Mr Jephson was a small wiry man, crowned by a vast acreage of bald head, and with the immobile countenance sometimes lovingly known as a 'poker face'. One felt he could watch the rain pour in torrents on the dowager duchess, Courtney Giles' waist expand visibly before his eyes, the statue of Nelson totter and fall on his shopkeeper, and never move a muscle of that face.

'I am delighted to meet your lordship,' said he to Harrowby. 'Knew your father, the earl, very well at one time. Had business dealings with him – often. A man after my own heart. Always ready to take a risk. I trust you left him well?'

'Quite, thank you,' Lord Harrowby answered. 'Although he will insist on playing polo. At his age – eighty-two – it is a dangerous sport.'

Mr Jephson smiled.

'Still taking chances,' he said. 'A splendid old gentleman. I understand that you. Lord Harrowby, have a proposition to make to me as an underwriter in Lloyds.'

They sat down. Alas, if Mr Burke, who compiled the well-known *Peerage*, could have seen Lord Harrowby then, what distress would have been his! For a most unlordly flush again mantled that British cheek. A nobleman was supremely rattled.

'I will try and explain,' said his lordship, gulping a plebeian gulp. 'My affairs have been for some time in rather a chaotic state. Idleness – the life of the town – you gentlemen will understand. Naturally, it has been suggested to me that I exchange my name and title for the millions of some American heiress. I have always violently objected to any such plan. I – I couldn't quite bring myself to do any such low trick as that. And then – a – few months ago on the Continent – I met a girl –'

He paused.

'I'm not a clever chap – really,' he went on. 'I'm afraid I can not describe her to you. Spirited – charming –' He looked toward the youngest of the trio. 'You, at least, understand,' he finished.

Mr Minot leaned back in his chair and smiled a most engaging smile.

'Perfectly,' he said.

'Thank you,' went on Lord Harrowby in all seriousness. 'It was only incidental – quite irrelevant – that this young woman happened to be very wealthy. I fell desperately in love. I am still in that – er – pleasing state. The young lady's name, gentlemen, is Cynthia Meyrick. She is the daughter of Spencer Meyrick, whose fortune has, I believe, been accumulated in oil.'

Mr Thacker's eyebrows rose respectfully.

'A week from next Tuesday,' said Lord Harrowby solemnly, 'at San Marco, on the east coast of Florida, this young woman and I are to be married.'

'And what,' asked Owen Jephson, 'is your proposition?'

Lord Harrowby shifted nervously in his chair.

'I say we are to be married,' he continued. 'But are we? That is the nightmare that haunts me. A slip. My – er – creditors coming down on me. And far more important, the dreadful agony of losing the dearest woman in the world.'

'What could happen?' Mr Jephson wanted to know.

'Did I say the young woman was vivacious?' inquired Lord Harrowby. 'She is. A thousand girls in one. Some untoward happening, and she might change her mind – in a flash.'

Silence within the room; outside the roar of New York and the clatter of the inevitable riveting machine making its points relentlessly.

'That,' said Lord Harrowby slowly, 'is what I wish you to insure me against, Mr Jephson.'

'You mean –'

'I mean the awful possibility of Miss Cynthia Meyrick's changing her mind.'

Again silence, save for the riveting machine outside. And three men looking unbelievingly at one another.

'Of course,' his lordship went on hastily, 'it is understood that I personally am very eager for this wedding to take place. It is understood that in the interval before the ceremony I shall do all in my power to keep Miss Meyrick to her present intention. Should the marriage be abandoned because of any act of mine, I would be ready to forfeit all claims on Lloyds.'

Mr Thacker recovered his breath and his voice at one and the same time.

'Preposterous,' he snorted. 'Begging your lordship's pardon, you can not expect hard-headed business men to listen seriously to any such proposition as that. Tushery, sir, tushery! Speaking as the American representative of Lloyds –'

'One moment,' interrupted Mr Jephson. In his eyes shone a queer light – a light such as one might expect to find in the eyes of Peter Pan, the boy who never grew up. 'One moment, please. What sum had you in mind, Lord Harrowby?'

'Well – say one hundred thousand pounds,' suggested his lordship. 'I realize that my proposition is fantastic. I really admitted as much. But –'

'One hundred thousand pounds.' Mr Jephson repeated it thoughtfully. 'I should have to charge your lordship a rather high rate. As high as ten per cent.'

Lord Harrowby seemed to be in the throes of mental arithmetic.

'I am afraid,' he said finally, 'I could not afford one hundred thousand at that rate. But I could afford – seventy-five thousand. Would that be satisfactory, Mr Jephson?'

'Jephson,' cried Mr Thacker wildly. 'Are you mad? Do you realize –'

'I realize everything, Thacker,' said Jephson calmly. 'I have your lordship's word that the young lady is at present determined on this alliance? And that you will do all in your power to keep her to her intention?'

'You have my word,' said Lord Harrowby. 'If you should care to telegraph –'

'Your word is sufficient,' said Jephson. 'Mr Minot, will you be kind enough to bring me a policy blank?'

'See here, Jephson,' foamed Thacker. 'What if this thing should get into the newspapers? We'd be the laughing-stock of the business world.'

'It mustn't,' said Jephson coolly.

'It might,' roared Thacker.

Mr Minot arrived with a blank policy, and Mr Jephson sat down at the young man's desk.

'One minute,' said Thacker. 'The faith of you two gentlemen in each other is touching, but I take it the millennium is still a few years off.' He drew toward him a blank sheet of paper, and wrote. 'I want this thing done in a businesslike way, if it's to be done in my office.' He handed the sheet of paper to Lord Harrowby. 'Will you read that, please?' he said.

'Certainly.' His lordship read: 'I hereby agree that in the interval until my wedding with Miss Cynthia Meyrick next Tuesday week I will do all in my power to put through the match, and that should the wedding be called off through any subsequent direct act of mine, I will forfeit all claims on Lloyds.'

'Will you sign that, please?' requested Mr Thacker.

'With pleasure.' His lordship reached for a pen.

'You and I, Richard,' said Mr Thacker, 'will sign as witnesses. Now, Jephson, go ahead with your fool policy.'

Mr Jephson looked up thoughtfully.

'Shall I say, your lordship,' he asked, 'that if, two weeks from today the wedding has not taken place, and has absolutely no prospect of taking place, I owe you seventy-five thousand pounds?'

'Yes.' His lordship nodded. 'Provided, of course, I have not forfeited by reason of this agreement. I shall write you a check, Mr Jephson.'

For a time there was no sound in the room save the scratching of two pens, while Mr Thacker gazed open-mouthed at Mr Minot, and Mr Minot light-heartedly smiled back. Then Mr Jephson reached for a blotter.

'I shall attend to the London end of this when I reach there five days hence,' he said. 'Perhaps I can find another underwriter to share the risk with me.'

The transaction was completed, and his lordship rose to go.

'I am at the Plaza,' he said, 'if any difficulty should arise. But I sail tonight for San Marco – on the yacht of a friend.' He crossed over and took Mr Jephson's hand. 'I can only hope, with all my heart,' he finished feelingly, 'that you never have to pay this policy.'

'We're with your lordship there,' said Mr Thacker sharply.

'Ah – you have been very kind,' replied Lord Harrowby. 'I wish you all – good day.'

And shivering no longer, he went away in his fine fur coat.

As the door closed upon the nobleman, Mr Thacker turned explosively on his friend from oversea.

'Jephson,' he thundered, 'you're an idiot! A rank unmitigated idiot!'

The Peter Pan light was bright in Jephson's eyes.

'So new,' he half-whispered. 'So original! Bless the boy's heart. I've been waiting forty years for a proposition like that.'

'Do you realize,' Thacker cried, 'that seventy-five thousand pounds of your good money depends on the honor of Lord Harrowby?'

'I do,' returned Jephson. 'And I would not be concerned if it were ten times that sum. I know the breed. Why, once – and you, Thacker, would have called me an idiot on that occasion, too – I insured his father against the loss of a polo game by a team on which the earl was playing. And he played like the devil – the earl did – won the game himself. Ah, I know the breed.'

'Oh, well,' sighed Thacker, 'I won't argue. But one thing is certain, Jephson. You can't go back to England now. Your place is in San Marco with one hand on the rope that rings the wedding bells.'

Jephson shook his great bald head.

'No,' he said. 'I must return today. It is absolutely necessary. My interests in San Marco are in the hands of Providence.'

Mr Thacker walked the floor wildly.

'Providence needs help in handling a woman,' he protested. 'Miss Meyrick must not change her mind. Someone must see that she doesn't. If you can't go yourself –' He paused, reflecting. 'Some young man, active, capable –'

Mr Richard Minot had risen from his chair, and was moving softly toward his overcoat. Looking over his shoulder, he beheld Mr Thacker's keen eyes upon him.

'Just going out to lunch,' he said guiltily.

'Sit down, Richard,' remarked Mr Thacker with decision.

Mr Minot sat, the dread of something impending in his heart.

'Jephson,' said Mr Thacker, 'this boy here is the son of a man of whom I was very fond. His father left him the means to squander his life on clubs and cocktails if he had chosen – but he picked out a business career instead. Five years ago I took him into this office, and he has repaid me by faithful, even brilliant service. I would trust him with – well, I'd trust him as far as you'd trust a member of your own peerage.'

'Yes?' said Mr Jephson.

Mr Thacker wheeled dramatically and faced his young assistant.

'Richard,' he ordered, 'go to San Marco. Go to San Marco and see to it that Miss Cynthia Meyrick does not change her mind.'

A gone feeling shot through Mr Minot in the vicinity of his stomach. It was possible that he really needed that lunch.

'Yes, sir,' he said faintly. 'Of course, it's up to me to do anything you say. If you insist, I'll go, but –'

'But what, Richard?'

'Isn't it a rather big order? Women – aren't they like an – er – April afternoon – or something of that sort? It seems to me I've read they were – in books.'

'Humph,' snorted Mr Thacker. 'Is your knowledge of the ways of women confined to books?'

A close observer might have noted the ghost of a smile in Mr Minot's clear blue eyes.

'In part, it is,' he admitted. 'And then again – in part, it isn't.'

'Well, put away your books, my boy,' said Mr Thacker. 'A nice, instructive little vacation has fallen on you from heaven. Mad old Jephson here must be saved from himself. That wedding must take place – positively, rain or shine. I trust you to see that it does, Richard.'

Mr Minot rose and stepped over to his hat and coat.

'I'm off for San Marco,' he announced blithely. His lips were firm but smiling. 'The land of sunshine and flowers – and orange blossoms or I know the reason why.'

'Jephson trusts Harrowby,' said Mr Thacker. 'All very well. But just the same if I were you I'd be aboard that yacht tonight when it leaves New York harbor. Invited or uninvited.'

'I must ask,' put in Mr Jephson hurriedly, 'that you do nothing to embarrass Lord Harrowby in any way.'

'No,' said Thacker. 'But keep an eye on him, my boy. A keen and busy eye.'

'I will,' agreed Mr Minot. 'Do I look like Cupid, gentlemen? No? Ah – it's the overcoat. Well, I'll get rid of that in Florida. I'll say goodbye –'

He shook hands with Jephson and with Thacker.

'Goodbye, Richard,' said the latter. 'I'm really fond of old Jephson here. He's been my friend in need – he mustn't lose. I trust you, my boy.'

'I won't disappoint you,' Dick Minot promised. A look of seriousness flashed across his face. 'Miss Cynthia Meyrick changes her mind only over my dead body.'

He paused for a second at the door, and his eyes grew suddenly thoughtful.

'I wonder what she's like?' he murmured.

Then, with a smile toward the two men left behind, he went out and down that stenographer-bordered lane to San Marco.

Chapter II
An Evening in The River

Though San Marco is a particularly gaudy tassel on the fringe of the tourist's South, it was to the north that Mr Richard Minot first turned. One hour later he made his appearance amid the gold braid and dignity of the Plaza lobby.

The young man behind the desk – an exquisite creature done in Charles Dana Gibson's best manner – knew when to be affable. He also knew when not to be affable. Upon Mr Minot he turned the cold fishy stare he kept for such as were not guests under his charge.

'What is your business with Lord Harrowby?' he inquired suspiciously.

'Since when,' asked Mr Minot brightly, 'have *you* been in his lordship's confidence?'

This was the young man's cue to wince. But hotel clerks are notoriously poor wincers.

'It is customary –' he began with perfect poise.

'I know,' said Mr Minot. 'But then, I'm a sort of a friend of his lordship.'

'A sort of a friend?' How well he lifted his eyebrows!

'Something like that. I believe I'm to be best man at his wedding.'

Ah, yes; that splendid young man knew when to be affable. Affability swamped him now.

'Boy!' he cried. 'Take this gentleman's card to Lord Harrowby.'

A bellboy in a Zenda uniform accepted the card, laid it upon a silver tray, glued it down with a large New York thumb, and strayed off down gilded corridors shouting, 'Lord Harrowby.'

Whereat all the pretty little debutantes who happened to be decorating the scene at the moment felt their pampered hearts go pit-a-pat and, closing their eyes, saw visions and dreamed dreams.

Lord Harrowby was at luncheon, and sent word for Mr Minot to join him. Entering the gay dining room, Minot saw at the far end the blond and noble head he sought. He threaded his way between the tables. Although he was an unusually attractive young man, he had never experienced anything like the array of stares turned upon him ere he had gone ten feet. 'What the devil's the matter?' he asked himself. 'I seem to be the cynosure of neighboring eyes, and then some.' He did not dream that it was because he was passing through a dining room of democrats to grasp the hand of a lord.

'My dear fellow, I'm delighted, I assure you –' Really, Lord Harrowby's face should have paid closer attention to his words. Just now it failed ignominiously in the matter of backing them up.

'Thank you,' Mr Minot replied. 'Your lordship is no doubt surprised at seeing me so soon –'

'Well – er – not at all. Shall I order luncheon?'

'No, thanks. I had a bite on the way up.'

And Mr Minot dropped into the chair which an eager waiter held ready. 'Lord Harrowby, I trust you are not going to be annoyed by what I have to tell you.'

His lordship's face clouded, and worry entered the mild blue eyes.

'I hope there's nothing wrong about the policy.'

'Nothing whatever. Lord Harrowby, Mr Jephson trusts you – implicitly.'

'So I perceived this morning. I was deeply touched.'

'It was – er – touching.' Minot smiled a bit cynically. 'Understanding as you do how Mr Jephson feels toward you, you will realize that it is in no sense a reflection on you that our office, viewing this matter in a purely business light, has decided that someone must go to San Marco with you. Someone who will protect Mr Jephson's interests.'

'Your office,' said his lordship, reflecting.

'You mean Mr Thacker, don't you?'

Could it be that the fellow was not so slow as he seemed?

'Mr Thacker is the head of our office,' smiled Mr Minot. 'It has been thought best that someone go with you, Lord Harrowby. Someone who will work night and day to see to it that Miss Meyrick does not change her mind. I – I am the someone. I hope you are not annoyed.'

'My dear chap! Not in the least. When I said this morning that I was quite set on this marriage, I was frightfully sincere.' And now his lordship's face, frank and boyish, in nowise belied his words. 'I shall be deeply grateful for any aid Lloyds can give me. And I am already grateful that Lloyds has selected you to be my ally.'

Really, very decent of him. Dick Minot bowed.

'You go south tonight?' he ventured.

'Yes. On the yacht *Lileth*, belonging to my friend, Mr Martin Wall. You have heard of him?'

'No. I can't say that I have.'

'Indeed! I understood he was very well-known here. A big, bluff, hearty chap. We met on the steamer coming over and became very good friends.'

A pause.

'You will enjoy meeting Mr Wall,' said his lordship meaningly, 'when I introduce you to him – in San Marco.'

'Lord Harrowby,' said Minot slowly, 'my instructions are to go south with you – on the yacht.'

For a moment the two men stared into each other's eyes. Then Lord Harrowby pursed his thin lips and gazed out at Fifth Avenue, gay and colorful in the February sun.

'How extremely unfortunate,' he drawled. 'It is not my boat, Mr Minot. If it were, nothing would give me greater pleasure than to extend an invitation to you.'

'I understand,' said Minot. 'But I am to go – invited or uninvited.'

'In my interests?' asked Harrowby sarcastically.

'As the personal conductor of the bridegroom.'

'Mr Minot – really –'

'I have no wish to be rude, Lord Harrowby. But it is our turn to be a little fantastic now. Could anything be more fantastic than boarding a yacht uninvited?'

'But Miss Meyrick – on whom, after all, Mr Jephson's fate depends – is already in Florida.'

'With her lamp trimmed and burning. How sad, your lordship, if some untoward event should interfere with the coming of the bridegroom.'

'I perceive,' smiled Lord Harrowby, 'that you do not share Mr Jephson's confidence in my motives.'

'This is New York, and a business proposition. Every man in New York is considered guilty until he proves himself innocent – and then we move for a new trial.'

'Nevertheless' – Lord Harrowby's mouth hardened – 'I must refuse to ask you to join me on the *Lileth*.'

'Would you mind telling me where the boat is anchored?'

'Somewhere in the North River, I believe. I don't know, really.'

'You don't know? Won't it be a bit difficult – boarding a yacht when you don't know where to find it?'

'My dear chap –' began Harrowby angrily.

'No matter.' Mr Minot stood up. 'I'll say *au revoir*, Lord Harrowby – until tonight.'

'Or until we meet in San Marco.' Lord Harrowby regained his good nature. 'I'm extremely sorry to be so impolite. But I believe we're going to be very good friends, nonetheless.'

'We're going to be very close to each other, at any rate,' Minot smiled. 'Once more – *au revoir*, your lordship.'

'Pardon me – goodbye,' answered Lord Harrowby with decision.

And Richard Minot was again threading his way between awed tables.

Walking slowly down Fifth Avenue, Mr Minot was forced to admit that he had not made a very auspicious beginning in his new role. Why had Lord Harrowby refused so determinedly to invite him aboard the yacht that was to bear the eager bridegroom south? And what was he to do now? Might he not discover where the yacht lay, board it at dusk, and conceal himself in a vacant cabin until the party was well under way? It sounded fairly simple.

But it proved otherwise. He was balked from the outset. For two hours, in the library of his club, in telephone booths and elsewhere, he sought for some tangible evidence of the existence of a wealthy American named Martin Wall and a yacht called the *Lileth*. City directories and yacht club year books alike were silent. Myth, myth, myth, ran through Dick Minot's mind.

Was Lord Harrowby – as they say at the Gaiety – spoofing him? He mounted to the top of a bus, and was churned up Riverside Drive. Along the banks of the river lay dozens of yachts, dismantled, swathed in winter coverings. Among the few that appeared ready to sail his keen eye discerned no *Lileth*.

Somewhat discouraged, he returned to his club and startled a waiter by demanding dinner at four-thirty in the afternoon. Going then to his rooms, he exchanged his overcoat for a sweater, his hat for a golf cap. At five-thirty, a spy for the first time in his eventful young life, he stood opposite the main entrance of the Plaza. Nearby ticked a taxi, engaged for the evening.

An hour passed. Lights, laughter, limousines, the cold moon adding its brilliance to that already brilliant square, the winter wind sighing through the bare trees of the park – New York seemed a city of dreams. Suddenly the chauffeur of Minot's taxi stood uneasily before him.

'Say, you ain't going to shoot anybody, are you?' he asked.

'Oh, no – you needn't be afraid of that.'

'I ain't afraid. I just thought I'd take off my license number if you was.'

Ah, yes – New York! City of beautiful dreams!

Another hour slipped by. And only the little taxi meter was busy, winking mechanically at the unresponsive moon.

At eight-fifteen a tall blond man, in a very expensive fur coat which impressed even the cab starter, came down the steps of the hotel. He ordered a limousine and was whirled away to the west. At eight-fifteen and a half Mr Minot followed.

Lord Harrowby's car proceeded to the drive and, turning, sped north between the moonlit river and the manlit apartment-houses. In the neighborhood of One Hundred and Tenth Street it came to a stop, and as Minot's car passed slowly by, he saw his lordship standing in the moonlight paying his chauffeur. Hastily dismissing his own car, he ran back in time to see Lord Harrowby disappear down one of the stone stairways into the gloom of the park that skirts the Hudson. He followed.

On and on down the steps and bare windswept paths he hurried, until finally the river, cold, silvery, serene, lay before him. Some thirty yards from shore he beheld the lights of a yacht flashing against the gloomy background of Jersey. The *Lileth*!

He watched Lord Harrowby cross the railroad tracks to a small landing, and leap from that into a boat in charge of a solitary rower. Then he heard the soft swish of oars, and watched the boat draw away from shore. He stood there in the shadow until he had seen his lordship run up the accommodation ladder to the *Lileth*'s deck.

He, too, must reach the *Lileth*, and at once. But how? He glanced quickly up and down the bank. A small boat was tethered near by – he ran to it, but a chain and padlock held it firmly. He must hurry. Aboard the yacht, dancing impatiently on the bosom of Hendrick Hudson's important discovery, he recognized the preparations for an early departure.

Minot stood for a moment looking at the wide wet river. It was February, yes, but February of the mildest winter New York had experienced in years. At the seashore he had always dashed boldly in while others stood on the sands and shivered. He dashed in now.

The water was cold, shockingly cold. He struck out swiftly for the yacht. Fortunately the accommodation ladder had not yet been taken up; in another moment he was clinging, a limp and dripping spectacle, to the rail of the *Lileth*.

Happily that side of the deck was just then deserted. A row of outside cabin doors in the bow met Minot's eye. Stealthily he swished toward them.

And, in the last analysis, the only thing between him and them proved to be a large commanding gentleman, whose silhouette was particularly militant and whose whole bearing was unfavorable.

'Mr Wall, I presume,' said Minot through noisy teeth.

'Correct,' said the gentleman. His voice was sharp, unfriendly. But the moonlight, falling on his face, revealed it as soft, genial, pudgy – the inviting sort of countenance to which, under the melting influence of Scotch and soda, one feels like relating the sad story of one's wasted life.

Though soaked and quaking, Mr Minot aimed at nonchalance.

'Well,' he said, 'you might be good enough to tell Lord Harrowby that I've arrived.'

'Who are you? What do you want?'

'I'm a friend of his lordship. He'll be delighted, I'm sure. Just tell him, if you'll be so kind.'

'Did he invite you aboard?'

'Not exactly. But he'll be glad to see me. Especially if you mention just one word to him.'

'What word?'

Mr Minot leaned airily against the rail.

'Lloyds,' he said.

An expression of mingled rage and dismay came into the pudgy face. It purpled in the moonlight. Its huge owner came threateningly toward the dripping Minot.

'Back into the river for yours,' he said savagely.

Almost lovingly – so it might have seemed to the casual observer – he wound his thick arms about the dripping Minot. Up and down the deck they turkey-trotted.

'Over the rail and into the river,' breathed Mr Wall on Minot's damp neck.

Two large and capable sailormen came at sound of the struggle.

'Here, boys,' Wall shouted. 'Help me toss this guy over.'

Willing hands seized Minot at opposite poles.

'One – two –' counted the sailormen.

'Well, good night, Mr Wall,' remarked Minot.

'Three!'

A splash, and he was ingloriously in the cold river again. He turned to the accommodation ladder, but quick hands drew it up. Evidently there was nothing to do but return once more to little old New York.

He rested for a moment, treading water, seeing dimly the tall homes of the cave dwellers, and over them the yellow glare of Broadway. Then he struck out. When he reached the shore, and turned, the *Lileth* was already under way, moving slowly down the silver path of the moon. An old man was launching the padlocked rowboat.

'Great night for a swim,' he remarked sarcastically.

'L-lovely,' chattered Minot. 'Say, do you know anything about the yacht that's just steamed out?'

'Not as much as I'd like ter. Used ter belong to a man in Chicago. Yesterday the caretaker told me she'd been rented fer the winter. Seen him tonight in a gin mill with money to throw to the birds. Looks funny to me.'

'Thanks.'

'Man came this afternoon and painted out her old name. Changed it t' *Lileth*. Mighty suspicious.'

'What was the old name?'

'The *Lady Evelyn*. If I was you, I'd get outside a drink, and quick. Goodnight.'

As Minot dashed up the bank, he heard the swish of the old man's oars behind. He ran all the way to his rooms, and after a hot bath and the liquid refreshment suggested by the waterman, called Mr Thacker on the telephone.

'Well, Richard?' that gentleman inquired.

'Sad news. Little Cupid's had a setback. Tossed into the Hudson when he tried to board the yacht that is taking Lord Harrowby south.'

'No? Is that so?' Mr Thacker's tone was contemplative. 'Well, Richard, the Palm Beach Special leaves at midnight. Better be on it. Better go down and help the bride with her trousseau.'

'Yes, sir. I'll do that. And I'll see to it that she has her lamp trimmed and burning. Considering that her father's in the oil business, that ought not to be –'

'I can't hear you, Richard. What are you saying?'

'Nothing – er – Mr Thacker. Look up a yacht called the *Lady Evelyn*. Chicago man, I think – find out if he's rented it, and to whom. It's the boat Harrowby went south on.'

'All right, Richard. Goodbye, my boy. Write me whenever you need money.'

'Perhaps I can't write as often as that. But I'll send you bulletins from time to time.'

'I depend on you, Richard. Jephson must not lose.'

'Leave it to me. The Palm Beach Special at midnight. And after that – Miss Cynthia Meyrick!'

Chapter III
Journeys End In – Taxi Bills

No matter how swiftly your train has sped through the Carolinas and Georgia, when it crosses the line into Florida a wasting languor overtakes it. Then it hesitates, sighs and creeps across the flat yellow landscape like an aged alligator. Now and again it stops completely in the midst of nothing, as who should say: 'You came down to see the South, didn't you? Well, look about you.'

The Palm Beach Special on which Mr Minot rode was no exception to this rule. It entered Florida and a state of innocuous desuetude at one and the same time. After a tremendous struggle, it gasped its way into Jacksonville about nine o'clock of the Monday morning following. Reluctant as Romeo in his famous exit from Juliet's boudoir, it got out of Jacksonville an hour later.

And San Marco was just two hours away, according to that excellent book of light fiction so widely read in the South – the timetable.

It seemed to Dick Minot that he had been looking out of a car window for a couple of eternities. Save for the diversion at Jacksonville, nothing had happened to brighten that long and wearisome journey. He wanted, now, to glance across the car aisle toward the diversion at Jacksonville. Yet it hardly seemed polite – so soon. Wherefore he continued to gaze out at the monotonous landscape.

For half a mile the train served its masters. Then, with a pathetic groan, it paused. Still Mr Minot gazed out the window. He gazed so long that he saw a family of razor-backs, passed a quarter of a mile back, catch up with the train and trot scornfully by. After that he kept his eyes on the live oaks and evergreens, to whose topmost branches hung gray moss like whiskers on a western senator.

Then he could stand it no longer. He turned and looked upon the diversion at Jacksonville. Gentlemen of the jury – she was beautiful. The custodian of a library of books on sociology could have seen that with half an astigmatic eye. Her copper-colored hair flashed alluringly in that sunny car; the curve of her cheek would have created a sensation in the neighborhood where burning Sappho loved and sang. Dick Minot's heart beat faster, repeating the performance it had staged when she boarded the train at Jacksonville.

Beautiful, yes – but she fidgeted. She had fidgeted madly in the station at Jacksonville during that hour's wait; now even more madly she bounced about on that plush seat. She opened and shut magazines, she straightened her pleasant little hat, she gazed in agony out the window. Beauty such as hers should have been framed in a serene and haughty dignity. Hers happened to be framed in a frenzy of fidget.

In its infinite wisdom, the train saw fit to start again. With a sigh of relief, the girl sank back upon her seat of torture. Mr Minot turned again to the uneventful landscape. More yellow sand, more bearded oaks and evergreens. And in a moment, the family of razor-backs, plodding along beside the track with a determined demeanor that said as plainly as words: 'You may go ahead – but we shall see what we shall see.'

Excellent train, it seemed fairly to fly. For a little while. Then another stop. Beauty wildly anxious on the seat of ancient plush. Another start – a stop – and a worried but musical voice in Dick Minot's ear:

'I beg your pardon – but what should you say are this train's chances for reaching San Marco by one o'clock?'

Minot turned. Brown eyes and troubled ones looked into his. A dimple twitched beside an adorable mouth. Fortunate Florida, peopled with girls like this.

'I should say,' smiled Mr Minot, 'about the same as those of the famous little snowball that strayed far from home.'

'Oh – you're right!' Why would she fidget so? 'And I'm in a frightfully uncomfortable position. I simply must reach San Marco for luncheon at one. I must!' She clenched her small hands. 'It's the most important luncheon of my life. What shall I do?'

Mr Minot glanced at his watch.

'It is now twenty minutes of twelve,' he said. 'My advice to you is to order lunch on the train.'

'It was so foolish of me,' cried the girl. 'I ran up to Jackson-ville in a friend's motor to do a little shopping. I should have known better. I'm always doing things like this.'

And she looked at Dick Minot accusingly, as though it were he who always put her up to them.

'I'm awfully sorry, really,' Minot said. He felt quite uncomfortable about it.

'And can't you suggest anything?' – pleadingly, almost tearfully.

'Not at this moment. I'll try, though. Look!' He pointed out the window. 'That family of razor-backs has caught up with us four times already.'

'What abominable service,' the girl cried. 'But – aren't they cunning? The little ones, I mean.'

And she stood looking out with a wonderful tenderness in her eyes, which, considering the small creatures upon which it was lavished, was almost ludicrous.

'Off again,' cried Minot.

And they were. The girl sat nervously on the edge of her seat, with the expression of one who meant to keep the train going by mental suggestion. Five cheerful minutes passed in rapid transit. And then – another abrupt stop.

'Almost like a football game,' said Minot blithely to the distressed lady across the aisle. 'Third down – five yards to go. Oh, by jove, there's a town on my side.'

'Not a trace of a town on mine,' she replied.

'It's the dreariest, saddest town I ever saw,' Minot remarked. 'So of course its name is Sunbeam. And look – what do you see – there beside the station!'

'An automobile!' the girl cried.

'Well, an automobile's ancestor, at any rate,' laughed Minot. 'Vintage of 1905. Say – I have a suggestion now. If the chauffeur thinks he can get you – I mean, us – to San Marco by one o'clock, shall we –'

But the girl was already on her way.

'Come on!' Her eyes were bright with excitement. 'We – oh, dear – the old train's started again.'

'No matter – I'll stop it!' Minot reached for the bell cord.

'But do you dare – can't you be arrested?'

'Too late – I've done it. Let me help you with those magazines. Quick! This way.'

On the platform they met an irate conductor, red and puffing.

'Say – who stopped this train?' he bellowed.

'I don't know – who usually stops it?' Minot replied, and he and the girl slid by the uniform to the safety of Sunbeam.

The lean, lank, weary native who lolled beside the passé automobile was startled speechless for a moment by the sight of two such attractive visitors in his unattractive town. Then he remembered.

'Want a taxi, mister?' he inquired. 'Take you up to the Sunbeam House for a quarter apiece –'

'Yes, we do want a taxi –' Minot began.

'To San Marco,' cried the girl breathlessly. 'Can you get us there by one o'clock?'

'To – to – say, lady,' stammered the rustic chauffeur. 'That train you just got off of is going to San Marco.'

'Oh, no, it isn't,' Minot explained. 'We know better. It's going out into the country to lie down under a shade tree and rest.'

'The train is too slow,' said the girl. 'I must be in San Marco before one o'clock. Can you get me – us – there by then? Speak quickly, please.'

The effect of this request on the chauffeur was to induce even greater confusion.

'T-to – to San Marco,' he stumbled. 'W–well, say, that's a new one on me. Never had this car out o' Sunbeam yet.'

'Please – please!' the girl pleaded.

'Lady,' said the chauffeur, 'I'd do anything I could, within reason –'

'Can you get us to San Marco by one o'clock?' she demanded.

'I ain't no prophet, lady.' A humorous gleam came into his eye. 'But ever since I got this car I been feelin' sort o' reckless. If you say so, I'll bid all my family and friends goodbye, and we'll take a chance on San Marco together.'

'That's the spirit,' laughed Minot. 'But forget the family and friends.'

He placed his baggage in the front of the car, and helped the girl into the tonneau. With a show of speed, the countryman went around to the front of the car and began to crank.

He continued to crank with agonized face. In the course of a few minutes, sounds of a terrific disturbance came from inside the car. Still, like a hurdy-gurdy musician, the man cranked.

'I say,' Minot inquired, 'has your machine got the Sextette from *Lucia*?'

'Well, there's been a lot of things wrong with it,' the man replied, 'but I don't think it's had that yet.'

The girl laughed, and such a laugh, Dick Minot was sure, had never been heard in Sunbeam before. At that moment the driver leaped to his seat, breathing hard, and had it out with the wheel.

'Exeunt, laughingly, from Sunbeam,' said Minot in the girl's ear.

The car rolled asthmatically from the little settlement, and out into the sand and heat of a narrow road.

'Eight miles to San Marco,' said the driver out of the corner of his mouth. 'Sit tight. I'm going to let her out some.'

Again Dick Minot glanced at the girl beside him. Fate was in a jovial mood today to grant him this odd ride in the company of one so charming! He could not have told what she wore, but he knew she was all in white, and he realized the wisdom of white on a girl who had, in her hair and eyes, colors to delight the most exacting. About her clung a perfume never captured in a bottle; her chin was the chin of a girl with a sense of humor; her eyes sparkled with the thrill of their adventure together. And the dimple, in repose now, became the champion dimple of the world.

Minot tried to think of some sprightly remark, but his usually agile tongue remained silent. What was the matter with him? Why should this girl seem different, somehow, from all the other girls he had ever met? When he looked into her eyes a flood of memories – a little sad – of all the happy times he had ever known overwhelmed him. Memories of a starlit sea – the red and white awnings of a yacht – the wind whispering through the trees on a hillside – an orchestra playing in the distance – memories of old, and happy, far-off things – of times when he was even younger, even more in love with life. Why should this be? he wondered.

And the girl, looking at him, wondered, too – was he suddenly bereft of his tongue?

'I haven't asked you the conventional question,' she said at last. 'How do you like Florida?'

'It's wonderful, isn't it?' Minot replied, coming to with a start. 'I can speak of it even more enthusiastically than any of the railroad folders do. And yet, it's only recent – my discovery of its charms.'

'Really?'

'Yes. When I was surveying it on that stopwatch of a train, my impression of it was quite unfavorable. It seemed

32

so monotonous. I told myself nothing exciting could ever happen here.'

'And – something has happened?'

'Yes – something certainly has happened.'

She blushed a little at his tone. Young men usually proposed to her the first time they saw her. Why shouldn't she blush – a little?

'Something very fine,' Minot went on. 'And I am surely very grateful to fate –'

'Would you mind looking at your watch – please?'

'Certainly. A quarter after twelve. As I was saying –'

'Do you think we can make it?'

'I am sure of it.'

'You see, it is so very important. I want so very much to be there by one o'clock.'

'And I want you to.'

'I wonder – if you really knew –'

'Knew what?'

'Nothing. I wish you would, please – but you just did look at your watch, didn't you?'

They rattled on down that road that was so sandy, so uninteresting, so lonely, with only a garage advertisement here and there to suggest a world outside. Suddenly the driver ventured a word over his shoulder.

'Don't worry, lady,' he said. 'We'll get there sure.'

And even as he spoke the car gave a roar of rage and came to a dead stop.

'Oh, dear – what is it now?' cried the girl.

'Acts like the train,' commented Minot.

The driver got out and surveyed the car without enthusiasm.

'I wonder what she's up to now?' he remarked. 'Fifteen years I drove horses, which are supposed to have brains, but this machine can think of things to do to me that the meanest horse never could.'

'You promised, driver,' pleaded the girl. 'We must reach San Marco on time. Mr – your watch?'

'Twenty-five past twelve,' smiled Minot .

The native descended to the dust and slid under the car. In a moment he emerged, triumphant.

'All O.K.,' he announced. 'Don't you worry, lady. It's San Marco or bust.'

'If only something doesn't bust,' Minot said.

Again they were plowing through the sand. The girl sat anxiously on the edge of the seat, her cheeks flaming, her eyes alight. Minot watched her. And suddenly all the happy, sad little memories melted into a golden glow – the glow of being alive – on this lonesome road – with her!

Then suddenly he knew! This was the one girl, the girl of all the world, the girl he should love while the memory of her lasted, which would be until the eyes that looked upon her now were dust.

A great exultation swept through him – 'What did you mean,' he asked, 'when you said you were always doing things like this?'

'I meant,' she answered, 'that I'm a silly little fool. Oh, if you could know me well –' and her eyes seemed to question the future – 'you'd see for yourself. Never looking ahead to calculate the consequences. It's the old story of fools rushing in –'

'You mean of angels rushing in, don't you? I never was good at old saws, but –'

'And once more, please – your watch?'

'Twenty minutes of one.'

'Oh, dear – can we' – A wild whoop from the driver interrupted. 'San Marco,' he cried, pointing to where red towers rose above the green of the country. 'It paid to take a chance with me. I sure did let her out. Where do you want to go, lady?'

'The Hotel de la Pax,' said the girl, and with a sigh of deep relief, sank back upon the cushions.

'And Salvator won,' quoted Mr Minot with a laugh.

'How can I ever thank you?' the girl asked.

'Don't try,' said Minot. 'That is – I mean – try, if you will, please.'

'It meant so very much to me –'

'No – you'd better not, after all. It makes me feel guilty. For I did nothing that doesn't come under the head of glorious privilege. A chance to serve you! Why, I'd travel to the ends of the earth for that.'

'But – it was good of you. You can hardly realize all it meant to me to reach this hotel by one o'clock. Perhaps I ought to tell you –'

'It doesn't matter,' Minot replied. 'That you have reached here is my reward.' His cheeks burned; his heart sang. Here was the one girl, and he built castles in Spain with lightning strokes. She should be his. She must be. Before him life stretched, glorious, with her at his side –

'I think I will tell you,' the girl was saying. 'This is to be the most important luncheon of my life because –'

'Yes?' smiled Mr Minot.

'Because it is the one at which I am going to announce my engagement!'

Minot's heart stopped beating. A hundred castles in Spain came tumbling about his ears, and the roar of their falling deafened him. He put out his hand blindly to open the door, for he realized that the car had come to a stop.

'Let me help you, please,' he said dully.

And even as he spoke a horrible possibility swept into his heart and overwhelmed him.

'I – I beg your pardon,' he stammered, 'but would you mind telling me one thing?'

'Of course not. But I really must fly –'

'The name of – the happy man.'

'Why – Allan, Lord Harrowby. Thank you so much – and goodbye.'

She was gone now – gone amid the palms of that gorgeous hotel courtyard. And out of the roar that enveloped him Minot heard a voice:

'Thirty-five dollars, mister.'

So promptly did he pay this grievous overcharge that the chauffeur asked hopefully:

'Now could I take you anywhere, sir?'

'Yes,' said Minot bitterly. 'Take me back to New York.'

'Well – if I had a new front tire I might try it.'

Two eager black boys were moving inside with Minot's bags, and he followed. As he passed the fountain tinkling gaily in the courtyard: 'What was it I promised Thacker?' he said to himself. '"Miss Cynthia Meyrick changes her mind only over my dead body." Ah, well – the good die young.'

Chapter IV
Mr Trimmer Limbers Up

At the desk of the De la Pax Mr Minot learned that for fifteen dollars a day he might board and lodge amid the splendors of that hotel. Gratefully he signed his name. One of the negro boys – who had matched coins for him with the other boy while he registered – led the way to his room.

It proved a long and devious journey. The Hotel de la Pax was a series of afterthoughts on the part of its builders. Up hill and down dale the boy led, through dark passageways, over narrow bridges, until at length they arrived at the door of 389.

'My boy,' muttered Minot feelingly, 'I congratulate you. Henry M. Stanley in the flower of his youth couldn't have done any better.'

'Yes, suh.' The boy threw open the door of a narrow cell, at the farther end of which a solitary window admitted the well-known Florida sunshine. Minot stepped over and glanced out. Where the gay courtyard with its green palms waving, its fountain tinkling? Not visible from 389. Instead Minot saw a narrow street, its ancient cobblestones partly obscured by flourishing grass, and bordered by quaint, top-heavy Spanish houses, their plaster walls a hundred colors from the indignities of the years.

'We seem to have strayed over into Spain,' he remarked.

The bellboy giggled.

'Yes, suh. We one block and a half from de hotel office.'

'I didn't notice any taxis in the corridors,' smiled Minot. 'Here – wait a minute.' He tossed the boy a coin. 'Your fare back home. If you get stranded on the way, telegraph.'

The boy departed, and Minot continued to gaze out. Directly across from his window, looking strangely out of place in that dead and buried street, stood a great stone house that bore on its front the sign 'Manhattan Club and Grill'. On the veranda, flush with the sidewalk and barely fifteen feet away, a huge red-faced man sat deep in slumber.

Many and strange pursuits had claimed the talents of old Tom Stacy, manager of the Manhattan Club, ere his advent in San Marco. A too active district attorney had forced the New York police to take a keen interest in his life and works, hence Mr Stacy's presence on that Florida porch. But such troubles were forgot for the moment. He slumbered peacefully, secure in the knowledge that the real business of the club would not require his attention until darkness fell. His great head fell gradually farther in the direction of his generous waist, and while there is no authentic evidence to offer, it is safe to assume that he dreamed of Broadway.

Suddenly Mr Stacy's head took another tilt downward, and his Panama hat slipped off to the veranda floor. To the gaze of Mr Minot, above, there was revealed a bald pate extensive and gleaming. The habitual smile fled from Minot's face. A feeling of impotent anger filled his soul. For a bald head could recall but one thing – Jephson.

He strode from the window, savagely kicking an innocent suitcase that got in his way. What mean trick was this fate had played him as he entered San Marco? To show to him the one girl in all her glory and sweetness, to thrill him through and through with his discovery – and then to send the girl scurrying off to announce her engagement to another man! Scurvy, he called it. But scurvier still, that it should be the very engagement he had hastened to San Marco to bring to its proper close – 'I do,' and Mendelssohn.

He sat gloomily down on the bed. What could he do? What save keep his word, given on the seventeenth floor of an office building in New York? No man had yet had reason to question the good faith of a Minot. His dead father, at the beginning of his career, had sacrificed his fortune to keep his word, and gone back with a smile to begin all over again. What could he do?

Nothing, save grit his teeth and see the thing through. He made up his mind to this as he bathed and shaved, and prepared himself for his debut in San Marco. So that, when he finally left the hotel and stepped out into San Sebastian Avenue, he was cheerful with a dogged, boy-stood-on-the-burning-deck cheerfulness.

A dozen negroes, their smiles reminiscent of tooth powder advertisements, vainly sought to cajole him into their shaky vehicles. With difficulty he avoided their pleas, and strolled down San Marco's main thoroughfare. On every side clever shopkeepers spread the net for the eagle on the dollar. Jewelers' shops flashed, modistes hinted, milliners begged to present their latest creations.

He came presently to a narrow cross street, where humbler merchants catered to the Coney instinct that lurks in even the most affluent of tourists. There gaudy souvenir stores abounded. The ugly and inevitable alligator, fallen from his proud estate to fireside slipper, wallet, cigar case, umbrella stand, photograph album and Lord-knows-what, was headlined in this street. Picture postcards hung in flocks, tin-type galleries besought, newsstands, soda-water fountains and cheap boarding houses stood side by side. And, every few feet, Mr Minot came upon 'The Oldest House in San Marco'.

On his way back to the hotel, in front of one of the more dazzling modiste's shops, he saw a limousine drawn up to the curb, and in it Jack Paddock, friend of his college days. Paddock leaped blithely from the machine and grasped Dick Minot by the hand.

'You here?' he cried.

'Foolish question,' commented Mr Minot.

'Yes, I know,' said Mr Paddock. 'Been here so long my brain's a little flabby. But I'm glad to see you, old man.'

'Same here.' Mr Minot stared at the car. 'I say. Jack, did you earn that writing fiction?'

Paddock laughed.

'I'm not writing much fiction now,' he replied. 'The car belongs to Mrs Helen Bruce, the wittiest hostess in San Marco.' He came closer. 'My boy,' he confided, 'I have struck something essentially soft. Sometime soon, in a room with all the doors and windows closed and the weatherstrips in place, I'll whisper it to you. I've been dying to tell somebody.'

'And the car –'

'Part of the graft, Dick. Here comes Mrs Bruce now. Did I mention she was the wittiest – of course I did. Want to meet her? Well, later then. You're at the Pax, I suppose. See you there.'

Mr Minot moved on from the imminence of Mrs Bruce. A moment later the limousine sped by him. One seat was generously filled by the wittiest hostess in San Marco. Seated opposite her, Mr Paddock waved an airy hand. Life had always been the gayest of jokes to Mr Paddock.

Life was at the moment quite the opposite to Dick Minot. He devoted the next hour to sad introspection in the lobby. It was not until he was on his way in to dinner that he again saw Cynthia Meyrick. Then, just outside the dining-room door, he encountered her, still all in white, lovelier than ever, in her cheek a flush of excitement no doubt put there by the most important luncheon of her life. He waited for her to recognize him – and he did not wait in vain.

'Ah, Mr –'

'Minot.'

'Of course. In the hurry of this noon I quite overlooked an introduction. I am –'

'Miss Cynthia Meyrick. I happen to know because I met his lordship in New York. May I ask – was the luncheon –'

'Quite without a flaw. So you know Lord Harrowby?'

'Er – slightly. May I offer my very best wishes?'

'So good of you.'

Formal, formal, formal. Was that how it must be between them hereafter? Well, it was better so. Miss Meyrick presented her father and her aunt, and that did not tend to lighten the formality. Icicles, both of them, though stocky puffing icicles. Aunt inquired if Mr Minot was related to the Minots of Detroit, and when he failed to qualify, at once lost all interest in him. Old Spencer Meyrick did not accord him even that much attention.

Yet – all was not formal, as it happened. For as Cynthia Meyrick moved away, she whispered: 'I must see you after dinner – on important business.' And her smile as she said it made Minot's own lonely dinner quite cheery.

At seven in the evening the hotel orchestra gathered in the lobby for its nightly concert, and after the way of orchestras, it was almost ready to begin when Minot left the dining room at eight. Sitting primly in straight backed chairs, an audience gathered for the most part from the more inexpensive hostelries waited patiently. Presumably these people were there for an hour with music, lovely maid. But it was the gowns of more material maids that interested the greater number of them, and many drab little women sat making furtive mental notes that should while away the hours conversationally when they got back to Akron or Terre Haute.

Minot sat down in a veranda chair and looked out at the courtyard. In the splendor of its evening colors, it was indeed the setting for romance. In the midst of the green palms and blooming things splashed a fountain which might well have been the one old Ponce de Leon sought. On three sides the lighted towers and turrets of that huge hotel climbed toward the bright, warm southern sky. A dazzling moon shamed Mr Edison's lamps, the breeze came tepid from the sea, the very latest in waltzes drifted out from the gorgeous lobby. Here romance, Minot thought, must have been born.

'Mr Minot – I've been looking everywhere –'

She was beside him now, a slim white figure in the dusk – the one thing lacking in that glittering picture. He leaped to meet her.

'Sitting here dreaming, I reckon,' she whispered, 'of somebody far away.'

'No.' He shook his head. 'I leave that to the newly engaged.'

She made no answer. He gave her his chair, and drew up another for himself.

'Mr Minot,' she said, 'I was terribly thoughtless this noon. But you must forgive me – I was so excited. Mr Minot – I owe you –'

She hesitated. Minot bit his lip savagely. Must he hear all that again? How much she owed him for his service – for getting her to that luncheon in time – that wonderful luncheon –

'I owe you,' finished the girl softly, 'the charges on that taxi.'

It was something of a shock to Minot. Was she making game of him?

'Don't,' he answered. 'Here in the moonlight, with that waltz playing, and the old palms whispering – is this a time to talk of taxi bills?'

'But – we must talk of something – oh, I mean – I insist. Won't you please tell me the figure?'

'All the time we were together this morning, I talked figures – the figures on the face of a watch. Let us find some pleasanter topic. I believe Lord Harrowby said you were to be married soon?'

'Next Tuesday. A week from tomorrow.'

'In San Marco?'

'Yes. It breaks auntie's heart that it can't be in Detroit. Lord Harrowby is her triumph, you see. But father can't go north in the winter – and Allan wishes to be married at once.'

Minot was thinking hard. So Harrowby was auntie's triumph? And was he not Cynthia Meyrick's as well? He would have given much to be able to inquire.

Suddenly, with the engaging frankness of a child, the girl asked:

'Has your engagement ever been announced, Mr Minot?'

'Why – er – not to my knowledge,' Minot laughed. 'Why?'

'I was just wondering – if it made everybody feel queer. The way it makes me feel. Ever since one o'clock – I ought never to say it – I've felt as though everything was over. I've seemed old! Old!' She clenched her fists, and spoke almost in terror. 'I don't want to grow old. I'd hate it.'

'It was here,' said Minot softly, 'Ponce de Leon sought the fountain of youth. When you came up I was pretending the one splashing out there was that very fountain itself –'

'If it only were,' the girl cried. 'Oh – you could never drag me away from it. But it isn't. It's supplied by the San Marco Water Works, and there's a meter ticking somewhere, I'm sure. And now – Mr Minot –'

'I know. You mean the thirty-five dollars I paid our driver. I wish you would write me a check. I've a reason.'

'Thank you. I wanted to – so much. I'll bring it to you soon.'

She was gone, and Minot sat staring into the palms, his lips firm, his hands gripping the arms of his chair. Suddenly, with a determined leap, he was on his feet.

A moment later he stood at the telegraph counter in the lobby, writing in bold flowing characters a message for Mr John Thacker, on a certain seventeenth floor, New York.

I resign. Will stay on the job until a substitute arrives, but start him when you get this.

Richard Minot.

The telegram sent, he returned to his veranda chair to think. Thacker would be upset, of course. But after all, Thacker's claim on him was not such that he must wreck his life's happiness to serve him. Even Thacker must see that. And the girl – was she madly in love with the lean and aristocratic Harrowby? Not by any means, to judge from her manner. Next Tuesday – a week. What couldn't happen in a – Minot stopped. No, that wouldn't do, either. Even if a substitute arrived, he could hardly with honor turn about and himself wreck the hopes of Thacker and Jephson. He lost, either way. It was a horrible mix-up. He cursed beneath his breath.

The red glow of a cigar near by drew closer as the smoker dragged his chair across the veranda floor. Minot saw behind the glow the keen face of a man eager for talk.

'Some scene, isn't it?' said the stranger. 'Sort of makes the musical comedies look cheap. All it needs is seven stately chorus ladies walking out from behind that palm down to the left, and it would have Broadway lashed to the mast.'

'Yes,' replied Minot absently. 'This is the real thing.'

'I've been sitting here thinking,' the other went on. 'It doesn't seem to me this place has been advertised right. Why, there are hundreds of people up north whose windows look out on sunset over the brewery – people with money, too – who'd take the first train for here if they realized the picture we're looking at now. Get some good hustler to tell 'em about it –' He paused. 'I hate to talk about myself, but say – ever hear of Cotrell's Ink Eraser? Nothing ever written Cotrell can't erase. Will not soil or scratch the paper. If the words Cotrell has erased were put side by side –'

'Selling it?' Minot inquired wearily.

'No. But I made that eraser. Put it on every desk between New York and the rolling Oregon. After that I landed Helot's Bottled Sauces. And then Patterson's Lime Juice. Puckered every mouth in America. Advertising is my specialty.'

'So I gather.'

'Sure as you sit here. Have a cigar. Trimmer is my name – never mind the jokes. Henry Trimmer. Advertising specialist. Is your business flabby? Does it need a tonic? Try Trimmer.

Quoting from my letterhead.' He leaned closer. 'Excuse a personal question, but didn't I see you talking with Miss Cynthia Meyrick a while back?'

'Possibly.'

Mr Trimmer came even closer.

'Engaged to Lord Harrowby, I understand.'

'I believe so –'

'Young fellow,' Mr Trimmer's tone was exultant, 'I can't keep in any longer. I got a proposition in tow so big it's bursting my brain cells – and it takes some strain to do that. No, I can't tell you the exact nature of it – but I will say this – tomorrow night this time I'll throw a bomb in this hotel so loud it'll be heard round the world.'

'An anarchist?'

'Not on your life. Advertiser. And I've got something to advertise this hot February, take it from me. Maybe you're a friend of Miss Meyrick. Well, I'm sorry. For when I spring my little surprise I reckon this Harrowby wedding is going to shrivel up and fade away.'

'You mean to say you – you're going to stop the wedding?'

'I mean to say nothing. Watch me. Watch Henry Trimmer. Just a tip, young fellow. Well, I guess I'll turn in. Get some of my best ideas in bed. See you later.'

And Mr Trimmer strode into the circle of light, a fine upstanding figure of a man, to pass triumphantly out of sight among the palms. Dazed, Dick Minot stared after him.

A voice spoke his name. He turned. The slim white presence again, holding toward him a slip of paper.

'The check, Mr Minot. Thirty-five dollars. Is that correct?'

'Correct. It's splendid. Because I'm never going to cash it – I'm going to keep it –'

'Really, Mr Minot, I must say good –'

He came closer. Thacker and Jephson faded. New York was far away. He was young, and the moon was shining –

'– going to keep it – always. The first letter you ever wrote me –'

'And the last, Mr Minot. Really – I must go. Goodnight.'

He stood alone, with the absurd check in his trembling fingers. Slowly the memory of Trimmer came back. A bomb? What sort of a bomb?

Well, he had given his word. There was no way out – he must protect old Jephson's interests. But might he not wish the enemy – success? He stared off in the direction the advertising wizard had gone.

'Trimmer, old boy,' he muttered, 'here's to your pitching arm!'

Chapter V
Mr Trimmer Throws His Bomb

Miss Cynthia Meyrick was a good many girls in one. So many, indeed, that it might truthfully be added that while most people are never so much alone as when in a crowd, Miss Meyrick was never so much in a crowd as when alone. Most of these girls were admirable, a few were more mischievous than admirable, but rely upon it that every single one of them was nice.

It happened to be as a very serious-minded girl that Miss Meyrick opened her eyes on Tuesday morning. She lay for a long time watching the Florida sunshine, spoken of so tenderly in the railroad's come-on books, as it danced across the foot of her bed. Today the *Lileth* was to steam into San Marco harbor! Today her bridegroom was to smile his slow British smile on her once more! She recalled these facts without the semblance of a thrill.

Where, she wondered, was the thrill? The frivolous girl who had met Lord Harrowby abroad, and dazzled by dreams of social triumphs to come had allowed her aunt to urge her into this betrothal, was not present at the moment. Had she been, she would have declared this Cynthia Meyrick a silly, and laughed her into gaiety again.

Into the room toddled the aunt who had stood so faithfully on the coaching line abroad. With heavy wit, she spoke of the coming of Lord Harrowby. Miss Cynthia did not smile. She turned grave eyes on her aunt.

'I'm wondering,' she confessed. 'Was it the thing to do, after all? Shall I be so very happy?'

'Nonsense. Ninety-nine out of a hundred engaged girls have doubts. It's natural.' Aunt Mary sat down on the bed, which groaned in agony. 'Of course you'll be happy. You'll take precedence over Marion Bishop – didn't we look that up? And after

the airs she's put on when she's come back to Detroit – well, you
ought to be the happiest of girls.'

'I know – but –' Miss Meyrick continued to gaze solemnly
at her aunt. She was accustomed to the apparition. To anyone
who knew Aunt Mary only in her public appearances, a view of
her now would have been startling. Not to go too deeply into
the matter, she had not yet been poured into the steel girders that
determined her public form. Her washed-out eyes were puffy,
and her gray hair was not so luxurious as it would be when
she appeared in the hotel dining room for lunch. There she
sat, a fat little lump of a woman who had all her life chased
will-o'-the-wisps.

'But what?' she demanded firmly.

'It seems as if all my fun were over. Didn't you feel that way
when you became engaged?'

'Hardly. But then – I hadn't enjoyed everything money will
buy, as you have. I've always said you had too much. There,
dear – cheer up. You don't seem to realize. Why, I can remember
when you were born – in the flat down on Second Street – and
your father wearing his old overcoat another year to pay the
doctor's bill. And now that little fluffy baby is to marry into
the peerage! Bless you, how proud your mother would be had
she lived –'

'Are you sure, Aunt Mary?'

'Positive.' Aunt Mary's eyes filled, and with a show of real, if
clumsy affection, she leaned over and kissed her niece. 'Come,
dear, get up. I've ordered breakfast in the rooms.'

Miss Cynthia sat up. And as if banished by that act, the
serious little mouse of a girl scampered into oblivion, and in
her place appeared a gay young rogue who sees the future lying
bright ahead.

'After all,' she smiled, 'I'm not married – yet.' And humming
brightly from a current musical comedy – 'Not just yet – just
yet – just yet –' she stretched forth one slim white arm to

throw aside the coverlet. At which point it is best discreetly to withdraw.

Mr Minot, after a lonesome if abundant breakfast, was at this moment strolling across the hotel courtyard toward yesterday morning's New York papers. As he walked, the pert promises of Mr Trimmer filled his mind. What was the proposition Mr Trimmer had in tow? How would it affect the approaching wedding? And what course of action should the representative of Jephson pursue when it was revealed? For in the sensible light of morning Dick Minot realized that while he remained in San Marco as the guardian of Jephson's interests, he must do his duty. Adorable Miss Meyrick might be, but any change of mind on her part must be over his dead body. A promise was a promise.

With this resolve firm, he proceeded along the hot sidewalk of San Sebastian Avenue. On his right the rich shops again, a dignified Spanish church as old as the town, a rambling lackadaisical 'opera house'. On his left the green and sand colored plaza, with the old Spanish governor's house in the center, now serving Uncle Sam as post office. A city of the past was this; 'other times, other manners' breathed in the air.

At the newsstand Minot met Jack Paddock, jaunty, with a gardenia in his buttonhole and the atmosphere of prosperity that goes with it.

'Come for a stroll,' Paddock suggested. 'I presume you want the giddy story of my life I promised you yesterday? Been down to the old Spanish fort yet? No? Come ahead, and there on the ramparts I'll impart.'

They went down the narrow and very modern street of the souvenir vendors. Suddenly the street ended, and they walked again in the past. The remnants of the old city gates restored, loomed in the sunlight. They stepped through the portals, and Minot gave a gasp.

There in the quiet morning stood the great gray fort that the early settlers had built to protect themselves from the gay dogs who roamed the seas. Its massive walls spoke clearly of romance, of bloody days of cutlass and spike, of bandaged heads and ready arms. Such things still stood! Still stood in the United States – land of steam radiators and men who marched in suffrage parades!

The old caretaker let them in, and they went up the stone steps to stand at last on the parapet looking down on the shimmering sea. To Minot, fresh from Broadway, it all seemed like a colorful dream. They climbed to the highest point and sat, swinging their legs over the edge. Far below the bright blue waters broke on the lower walls.

'It's a funny country down here,' Paddock said slowly. 'A sort of too-good-to-be-true, who-believes-it place. Bright and gay and full of green palms, and so much like a musical comedy you keep waiting all the time for the curtain to go down and the male population to begin its march up the aisle. I've been here three months, and I don't yet think it's really true.'

He shifted on the cold stones.

'Ever since white men hit on it,' he went on, 'it's sort of kept luring them here on fool dream hunts – like a woman. Along about the time old Ponce de Leon came over here prospecting for the fountain that nobody but Lillian Russell has located yet, another Spaniard – I forget his name – had a pipe dream, too. He came over hot-foot looking for a mountain of gold he dreamed was here. I'm sorry for that old boy.'

'Sorry for him?' repeated Minot.

'Yes – sorry. He had the right idea, but he arrived several hundred years too soon. He should have waited until the yellow rich from the North showed up here. Then he'd have found his mountain – he'd have found a whole range of them.'

'I suppose I'm to infer,' Mr Minot said, 'that where he failed, you've landed.'

'Yes, Dick. I am right on the mountain with my little alpenstock in hand.'

'I'm sorry,' replied Minot frankly. 'You might have amounted to something if you'd been separated from money long enough.'

'So I've heard,' Paddock said with a yawn. 'But it wasn't to be. I haven't seen you since we left college, have I? Well, Dick, for a couple of years I tried to make good doing fiction. I turned them out by the yard – nice quiet little tea-table yarns with snappy dialogue. Once I got eighty dollars for a story. It was hard work – and I always did yearn for the purple, you know.'

'I know,' said Minot gravely.

'Well, I've struck it, Dick. I've struck the deep purple with a loud if sickening thud. Hist! The graft I mentioned yesterday.' He glanced over his shoulder. 'Remember Mrs. Bruce, the wittiest hostess in San Marco?'

'Of course I do.'

'Well, I write her repartee for her.'

'Her – what?'

'Her repartee – her dialogue – the bright talk she convulses dinner tables with. Instead of putting my smart stuff into stories at eighty per, I sell it to Mrs Bruce at – I'd be ashamed to tell you, old man. I remarked that it was essentially soft. It is.'

'This is a new one on me,' said Minot, dazed.

A delighted smile spread over Mr Paddock's handsome face.

'Thanks. That's the beauty of it. I'm a pioneer. There'll be others, but I was the first. Consider the situation. Here's Mrs Bruce, loaded with diamonds and money, but tongue-tied in company, with a wit developed in Zanesville, Ohio. Bright, but struggling, young author comes to her – offers to make her conversation the sensation of the place for a few pesos.'

'You did that?'

'Yes – I ask posterity to remember it was I who invented the graft. Mrs Bruce fell on my fair young neck. Now, she gives me in advance a list of her engagements, and for the important ones I devise her line of talk. Then, as I'm usually present at the occasion, I swing things round for her and give her her cues.

If I'm not there, she has to manage it herself. It's a great life – only a bit of a strain on me. I have to remember not to be clever in company. If I forget and spring a good one, she jumps on me proper afterward for not giving it to her.'

'Jack,' said Minot slowly, 'come away from here with me. Come north. This place will finish you sure.'

'Sorry, old man,' laughed Paddock, 'but I've had a nip of the lotus. This lazy old land suits me. I like to sit on a veranda while a dusky menial in a white coat hands me the tinkle-tinkle in a tall cool glass. Come away. Oh, no – I couldn't do that.'

'You'll marry down here,' sighed Minot. 'Some girl with money. And the career we all hoped you'd make for yourself will go up in a golden cloud.'

'I met a girl,' Paddock replied, half closing his eyes and smiling cynically at the sea – 'little thing from the Middle West, stopping at a back street boarding-house – father in the hardware business, nobody at all – but eyes like the sea there, hands like butterflies – sort of – got me. That's how I happen to know I'll never marry. For if I married anybody it would have to be her – and I let her go home without saying a word because I was selfish and like this easy game and intend to stick to it until I'm smothered in rose-leaves. Shall we wander back?'

'See here. Jack – I don't want to preach' – Minot tried to conceal his seriousness with a smile – 'but if I were you I'd stick to this girl, and make good –'

'And leave this?' Paddock laughed. 'Dick, you old idiot, this is meat and drink to me. This nice old land of loiter in the sun. Nay, nay. Now, I've really got to get back. Mrs Bruce is giving a tango tea this afternoon – informal, but something has to be said – These fellows who write a daily humorous column must lead a devil of a life.'

With a laugh, Minot followed his irresponsible friend down the steps. They crossed the bridge over the empty moat and came through the city gates again to the street of the alligator.

'By the way,' Paddock said as they went up the hotel steps, 'you haven't told me what brought you south?'

'Business, Jack,' said Minot. 'It's a secret – perhaps I can tell you later.'

'Business? I thought, of course, you came for pleasure.'

'There'll be no pleasure in this trip for me,' said Minot bitterly.

'Oh, won't there?' Paddock laughed. 'Wait till you hear Mrs Bruce talk. See you later, old man.'

At luncheon they brought Mr Minot a telegram from a certain seventeenth floor in New York. An explosive telegram. It read:

Nonsense nobody here to take your place, see it through, you've given your word.
Thacker.

Gloomily Mr Minot considered. What was there to do but see it through? Even though Thacker should send another to take his place, could he stay to woo the lady he adored?

Hardly. In that event he would have to go away – never see her again – never hear her voice –

If he stayed as Jephson's representative he might know the glory of her nearness for a week, might thrill at her smile – even while he worked to wed her to Lord Harrowby. And perhaps – Who could say? Hard as he might work, might he not be thwarted? It was possible.

So after lunch he sent Thacker a reassuring message, promising to stay. And at the end of a dull hour in the lobby, he set out to explore the town.

The Mermaid Tea House stood on the waterfront, with a small second-floor balcony that looked out on the harbor. Passing that way at four-thirty that afternoon, Minot heard a voice call to him. He glanced up.

'Oh, Mr Minot – won't you come into my parlor?' Cynthia Meyrick smiled down on him.

'Splendid,' Minot laughed. 'I walk forlorn through this old Spanish town – suddenly a lattice is thrown wide, a fair hand beckons. I dash within.'

'Thanks for dashing,' Miss Meyrick greeted him, on the balcony. 'I was finding it dreadfully dull. But I'm afraid the Spanish romance is a little lacking. There is no moonlight, no lattice, no mantilla, no Spanish beauty.'

'No matter,' Minot answered. 'I never did care for Spanish types. They flash like a sky-rocket – then tumble in the dark. Now, the home-grown girls –'

'And nothing but tea,' she interrupted. 'Will you have a cup?'

'Thanks. Was it really very dull?'

'Yes. This book was to blame.' She held up a novel.

'What's the matter with it?'

'Oh – it's one of those books in which the hero and heroine are forever "gazing into each other's eyes". And they understand perfectly. But the reader doesn't. I've reached one of those gazing matches now.'

'But isn't it so in real life – when people gaze into each other's eyes, don't they usually understand?'

'Do they?'

'Don't they? You surely have had more experience than I.'

'What makes you think so?' she smiled.

'Because your eyes are so very easy to gaze into.'

'Mr Minot – you're gazing into them – brazenly. And neither of us understand do we?'

'Oh, no – we're both completely at sea.'

'There,' she cried triumphantly. 'I told you these authors were all wrong.'

Minot, having begun to gaze, found difficulty in stopping. She was near, she was beautiful – and a promise made in New York was a dim and distant thing.

'The railroad folders try to make you believe Florida is an annex to Heaven,' he said. 'I used to think they were lying. But –'

She blushed.

'But what, Mr Minot?'

He leaned close, a strange light in his eyes. He opened his mouth to speak.

Suddenly he glanced over her shoulder, and the light died from his eyes. His lips set in a bitter curve.

'Nothing,' he said. A silence.

'Mr Minot – you've grown awfully dull.'

'Have I? I'm sorry.'

'Must I go back to my book –'

She was interrupted by the shrill triumphant cry of a yacht's siren at her back. She turned her head.

'The *Lileth*,' she said.

'Exactly,' said Minot. 'The bridegroom cometh.'

Another silence.

'You'll want to go to meet him,' Minot said, rising. He stood looking at the boat, flashing gaily in the sunshine. 'I'll go with you as far as the street.'

'But – you know Lord Harrowby. Meet him with me.'

'It seems hardly the thing –'

'But I'm not sentimental. And surely Allan's not.'

'Then I must be,' said Minot. 'Really – I'd rather not –'

They went together to the street. At the parting of the ways, Minot turned to her.

'I promised Lord Harrowby in New York,' he told her, 'that you would have your lamp trimmed and burning.'

She looked up at him. A mischievous light came into her eyes.

'Please – have you a match?' she asked.

It was too much. Minot turned and fled down the street. He did not once look back, though it seemed to him that he felt every step the girl took across that narrow pier to her fiancé's side.

As he dressed for dinner that night his telephone rang, and Miss Meyrick's voice sounded over the wire.

'Harrowby remembers you very pleasantly. Won't you join us at dinner?'

'Are you sure an outsider –' he began.

'Nonsense. Mr Martin Wall is to be there.'

'Ah – thank you – I'll be delighted,' Minot replied.

In the lobby Harrowby seized his hand.

'My dear chap – you're looking fit. Great to see you again. By the way – do you know Martin Wall?'

'Yes – Mr Wall and I met just before the splash!' Minot smiled. He shook hands with Wall, unaccountably genial and beaming. 'The Hudson, Mr Wall, is a bit chilly in February.'

'My dear fellow,' said Wall, 'can you ever forgive me? A thousand apologies. It was all a mistake – a horrible mistake.'

'I felt like a rotter when I heard about it,' Harrowby put in. 'Martin mistook you for someone else. You must forgive us both.'

'Freely,' said Minot. 'And I want to apologize for my suspicions of you, Lord Harrowby.'

'Thanks, old chap.'

'I never doubted you would come – after I saw Miss Meyrick.'

'She is a ripper, isn't she?' said Harrowby enthusiastically.

Martin Wall shot a quick, almost hostile glance at Minot.

'You've noticed that yourself, haven't you?' he said in Minot's ear.

At which point the Meyrick family arrived, and they all went in to dinner.

That function could hardly be described as hilarious. Aunt Mary fluttered and gasped in her triumph, and spoke often of her horror of the new. The recent admission of automobiles to the sacred precincts of Bar Harbor seemed to be the great and disturbing fact in life for her. Spencer Meyrick said little; his thoughts were far away. The rush and scramble of a business office, the click of typewriters, the excitement of the dollar chase – these things had been his life. Deprived of them, like many another exile in the South, he moved in a dim world of unrealities and wished that he were home. Minot, too, had little to say. On Martin Wall fell the burden of entertainment, and he bore it as one trained for the work. Blithely he gossiped of queer corners that had known him and amid the flow of his oratory the dinner progressed.

It was after dinner, when they all stood together in the lobby a moment before separating, that Mr Henry Trimmer made good his promise out of a clear sky.

Cynthia Meyrick stood facing the others, talking brightly, when suddenly her face paled and the flippant words died on her lips. They all turned instantly.

Through the lobby, in a buzz of excited comment, a man walked slowly, his eyes on the ground. He was a tall blond Englishman, not unlike Lord Harrowby in appearance. His gray eyes, when he raised them for a moment, were listless, his shoulders stooped and weary, and he had a long drooping mustache that hung like a weeping willow above a particularly cheerless stream.

However, it was not his appearance that excited comment and caused Miss Meyrick to pale. Hung over his shoulders was a pair of sandwich boards such as the outcasts of a great city carry up and down the streets. And on the front board, turned full toward Miss Meyrick's dinner party, was printed in bold black letters:

I

AM

THE

REAL

LORD

HARROWBY

With a little gasp and a murmured apology, Miss Meyrick turned quickly and entered the elevator. Lord Harrowby stood like a man of stone, gazing at the sandwich boards.

It was at this point that the hotel detective sufficiently recovered himself to lay eager hands on the audacious sandwich man and propel him violently from the scene.

In the background Mr Minot perceived Henry Trimmer, puffing excitedly on a big black cigar, a triumphant look on his face.

Mr Trimmer's bomb was thrown.

Chapter VI
Ten Minutes of Agony

'All I ask, Mister Harrowby, is that you consent to a short interview with your brother.'

Mr Trimmer was speaking. The time was noon of the following day, and Trimmer faced Lord Harrowby in the sitting room of his lordship's hotel suite. Also present – at Harrowby's invitation – were Martin Wall and Mr Minot.

His lordship turned his gray eyes on Trimmer's eager face. He could make those eyes fishy when he liked – he made them so now.

'He is not my brother,' he said coldly, 'and I shall not see him. May I ask you not to call me Mr Harrowby?'

'You may ask till you're red in your noble face,' replied Trimmer, firm in his disrespect.

'But I shall go on calling you "Mister" just the same. I call you that because I know the facts. Just as I call your poor cheated brother, who was in this hotel last night between sandwich boards, Lord Harrowby.'

'Really,' said his lordship, 'I see no occasion for prolonging this interview.'

Mr Trimmer leaned forward. He was a big man, but his face was incongruously thin – almost ax-like. The very best sort of face to thrust in anywhere – and Trimmer was the very man to do the thrusting without batting an eye.

'Do you deny,' he demanded with the air of a prosecutor, 'that you had an older brother by the name of George?'

'I certainly do not,' answered Lord Harrowby. 'George ran off to America some twenty-two years ago. He died in a mining camp in Arizona twelve years back. There is no question whatever about that. We had it on the most reliable authority.'

'A lot of lies,' said Trimmer, 'can be had on good authority. This situation illustrates that. Do you think, Mr Harrowby, that I'd be wasting my time on this proposition if I wasn't dead sure of my facts. Why, poor old George has the evidence in his possession. Incontrovertible proofs. It wouldn't hurt you to see him and look over what he has to offer.'

'Your lordship,' Minot suggested, 'you know that I am your friend and that my great desire is to see you happily married next week. In order that nothing may happen to prevent, I think you ought to see –'

'This impostor,' cut in his lordship haughtily. 'No, I can not. This is not the first time adventurers have questioned the Harrowby title. The dignity of our family demands that I refuse to take any notice whatsoever.'

'Go on,' sneered Trimmer. 'Hide behind your dignity. When I get through with you you won't have enough left to conceal your stick-pin.'

'Trimmer,' said Martin Wall, speaking for the first time, 'how much money do you want?'

Mr Trimmer kept his temper admirably.

'Your society has not corrupted me, Mr Wall,' he said sweetly. 'I am not a blackmailer. I am simply a publicity man. I'm working on a salary which Lord Harrowby – the real Lord Harrowby – is to pay me when he comes into his own. I've handled successfully in publicity campaigns prima donnas, pills, erasers, perfumes, holding companies, race horses, soups and society leaders. It isn't likely that I shall fall down on this proposition. For the last time, Mr Allan Harrowby, will you see your brother?'

'Lord Harrowby, if I were you –' Minot began.

'My dear fellow.' His lordship raised one slim hand. 'It is quite impossible. Which, I take it, terminates our talk with Mr Trimmer.'

'Yes,' said Mr Trimmer, rising. 'Except for one thing. Our young friend here, when he urges you to grant my request, is giving a correct imitation of a wise head on youthful shoulders. He's an American, and he knows about me – about Henry Trimmer. I guess you never heard, Mr Harrowby, what I did for Cotrell's Ink Eraser –'

'Come on,' said Mr Wall militantly, 'erase yourself.'

'For the moment, I will,' smiled Mr Trimmer. 'But I warn you, Mr Harrowby, you are going to be sorry. You aren't up against any piker in publicity – no siree. That little sandwich-board stunt of mine last night was just a starter. I'm going to take the public into partnership. Put it up to the people – that's my motto.'

'Good day, sir,' snapped Lord Harrowby.

'Put it up to the people. And when I pull off the little trick I thought of this morning, you're going to get down before me on your noble knees, and beg off. I warn you. Good day, gentlemen. And may I add one simple request on parting? Watch Trimmer!'

He went out, slamming the door behind him. Mr Wall rose and walked rapidly toward a decanter.

'Rather tough on you, Lord Harrowby,' he remarked, pouring himself a drink. 'Especially just now. The fresh bounder! Ought to have been kicked out of the room.'

'An impostor,' snorted Harrowby. 'A rank impostor.'

'Of course.' Mr Wall set down his glass. 'But don't worry. If Trimmer gets too obstreperous, I'll take care of him myself. I guess I'll be going back to the yacht.'

After Wall's departure, Minot and Harrowby sat staring at each other for a long moment.

'See here, your lordship,' said Minot at last. 'You know why I'm in San Marco. That wedding next Tuesday must take place without fail. And I can't say that I approve of your action just now –'

'My dear boy,' Harrowby interrupted soothingly, 'I appreciate your position. But there was nothing to be gained by seeing Mr Trimmer's friend. The Meyricks were distressed, naturally, by that ridiculous sandwich-board affair last evening, but they have made no move to call off the wedding on account of it. The best thing to do, I'm sure, is to let matters take their course. I might be able to prove that chap's claims false – and then again I mightn't, even if I knew they were false. And – there is a third possibility.'

'What is that?'

'He might really be – George.'

'But you said your brother died, twelve years ago.'

'That is what we heard. But – one can not be sure. And, delighted as I should be to know that George is alive, naturally I should prefer to know it after next Tuesday.'

Anger surged into Minot's heart.

'Is that fair to the young lady who –'

'Who is to become my wife?' Lord Harrowby waved his hand. 'It is. Miss Meyrick is not marrying me for my title. As for her father and aunt, I can not be so sure. I want no disturbance. You want none. I am sure it is better to let things take their course.'

'All right,' said Minot. 'Only I intend to do everything in my power to put this wedding through.'

'My dear chap – your cause is mine,' answered his lordship.

Minot returned to the narrow confines of his room. On the bureau, where he had thrown it earlier in the day, lay an invitation to dine that night with Mrs Bruce. Thus was Jack Paddock's hand shown. The dinner was to be in Miss Meyrick's honor, and Mr Minot was not sorry he was to go. He took up the invitation and reread it smilingly. So he was to hear Mrs Bruce at her own table – the wittiest hostess in San Marco – bar none.

The drowsiness of a Florida midday was in the air. Mr Minot lay down on his bed. A hundred thoughts were his: the brown of Miss Meyrick's eyes, the sincerity of Mr Trimmer's voice when he spoke of his proposition, the fishy look of Lord Harrowby refusing to meet his long lost brother. Things grew hazy. Mr Minot slept.

On leaving Lord Harrowby's rooms, Mr Martin Wall did not immediately set out for the *Lileth*, on which he lived in preference to the hotel. Instead he took a brisk turn about the spacious lobby of the De la Pax.

People turned to look at him as he passed. They noted that his large, placid, rather jovial face was lighted by an eye sharp and queer, and a bit out of place amid its surroundings. Mr Wall considered himself the true cosmopolite, and his history rather bore out the boast. Many and odd were the lands that had known him. He had loaned money to a prince of Algiers (on excellent security), broken bread with a sultan, organized a baseball nine in Cuba, and coming home from the East via the Indian ports, had flirted on shipboard with the wife of a Russian grand duke. As he passed through that cool lobby it was not to be wondered at that middle west merchants and their wives found him worthy of a second glance.

The courtyard of the Hotel de la Pax was fringed by a series of modish shops, with doors opening both on the courtyard and on the narrow street outside. Among these, occupying a corner room was the very smart jewel shop of Ostby and Blake. Occasionally in the winter resorts of the South one may find jewelry shops whose stock would bear favorably competition with Fifth Avenue. Ostby and Blake conducted such an establishment.

For a moment before the show-window of this shop Mr Wall paused, and with the eye of a connoisseur studied the brilliant display within. His whole manner changed. The air of boredom with which he had surveyed his fellow travelers of the lobby disappeared; on the instant he was alert, alive, almost eager. Jauntily he strolled into the store.

One clerk only – a tall thin man with a sallow complexion and hair the color of a lemon – was in charge. Mr Wall asked to be shown the stock of unset diamonds.

The trays that the man set before him caused the eyes of Mr Wall to brighten still more. With a manner almost reverent he stooped over and passed his fingers lovingly over the stones. For an instant the tall man glanced outside, and smiled a sallow smile. A little girl in a pink dress was crossing the street, and it was at her that he smiled.

'There's a flaw in that stone,' said Mr Wall, in a voice of sorrow. 'See –'

From outside came the shrill scream of a child, interrupting. The tall man turned quickly to the window.

'My God –' he moaned.

'What is it?' Mr Wall sought to look over his shoulder. 'Automobile –'

'My little girl,' cried the clerk in agony. He turned to Martin Wall, hesitating. His sallow face was white now, his lips trembled. Doubtfully he gazed into the frank open countenance of Martin Wall. And then –

'I leave you in charge,' he shouted, and fled past Mr Wall to the street.

For a moment Martin Wall stood, frozen to the spot. His eyes were unbelieving; his little Cupid's bow mouth was wide open.

'Here – come back –' he shouted, when he could find his voice.

No one heeded. No one heard. Outside in the street a crowd had gathered. Martin Wall wet his dry lips with his tongue. An unaccountable shudder swept his huge frame.

'My God –' he cried in a voice of terror, 'I'm alone!'

For the first time he dared to move. His elbow bumped a hundred thousand dollars' worth of unset diamonds. Frightened, he drew back.

He collided with a showcase rich in emeralds, rubies and aquamarines. He put out a plump hand to steady himself. It rested on a display case of French, Russian and Dutch silver.

Mr Wall's knees grew weak. He felt a strange prickly sensation all over him. He took a step – and was staring at the finest display of black pearls south of Maiden Lane, New York.

Quickly he turned away. His eyes fell upon the door of a huge safety vault! It was swinging open!

Little beads of perspiration began to pop out on the forehead of Martin Wall. His heart was hammering like that of a youth who sees after a long separation his lady love. His eyes grew glassy.

He took out a silk handkerchief and passed it slowly across his damp forehead.

Staggering slightly, he stepped again to the trays of unset stones. The glassy eyes had grown greedy now. He put out one huge hand as the lover aforesaid might reach toward his lady's hair.

Then Mr Wall shut his lips firmly, and thrust both of his hands deep into his trousers pockets.

He stood there in the middle of that gorgeous room – a fat figure of a man suffering a cruel inhuman agony.

He was still standing thus when the tall man came running back. Apprehension clouded that sallow face.

'It was very kind of you.' The small eyes of the clerk darted everywhere; then came back to Martin Wall. 'I'm obliged – why, what's the matter, sir?'

Martin Wall passed his hand across his eyes, as a man banishing a terrible dream.

'The little girl?' he asked.

'Hardly a scratch,' said the clerk, pointing to the smiling child at his side. 'It was lucky, wasn't it?' He was behind the counter now, studying the trays unprotected on the show-case.

'Very lucky.' Martin Wall still had to steady himself. 'Perhaps you'd like to look about a bit before I go –'

'Oh, no, sir. Everything's all right, I'm sure. You were looking at these stones –'

'Some other time,' said Wall weakly. 'I only wanted an idea of what you had.'

'Good day, sir. And thank you very much.'

'Not at all.' And the limp ex-guardian passed unsteadily from the store into the glare of the street.

Mr Tom Stacy, of the Manhattan Club, half dozing on the veranda of his establishment, was rejoiced to see his old friend Martin Wall crossing the pavement toward him.

'Well, Martin –' he began. And then a look of concern came into his face. 'Good lord, man – what ails you?'

Mr Wall sank like a wet rag to the steps.

'Tom,' he said, 'a terrible thing has just happened. I was left alone in Ostby and Blake's jewelry shop.'

'Alone?' cried Mr Stacy. 'You – alone?'

'Absolutely alone.'

Mr Stacy leaned over.

'Are you leaving town – in a hurry?' he asked.

Gloomily Mr Wall shook his head.

'He put me on my honor,' he complained. 'Left me in charge of the shop. Can you beat it? Of course after that, I – well – you know, somehow I couldn't do it. I tried, but I couldn't.'

Mr Stacy threw back his head, and his raucous laughter smote the lazy summer afternoon.

'I can't help it,' he gasped. 'The funniest thing I ever – you – the best stone thief in America alone in charge of three million dollars' worth of the stuff!'

'Good heavens, man,' whispered Wall. 'Not so loud!' And well might he protest, for Mr Stacy's indiscreet and mirthful tone carried far. It carried, for example, to Mr Richard Minot, standing hidden behind the curtains of his little room over-head.

'Come inside, Martin,' said Stacy. 'Come inside and have a bracer. You sure must need it, after that.'

'I do,' replied Mr Wall, in heartfelt tones. He rose and followed Tom Stacy.

Cheeks burning, eyes popping, Mr Minot watched them disappear into the Manhattan Club.

Here was news indeed. Lord Harrowby's boon companion the ablest jewel thief in America! Just what did that mean?

Putting on coat and hat, he hurried to the hotel office and there wrote a cablegram:

Situation suspicious are you dead certain H. is on the level?

An hour later, in his London office, Mr Jephson read this message carefully three times.

Chapter VII
Chain Lightning's Collar

The Villa Jasmine, Mrs Bruce's winter home, stood in a park of palms and shrubbery some two blocks from the Hotel de la Pax. Mr Minot walked thither that evening in the resplendent company of Jack Paddock.

'You'll enjoy Mrs Bruce tonight,' Paddock confided. 'I've done her some rather good lines, if I do say it as shouldn't.'

'On what topics?' asked Minot, with a smile.

'International marriage – jewels – by the way, I don't suppose you know that Miss Cynthia Meyrick is to appear for the first time wearing the famous Harrowby necklace?'

'I didn't even know there was a necklace,' Minot returned.

'Ah, such ignorance. But then, you don't wander much in feminine society, do you? Mrs Bruce told me about it this morning. Chain Lightning's Collar.'

'Chain Lightning's what?'

'Ah, my boy –' Mr Paddock lighted a cigarette. 'You should go round more in royal circles. List, commoner, while I relate. It seems that the Earl of Raybrook is a giddy old sport with a gambling streak a yard wide. In his young days he loved the Lady Evelyn Holloway. Lady Evelyn had a horse entered in a derby about that time – name, Chain Lightning. And the Earl of Raybrook wagered a diamond necklace against a kiss that Chain Lightning would lose.'

'Wasn't that giving big odds?' inquired Minot.

'Not if you believe the stories of Lady Evelyn's beauty. Well, it happened before Tammany politicians began avenging Ireland on Derby Day. Chain Lightning won. And the earl came across with the necklace. Afterward he married Lady Evelyn –'

'To get back the necklace?'

'Cynic. And being a rather racy old boy, he referred to the necklace thereafter as Chain Lightning's Collar. It got to be pretty well known in England by that name. I believe it is considered a rather neat piece of jewelry among the English nobility – whose sparklers aren't what they were before the steel business in Pittsburgh turned out a good thing.'

'Chain Lightning's Collar,' mused Minot. 'I presume Lady Evelyn was the mother of the present Lord Harrowby?'

'So 'tis rumored,' smiled Paddock. 'Though I take it his lordship favors his father in looks.'

They walked along for a moment in silence. The story of this necklace of diamonds could bring but one thing to Minot's thoughts – Martin Wall drooping on the steps of the Manhattan Club while old Stacy roared with joy. He considered. Should he tell Mr Paddock? No, he decided he would wait.

'As I said,' Paddock ran on, 'you'll enjoy Mrs Bruce tonight. Her lines are good, but somehow – it's really a great problem to me – she doesn't sound human and natural when she gets them off. I looked up her beauty doctor and asked him if he couldn't put a witty gleam in her eye, but he told me he didn't care to go that far in correcting Mrs Bruce's Maker.'

They had reached the Villa Jasmine now, a great white palace in a flowery setting more like a dream than a reality. The evening breeze murmured whisperingly through the palms, a hundred gorgeous colors shone in the moonlight, fountains splashed coolly amid the greenery.

'Act Two,' muttered Minot. 'The grounds surrounding the castle of the fairy princess.'

'You have to come down here, don't you,' replied Paddock, 'to realize that old Mother Nature has a little on Belasco, after all?'

The whir of a motor behind them caused the two young men to turn. Then Mr Minot saw her coming up the path toward him – coming up that fantastic avenue of palms – tall, fair, white, a lovely figure in a lovely setting –

Ah, yes – Lord Harrowby! He walked at her side, nonchalant, distinguished, almost as tall as a popular illustrator thinks a man in evening clothes should be. Truly, they made a handsome couple. They were to wed. Mr Minot himself had sworn they were to wed.

He kept the bitterness from his tone as he greeted them there amid the soft magic of the Florida night. Together they went inside. In the center of a magnificent hallway they found Mrs Bruce standing, like stout Cortez on his Darien peak, triumphant amid the glory of her gold.

Mr Minot thought Mrs Bruce's manner of greeting somewhat harried and oppressed. Poor lady, every function was a first night for her. Would the glare of the footlights frighten her? Would she falter in her lines – forget them completely? Only her sisters of the stage could sympathize with her understandingly now.

'So you are to carry Cynthia away?' Minot heard her saying to Lord Harrowby. 'Such a lot of my friends have married into the peerage. Indeed, I have sometimes thought you English have no other pastime save that of slipping engagement rings on hands across the sea.'

A soft voice spoke in Minot's ear.

'Mine,' Mr Paddock was saying. 'Not bad, eh? But look at that Englishman. Why should I have sat up all last night writing lines to try on him? Can you tell me that?'

Lord Harrowby, indeed, seemed oblivious of Mrs Bruce's little bon mot. He hemmed and hawed, and said he was a lucky man. But he did not mean that he was a lucky man because he had the privilege of hearing Mrs Bruce.

Mr Bruce slipped out of the shadows into the weariness of another formal dinner. Mrs Bruce glittered, and he wrote the checks. He was a scraggly little man who sometimes sat for hours at a time in silence. There were those unkind enough to say that he sought back, trying to recall the reason that had led him to marry Mrs Bruce.

When he beheld Miss Cynthia Meyrick, and knew that he was to take her in to dinner, Mr Bruce brightened perceptibly. None save a blind and deaf man could have failed to. Cocktails consumed, the party turned toward the dining room. Except for the Meyricks, Martin Wall, Lord Harrowby and Paddock, Dick Minot knew none of them. There were a couple of colorless men from New York who, when they died, would be referred to as 'prominent club men', a horsy girl from Westchester, an ex-ambassador's wife and daughter, a number of names from Boston and Philadelphia with their respective bearers. And last but not least the two Bond girls from Omaha – blond, lovely, but inclined to be snobbish even in that company, for their mother was a Van Reypan, and Van Reypans are rare birds in Omaha and elsewhere.

Mr Minot took in the elder of the Bond girls, and found that Cynthia Meyrick sat on his left. He glanced at her throat as they sat down. It was bare of ornament. And then he beheld, sparkling in her lovely hair, the perfect diamonds of Chain Lightning's Collar. As he turned back to the table he caught the eye of Mr Martin Wall. Mr Wall's eye happened to be coming away from the same locality.

The girl from Omaha gossiped of plays and players, like a dramatic page from some old Sunday newspaper.

'I'm mad about the stage,' she confided. 'Of course, we get all the best shows in Omaha. Why, Maxine Elliott and Nat Goodwin come there every year.'

Mr Minot, New Yorker, shuddered. Should he tell her of the many and active years in the lives of these two since they visited any town together? No. What use? On the other side of him a sweet voice spoke:

'I presume you know, Mr Minot, that Mrs Bruce has the reputation of being the wittiest hostess in San Marco?'

'I have heard as much.' Minot smiled into Cynthia Meyrick's eyes. 'When does her act go on?'

Mrs Bruce was wondering the same thing. She knew her lines; she was ready. True, she understood few of those lines. Wit was not her specialty. Until Mr Paddock took charge of her, she had thought colored newspaper supplements humorous in the extreme. However, the lines Mr Paddock taught her seemed to go well, and she continued to patronize the old stand.

She looked up now from her conversation with her dinner partner, and silence fell as at a curtain ascending.

'I was just saying to Lord Harrowby,' Mrs, Bruce began, smiling about her, 'how picturesque our business streets are here. What with the Greek merchants in their native costumes –'

'Bandits, every one of them,' growled Mr Bruce, bravely interrupting. His wife frowned.

'Only the other day,' she continued, 'I bought a rug from a man who claimed to be a Persian prince. He said it was a prayer-rug, and I think it must have been, for ever since I got it I've been praying it's genuine.'

A little ripple of amusement ran about the table. The redoubtable Mrs Bruce was under way. People spoke to one another in undertones – little conversational nudges of anticipation.

'By the way, Cynthia,' the hostess inquired, 'have you heard from Helen Arden lately?'

'Not for some time,' responded Miss Meyrick, 'although I have her promise that she and the duke will be here – next Tuesday.'

'Splendid.' Mrs Bruce turned to his lordship. 'I think of Helen, Lord Harrowby, because she, too, married into your nobility. Her father made his money in sausage in the Middle West. In his youth he'd had trouble in finding a pair of ready-made trousers, but as soon as the money began to roll in, Helen started to look him up a coat of arms. And a family motto. I remember suggesting at the time, in view of the sausage: A family is no stronger than its weakest link.'

Mrs. Bruce knew when to pause. She paused now. The ripple became an outright laugh. Mr Paddock sipped languorously from his wine glass. He saw that his lines 'got over'.

'Went into society head foremost, Helen did,' Mrs Bruce continued. 'Thought herself a clever amateur actress. Used to act often for charity – though I don't recall that she ever got it.'

'The beauty of Mrs Bruce's wit,' said Miss Meyrick in Mr Minot's ear, 'is that it is so unconscious. She doesn't appear to realize when she has said a good thing.'

'There's just a chance that she doesn't realize it,' suggested Minot.

'Then Helen met the Duke of Lismore,' Mrs Bruce was speaking once more. 'Perhaps you know him, Lord Harrowby?'

'No – er – sorry to say I don't –'

'A charming chap. In some ways. Helen was a Shavian in considering marriage the chief pursuit of women. She pursued. Followed Lismore to Italy, where he proposed. I presume he thought that being in Rome, he must do as the Romeos do.'

'But, my dear lady,' said Harrowby in a daze, 'isn't it the Romans?'

'Isn't what the Romans?' asked Mrs Bruce blankly.

'Your lordship is correct,' said Mr Paddock hastily. 'Mrs Bruce misquoted purposely – in jest, you know. Jibe – japery.'

'Oh – er – pardon me,' returned his lordship.

'I saw Helen in London last spring,' Mrs Bruce went on. 'She confided to me that she considers her husband a genius. And if genius really be nothing but an infinite capacity for taking champagnes, I am sure the poor child is right.'

Little murmurs of joy, and the dinner proceeded. The guests bent over their food, shipped to Mrs Bruce in a refrigerating car from New York, and very little wearied by its long trip. Here and there two talked together. It was like an intermission between the acts.

Mr Minot turned to the Omaha girl. Even though she was two wives behind on Mr Nat Goodwin's career, one must be polite.

It was at the close of the dinner that Mrs Bruce scored her most telling point. She and Lord Harrowby were conversing about a famous English author, and when she was sure she had the attention of the table, she remarked:

'Yes, we met his wife at the Masonbys'. But I have always felt that the wife of a celebrity is like the coupon on one's railway ticket.'

'How's that, Mrs Bruce?' Minot inquired. After all, Paddock had been kind to him.

'Not good if detached,' said Mrs Bruce.

She stood. Her guests followed suit. It was by this bon mot that she chose to have her dinner live in the gossip of San Marco. Hence with it she closed the ceremony.

'Witty woman, your wife,' said one of the colorless New Yorkers to Mr Bruce, when the men were left alone.

Mr Bruce only grunted, but Mr Paddock answered brightly: 'Do you really think so?'

'Yes. Don't you?'

'Why – er – really –' Mr Paddock blushed. Modest author, he.

A servant appeared to say that Lord Harrowby was wanted at once outside, and excusing himself, Harrowby departed. He found his valet, a plump, round-faced, serious man, waiting in the shadows on the veranda. For a time they talked together in low tones. When Harrowby returned to the dining room, his never cheerful face was even gloomier than usual.

Spencer Meyrick and Bruce, exiles both of them, talked joyously of business and the rush of the day's work for which both longed. The New York man and a sapling from Boston conversed of chamber music. Martin Wall sat silent, contemplative. Perhaps had he spoken his thoughts they would have been of a rich jewel shop at noon – deserted.

A half-hour later Mrs Bruce's dinner party was scattered among the palms and flowers of her gorgeous lawn. Mr Minot had fallen again to the elder girl from Omaha, and blithely for her he was displaying his Broadway ignorance of horticulture. Suddenly out of the night came a scream. Instantly when he heard it, Mr Minot knew who had uttered it.

Unceremoniously he parted from the Omaha beauty and sped over the lawn. But quick as he was, Lord Harrowby was quicker. For when Minot came up, he saw Harrowby bending over Miss Meyrick, who sat upon a wicker bench.

'Cynthia – what is it?' Harrowby was saying.

Cynthia Meyrick felt wildly of her shining hair.

'Your necklace,' she gasped. 'Chain Lightning's Collar. He took it! He took it!'

'Who?'

'I don't know. A man!'

'A man!' Reverent repetition by feminine voices out of the excited group.

'He leaped out at me there – by that tree – pinioned my arms – snatched the necklace. I couldn't see his face. It happened in the shadow.'

'No matter,' Harrowby replied. 'Don't give it another thought, my child.'

'But how can I help –'

'I shall telephone the police at once,' announced Spencer Meyrick.

'I beg you'll do nothing of the sort,' expostulated Lord Harrowby. 'It would be a great inconvenience – the thing wasn't worth the publicity that would result. I insist that the police be kept out of this.'

Argument – loud on Mr Meyrick's part – ensued. Suggestions galore were offered by the guests. But in the end Lord Harrowby had his way. It was agreed not to call in the police.

Mr Minot, looking up, saw a sneering smile on the face of Martin Wall. In a flash he knew the truth.

With Aunt Mary calling loudly for smelling salts, and the whole party more or less in confusion, the return to the house started. Mr Paddock walked at Minot's side.

'Rather looks as though Chain Lightning's Collar had choked off our gaiety,' he mumbled. 'Serves her right for wearing the thing in her hair. She spoiled two corking lines for me by not wearing it where you'd naturally expect a necklace to be worn.'

Minot maneuvered so as to intercept Lord Harrowby under the portico.

'May I speak with you a moment?' he inquired. Harrowby bowed, and they stepped into the shadows of the drive.

'Lord Harrowby,' said Minot, trying to keep the excitement from his voice, 'I have certain information about one of the guests here this evening that I believe would interest you. Your lordship has been badly buffaloed. One of our fellow diners at Mrs Bruce's table holds the title of the ablest jewel thief in America!'

He watched keenly to catch Lord Harrowby's start of surprise. Alas, he caught nothing of the sort.

'Nonsense,' said his lordship nonchalantly. 'You mustn't let your imagination carry you away, dear chap.'

'Imagination nothing! I know what I'm talking about.' And then Minot added sarcastically: 'Sorry to bore you with this.'

His lordship laughed.

'Right-o, old fellow. I'm not interested.'

'But haven't you just lost –'

'A diamond necklace? Yes.' They had reached a particularly dark and secluded spot beneath the canopy of palm leaves. Harrowby turned suddenly and put his hands on Minot's shoulders. 'Mr Minot,' he said, 'you are here to see that nothing interferes with my marriage to Miss Meyrick. I trust you are determined to do your duty to your employers?'

'Absolutely. That is why –'

'Then,' replied Harrowby quickly, 'I am going to ask you to take charge of this for me.'

Suddenly Minot felt something cold and glassy in his hand. Startled, he looked down. Even in the dark, Chain Lightning's Collar sparkled like the famous toy that it was.

'Your lordship!'

'I can not explain now. I can only tell you it is quite necessary that you help me at this time. If you wish to do your full duty by Mr Jephson.'

'Who took this necklace from Miss Meyrick's hair?' asked Minot hotly.

'I did. I assure you it was the only way to prevent our plans from going awry. Please keep it until I ask you for it.'

And turning, Lord Harrowby walked rapidly toward the house.

'The brute!' Angrily Mr Minot stood turning the necklace over in his hand. 'So he frightened the girl he is to marry – the girl he is supposed to love –'

What should he do? Go to her, and tell her of Harrowby's amiable eccentricities? He could hardly do that – Harrowby had taken him into his confidence – and besides there was Jephson of the great bald head, the Peter Pan eyes. Nothing to do but wait.

Returning to the hotel from Mrs Bruce's villa, he found awaiting him a cable from Jephson. The cable assured him that beyond any question the man in San Marco was Allan Harrowby and, like Caesar's wife, above suspicion.

Yet even as he read, Lord Harrowby walked through the lobby, and at his side was Mr James O'Malley, house detective of the Hotel de la Pax. They came from the manager's office, where they had evidently been closeted.

With the cablegram in his hand, Minot entered the elevator and ascended to his room. The other hand was in the pocket of his top coat, closed tightly upon Chain Lightning's Collar – the bauble that the Earl of Raybrook had once wagered against a kiss.

78

Chapter VIII
After The Trained Seals

Mr Minot opened his eyes on Thursday morning with the uncomfortable feeling that he was far from his beloved New York. For a moment he lay dazed, wandering in that dim borderland between sleep and waking. Then, suddenly, he remembered.

'Oh, yes, by jove,' he muttered, 'I've been knighted. Groom of the Back-Stairs Scandals and Keeper of the Royal Jewels – that's me.'

He lifted his pillow. There on the white sheet sparkled the necklace of which the whole British nobility was proud – Chain Lightning's Collar. Some seventy-five blue-white diamonds, pear-shaped, perfectly graduated. His for the moment!

'What's Harrowby up to, I wonder?' he reflected. 'The dear old top! Nice, pleasant little party if a policeman should find this in my pocket.'

Another perfect day shone in that narrow Spanish street. Up in Manhattan theatrical press agents were crowning huge piles of snow with posters announcing their attractions. Ferries were held up by ice in the river. A breeze from the Arctic swept round the Flatiron building. Here lazy summer lolled on the bosom of the town.

In the hotel dining room Mr Minot encountered Jack Paddock, superb in white flannels above his grapefruit. He accepted Paddock's invitation to join him.

'By the way,' said Mrs Bruce's jester, holding up a small, badly printed newspaper, 'have you made the acquaintance of the *San Marco Mail* yet.'

'No – what's that?'

'A morning newspaper – by courtesy. Started here a few weeks back by a noiseless little Spaniard from Havana named Manuel Gonzale. Slipped in here on his rubber soles, Gonzale did – dressed all in white – lovely lemon face – shifty, can't-catch-me eyes. And his newspaper – hot stuff, my boy. It has Town Topics looking like a consular report from Greenland.'

'Scandals?' asked Mr Minot, also attacking a grapefruit.

'Scandals and rumors of scandals. Mostly hints, you know. Several references this morning to our proud and haughty friend, Lord Harrowby. For example, Madame On Dit, writing in her column on page one, has this to say: "The impecunious but titled Englishman who has arrived in our midst recently with the idea of connecting with certain American dollars has an interesting time ahead of him, if rumor speaks true. The little incident in the lobby of a local hotel the other evening – which was duly reported in this column at the time – was but a mild beginning. The gentleman in charge of the claimant to the title held so jealously by our British friend promises immediate developments which will be rich, rare and racy."'

'Rich, rare and racy,' repeated Minot thoughtfully. 'Ah, yes – we were to watch Mr Trimmer. I had almost forgot him in the excitement of last evening. By the way, does the *Mail* know anything about the disappearance of Chain Lightning's Collar?'

'Not as yet,' smiled Mr Paddock, 'although Madame On Dit claims to have been a guest at the dinner. By the way, what do you make of last night's melodramatic farce?'

'I don't know what to make of it,' answered Minot truthfully. He was suddenly conscious of the necklace in his inside coat pocket.

'Then all I can say, my dear Watson,' replied Mr Paddock with burlesque seriousness, 'is that you are unmistakably lacking in my powers of deduction. Give me a cigarette, and I'll tell you the name of the man who is gloating over those diamonds today.'

'All right,' smiled Minot. 'Go ahead.'

Mr Paddock, reaching for a match tray, spoke in a low tone in Minot's ear.

'Martin Wall,' he said. He leaned back.

'You ask how I arrived at my conclusion. Simple enough. I went through the list of guests for possible crooks, and eliminated them one by one. The man I have mentioned alone was left. Ever notice his eyes – remind me of Manuel Gonzale's. He's too polished, too slick, too good to be true. He's traveled too much – nobody travels as much as he has except for the very good reason that a detective is on the trail. And he made friends with simple old Harrowby on an Atlantic liner – that, if you read popular fiction, is alone enough to condemn him. Believe me, Dick, Martin Wall should be watched.'

'All right,' laughed Minot, 'you watch him.'

'I've a notion to. Harrowby makes me wary. Won't call in a solitary detective. Anyone might think he doesn't want the necklace back.'

After breakfast Minot and Paddock played five sets of tennis on the hotel courts. And Mr Minot won, despite the Harrowby diamonds in his trousers pocket, weighing him down. Luncheon over, Mr Paddock suggested a drive to Tarragona Island.

'A little bit of nowhere a mile offshore,' he said. 'No man can ever know the true inwardness of the word lonesome until he's seen Tarragona.'

Minot hesitated. Ought he to leave the scene of action? Of action? He glanced about him. There was less action here than in a Henry James novel. The tangle of events in which he was involved rested for a siesta.

So he and Mr Paddock drove along the narrow neck of land that led from the mainland to Tarragona Island. They entered the kingdom of the lonely. Sandy beach with the ocean on one side, swamps on the other. Scrubby palms, disreputable foliage, here and there a cluster of seemingly deserted cottages – the world and its works apparently a million miles away. Yet out on one corner of that bleak forgotten acre stood the slim outline of a wireless, and in a little white house lived a man who, amid the seagulls and the sand dunes, talked daily with great ships and cities far away.

'I told you it was lonesome,' said Mr Paddock.

'Lonesome,' shivered Minot. 'Even God has forgot this place. Only Marconi has remembered.'

And even as they wandered there amid the swamps, where alligators and rattlesnakes alone saw fit to dwell, back in San Marco the capable Mr Trimmer was busy. By poster and by handbill he was spreading word of his newest coup, so that by evening no one in town – save the few who were most concerned – was unaware of a development rich, rare and racy.

Minot and Paddock returned late, and their dinner was correspondingly delayed. It was eight-thirty o'clock when they at last strolled into the lobby of the De la Pax. There they encountered Miss Meyrick, her father and Lord Harrowby.

'We're taking Harrowby to the movies,' said Miss Meyrick. 'He confesses he's never been. Won't you come along?'

She was one of her gay selves tonight, white, slim, laughing, irresistible. Minot, looking at her, thought that she could make even Tarragona Island bearable. He knew of no greater tribute to her charm.

The girl and Harrowby led the way, and Minot and Paddock followed with Spencer Meyrick. The old man was an imposing figure in his white serge, which accentuated the floridness of his face. He talked of an administration that did not please him, of a railroad fallen on evil days. Now and again he paused and seemed to lose the thread of what he was saying, while his eyes dwelt on his daughter, walking ahead.

They arrived shortly at the San Marco Opera House, devoted each evening to three acts of 'refined vaudeville' and six of the newest film releases. It was here that the rich loitering in San Marco found their only theatrical amusement, and forgetting Broadway, laughed and were thrilled with simpler folk. A large crowd was fairly fighting to get in and Mr Paddock, who volunteered to buy the tickets, was forced to take his place at the end of a long line.

Finally they reached the dim interior of the opera house, and were shown to seats far down in front. By hanging back in the dusk Minot managed to secure the end seat, with Miss Meyrick at his side. Beyond her sat Lord Harrowby, gazing with rapt British seriousness at the humorous film that was being flashed on the screen.

Between pictures Harrowby offered an opinion.

'You in America are a jolly lot,' he said. 'Just fancy our best people in England attending a cinematograph exhibition.'

They tried to fancy it, but with his lordship there, they couldn't. Two more pictures ran their filmy lengths, while Mr Minot sat entranced there in the half dark. It was not the pictures that entranced him. Rather, was it a lady's nearness, the flash of her smile, the hundred and one tones of her voice – all, all again as it had been in that ridiculous automobile – just before the awakening.

After the third picture the lights of the auditorium were turned up, and the hour of vaudeville arrived. On to the stage strolled a pert confident youth garbed in shabby grandeur, who attempted sidewalk repartee. He clipped his jests from barber-shop periodicals, bought his songs from an ex-barroom song writer, and would have gone to the mat with anyone who denied that his act was 'refined'. Mr Minot, listening to his gibes, thought of the Paddock jest factory and Mrs Bruce.

When the young man had wrung the last encore from a kindly audience, the drop-curtain was raised and revealed on the stage in gleaming splendor Captain Ponsonby's troupe of trained seals. An intelligent aggregation they proved, balancing balls on their small heads, juggling flaming torches, and taking as their just due lumps of sugar from the captain's hand as they finished each feat. The audience recalled them again and again, and even the peerage was captivated.

'Clever beasts, aren't they?' Lord Harrowby remarked. And as Captain Ponsonby took his final curtain, his lordship added:

'Er – what follows the trained seals?'

The answer to Harrowby's query came almost immediately, and a startling answer it proved to be.

Into the glare of the footlights stepped Mr Henry Trimmer. His manner was that of the conquering hero. For a moment he stood smiling and bowing before the approving multitude. Then he raised a hand commanding silence.

'My dear friends,' he said, 'I appreciate this reception. As I said in my handbill of this afternoon, I am working in the interests of justice. The gentleman who accompanies me to your delightful little city is beyond any question whatsoever George Harrowby, the eldest son of the Earl of Raybrook, and as such he is entitled to call himself Lord Harrowby. I know the American people well enough to feel sure that when they realize the facts they will demand that justice be done. That is why I have prevailed upon Lord Harrowby to meet you here in this, your temple of amusement, and put his case before you. His lordship will talk to you for a time with a view to getting acquainted. He has chosen for the subject of his discourse *The Old Days at Rakedale Hall*. Ladies and gentlemen, I have the honor to introduce – the real Lord Harrowby.'

Out of the wings shuffled the lean and gloomy Englishman whom Mr Trimmer had snatched from the unknown to cloud a certain wedding day. The applause burst forth. It shook the building. From the gallery descended a shrill penetrating whistle of acclaim.

Mr Minot glanced at the face of the girl beside him. She was looking straight ahead, her cheeks bright red, her eyes flashing with anger. Beyond, the face of Harrowby loomed, frozen, terrible.

'Shall we – go?' Minot whispered.

'By no means,' the girl answered. 'We should only call attention to our presence here. I know at least fifty people in this
audience. We must see it through.'

The applause was stilled at last and, supremely fussed, the
'real Lord Harrowby' faced that friendly throng.

'Dear – er – people,' he said. 'As Mr Trimmer has told you,
we seek only justice. I am not here to argue my right to the title
I claim – that I can do at the proper time and place. I am simply
proposing to go back – back into the past many years – back to
the days when I was a boy at Rakedale Hall. I shall picture those
days as no impostor could picture them – and when I have done
I shall allow you to judge.'

And there in that crowded little southern opera house on that
hot February night, the actor who followed the trained seals
proceeded to go back. With unfaltering touch he sketched for
his audience the great stone country seat called Rakedale Hall,
where for centuries the Harrowbys had dwelt. It was as though
he took his audience there to visit – through the massive iron
gates up the broad avenue bordered with limes, until the high
chimneys, the pointed gables, the mullioned windows, and
the walls half hidden by ivy, creeping roses and honeysuckles
were revealed to them. He took them through the house to the
servants' quarters – which he called 'the offices' – out into the
kitchen gardens, thence to the paved quadrangle of the stables
with its arched gateway and the chiming clock above. Tennis
courts, grape houses, conservatories, they visited breathlessly;
they saw over the brow of the hill the low square tower of the
old church and the chimneys of the vicar's modest house.

And far away, they beheld the trees that furnished cover to
the little beasts it was the Earl of Raybrook's pleasure to hunt
in the season.

Becoming more specific, he spoke of the neighbors, and a bit
of romance crept in in the person of the fair-haired Honorable
Edith Townshend, who lived to the west of Rakedale Hall. He

described at length the picturesque personality of the 'racing parson', neighbor on the south, and in full accord with the ideas of the sporting Earl of Raybrook.

The events of his youth, he said, crowded back upon him as he recalled this happy scene, and emotion well-nigh choked him. However, he managed to tell of a few of the celebrities who came to dinner, of their bon mots, their preferences in cuisine. He mentioned the thrilling morning when he was nearly drowned in the brook that skirted the 'purple meadow'; also the thrilling afternoon when he hid his mother's famous necklace in the biscuit box on the sideboard, and upset a whole household. And he narrated a dozen similar exploits, each garnished with small illuminating details.

His audience sat fascinated. All who listened felt that his words rang true – even Lord Harrowby himself, sitting far forward, his hand gripping the seat in front of him until the white of his knuckles showed through.

Next the speaker shifted his scene to Eton, thrilled his hearers with the story of his revolt against Oxford, of his flight to the States, his wild days in Arizona. And he pulled out of his pocket a letter written by the old Earl of Raybrook himself, profanely expostulating with him for his madness, and begging that he return to ascend to the earldom when the old man was no more.

The 'real Lord Harrowby' finished reading this somewhat pathetic appeal with a little break in his voice, and stood looking out at the audience.

'If my brother Allan himself were in the house,' he said, 'he would have to admit that it is our father speaking in that letter.'

A rustle of interest ran through the auditorium. The few who had recognized Harrowby turned to stare at him now. For a moment he sat silent, his face a variety of colors in the dim light. Then with a cry of rage he leaped to his feet.

'You stole that letter, you cur,' he cried. 'You are a liar, a fraud, an impostor.'

The man on the stage stood shading his eyes with his hand.

'Ah, Allan,' he answered, 'so you are here, after all? Is that quite the proper greeting – after all these years?'

A roar of sympathetic applause greeted this sally. There was no doubt as to whose side Mr Trimmer's friend, the public, was on. Harrowby stood in his place, his lips twitching, his eyes for once blazing and angry.

Dick Minot was by this time escorting Miss Meyrick up the aisle, and they came quickly to the cool street. Harrowby, Paddock and Spencer Meyrick followed immediately. His lordship was most contrite.

'A thousand pardons,' he pleaded. 'Really I can't tell you how sorry I am, Cynthia. To have made you conspicuous – what was I thinking of? But he maddened me – I –'

'Don't worry, Allan,' said Miss Meyrick gently. 'I like you the better for being maddened.'

Old Spencer Meyrick said nothing, but Minot noted that his face was rather red, and his eyes were somewhat dangerous. They all walked back to the hotel in silence.

From the hotel lobby, as if by prearrangement, Harrowby followed Miss Meyrick and her father into a parlor. Minot and Paddock were left alone.

'My word, old top,' said Mr Paddock facetiously, 'a rough night for the nobility. What do you think? That lad's story sounded like a little bit of all right to me. Eh, what?'

'It did sound convincing,' returned the troubled Minot. 'But then – a servant at Rakedale Hall could have concocted it.'

'Mayhap,' said Mr Paddock. 'However, old Spencer Meyrick looked to me like a volcano I'd want to get out from under. Poor old Harrowby! I'm afraid there's a rift within the loot – nay, no loot at all.'

'Jack,' said Minot firmly, 'that wedding has got to take place.'

'Why, what's it to you?'

'It happens to be everything. But keep it under your hat.'

'Great Scott – does Harrowby owe you money?'

'I can't explain just at present, Jack.'

'Oh, very well,' replied Mr Paddock. 'But take it from me, old man – she's a million times too good for him.'

'A million,' laughed Mr Minot bitterly. 'You underestimate.'

Paddock stood staring with wonder at his friend.

'You lisp in riddles, my boy,' he said.

'Do I?' returned Minot. 'Maybe some day I'll make it all clear.'

He parted from Paddock and ascended to the third floor. As he wandered through the dark passageways in search of his room, he bumped suddenly into a heavy man, walking softly. Something about the contour of the man in the dark gave him a suggestion.

'Good evening, Mr Wall,' he said.

The scurry of hurrying footsteps, but no answer. Minot went on to 389, and placed his key in the lock. It would not turn. He twisted the knob of the door – it was unlocked. He stepped inside and flashed on the light.

His small abode was in a mad disorder. The chiffonier drawers had been emptied on the floor, the bed was torn to pieces, the rug thrown in a corner. Minot smiled to himself.

Someone had been searching – searching for Chain Lightning's Collar. Who? Who but the man he had bumped against in that dark passageway?

Chapter IX
'Wanted: Board And Room'

As Dick Minot bent over to pick up his scattered property, a knock sounded on the half-open door, and Lord Harrowby drooped in. The nobleman was gloom personified. He threw himself despondently down on the bed.

'Minot, old chap,' he drawled, 'it's all over.' His eyes took in the wreckage. 'Eh? What the deuce have you been doing, old boy?'

'I haven't been doing anything,' Minot answered. 'But others have been busy. While we were at the – er – theater, fond fingers have been searching for Chain Lightning's Collar.'

'The devil! You haven't lost it?'

'No – not yet, I believe.' Minot took the envelope from his pocket and drew out the gleaming necklace. 'Ah, it's still safe –'

Harrowby leaped from the bed and slammed shut the door.

'Dear old boy,' he cried, 'keep the accursed thing in your pocket. No one must see it. I say, who's been searching here? Do you think it could have been O'Malley?'

'What is O'Malley's interest in your necklace?'

'Some other time, please. Sorry to inconvenience you with the thing. Do hang on to it, won't you? Awful mix-up if you didn't. Bad mix-up as it is. As I said when I came in, it's all over.'

'What's all over?'

'Everything. The marriage – my chance for happiness – Minot, I'm a most unlucky chap. Meyrick has just postponed the wedding in a frightfully loud tone of voice.'

'Postponed it?' Sad news for Jephson this, yet as he spoke Mr Minot felt a thrill of joy in his heart. He smiled the pleasantest smile he had so far shown San Marco.

'Exactly. He was fearfully rattled, was Meyrick. My word, how he did go on. Considers his daughter humiliated by the antics of that creature we saw on the stage tonight. Can't say I blame him, either. The wedding is indefinitely postponed, unless that impostor is removed from the scene immediately.'

'Oh – unless,' said Minot. His heart sank. His smile vanished.

'Unless was the word, I fancy,' said Harrowby, blinking wisely.

'Lord Harrowby,' Minot began, 'you intimated the other day that this man might really be your brother –'

'No,' Harrowby broke in. 'Impossible. I got a good look at the chap tonight. He's no more a Harrowby than you are.'

'You give me your word for that?'

'Absolutely. Even after twenty years of America no Harrowby would drag his father's name on to the vaudeville stage. No, he is an impostor, and as such he deserves no consideration whatever. And by the by, Minot – you will note that the postponement is through no fault of mine.'

Minot made a wry face.

'I have noted it,' he said. 'In other words, I go on to the stage now – following the man who followed the trained seals. I thought my role was that of Cupid, but it begins to look more like Captain Kidd. Ah, well – I'll do my best.' He stood up. 'I'm going out into the soft moonlight for a little while, Lord Harrowby. While I'm gone you might call Spencer Meyrick up and ask him to do nothing definite in the way of postponement until he hears from me – us – er – you.'

'Splendid of you, really,' said Harrowby enthusiastically, as Minot held open the door for him. 'I had the feeling I could fall back on you.'

'And I have the feeling that you've fallen,' smiled Minot. 'So long – better wait up for my report.'

Fifteen minutes later, seated in a small rowboat on the starry waters of the harbor, Minot was loudly saluting the yacht *Lileth*. Finally Mr Martin Wall appeared at the rail.

'Well – what d'you want?' he demanded.

'A word with you, Mr Wall,' Minot answered. 'Will you be good enough to let down your accommodation ladder?'

For a moment Wall hesitated. And Minot, watching him, knew why he hesitated. He suspected that the young man in the tiny boat there on the calm bright waters had come to repay a call earlier in the evening – a call made while the host was out. At last he decided to let down the ladder.

'Glad to see you,' he announced genially as Minot came on deck.

'Awfully nice of you to say that,' Minot laughed. 'Reassures me. Because I've heard there are sharks in these waters.'

They sat down in wicker chairs on the forward deck. Minot stared at the cluster of lights that was San Marco by night.

'Corking view you have of that tourist-haunted town,' he commented.

'Ah – yes,' Mr Wall's queer eyes narrowed. 'Did you row out here to tell me that?' he inquired.

'A deserved rebuke,' Minot returned. 'Time flies and my errand is a pressing one. Am I right in assuming, Mr Wall, that you are Lord Harrowby's friend?'

'I am.'

'Good. Then you will want to help him in the very serious difficulty in which he now finds himself. Mr Wall, the man who calls himself the real Lord Harrowby made his debut on a vaudeville stage tonight.'

'So I've heard,' said Wall, with a short laugh.

'Lord Harrowby's fiancée and her father are greatly disturbed. They insist that this impostor must be removed from the scene at once, or there will be no wedding. Mr Wall – it is up to you and me to remove him –'

'Just what is your interest in the matter?' Wall inquired.

'The same as yours. I am Harrowby's friend. Now, Mr Wall, this is the situation as I see it – wanted, board and room in a quiet neighborhood for Mr George Harrowby. Far from the street-cars, the vaudeville stage, the wedding march and other disturbing elements. And what is more, I think I've found the quiet neighborhood. I think it's right here aboard the *Lileth*.'

'Oh – indeed!'

'Yes. A simple affair to arrange, Mr Wall. Trimmer and his live proposition are just about due for their final appearance of the night at the opera house right now. I will call at the stage door and lead Mr Trimmer away after his little introductory speech. I will keep him away until you and a couple of your sailors – I suggest the two I met so informally in the North River – have met the vaudeville lord at the stage door and gently, but firmly, persuaded him to come aboard this boat.'

Mr Wall regarded Minot with a cynical smile.

'A clever scheme,' he said. 'What would you say was the penalty for kidnaping in this state?'

'Oh, why look it up?' asked Minot carelessly. 'Surely Martin Wall is not afraid of a backwoods constable.'

'What do you mean by that, my boy?' said Wall, with an ugly stare.

'What do you think I mean?' Minot smiled back. 'I'd be very glad to take the role I've assigned you – I can't help feeling that it will be more entertaining than the one I have. The difficulty in the way is Trimmer. I believe I am better fitted to engage his attention. I know him better than you do, and he trusts me – begging your pardon – further.'

'He did give me a nasty dig,' said Wall, flaming at the recollection. 'The noisy mountebank! Well, my boy, your young enthusiasm has won me. I'll do what I can.'

'And you can do a lot. Watch me until you see me lead Trimmer away. Then get his pet. I'll steer Trimmer somewhere near the beach, and keep an eye on the *Lileth*. When you get George safely aboard, wave a red light in the bow. Then Trimmer and I shall part company for the night.'

'I'm on,' said Wall, rising. 'Anything to help Harrowby. And – this won't be the first time I've waited at the stage door.'

'Right-o,' said Minot. 'But don't stop to buy a champagne supper for a trained seal, will you? I don't want to have to listen to Mr Trimmer all night.'

They rowed ashore in company with two husky members of the yacht's crew, and ten minutes later Minot was walking with the pompous Mr Trimmer through the quiet plaza. He had told that gentleman that he came from Allan Harrowby to talk terms, and Trimmer was puffed with pride accordingly.

'So Mr Harrowby has come to his senses at last,' he said. 'Well, I thought this vaudeville business would bring him round. Although I must say I'm a bit disappointed – down in my heart. My publicity campaign has hardly started. I had so many lovely little plans for the future – say, it makes me sad to win so soon.'

'Sorry,' laughed Minot. 'Lord Harrowby, however, deems it best to call a halt. He sug–'

'Pardon me,' interrupted Mr Trimmer grandiloquently. 'As the victor in the contest, I shall do any suggesting that is done. And what I suggest is this – tomorrow morning I shall call upon Allan Harrowby at his hotel. I shall bring George with me, also some newspaper friends of mine. In front of the crowd Allan Harrowby must acknowledge his brother as the future heir to the earldom of Raybrook.'

'Why the newspaper men?' Minot inquired.

'Publicity,' said Trimmer. 'It's the breath of life to me – my business, my first love, my last. Frankly, I want all the advertisement out of this thing I can get. At what hour shall we call?'

'You would not consider a delay of a few days?' Minot asked.

'Save your breath,' advised Trimmer promptly.

'Ah – I feared it,' laughed Minot. 'Well then – shall we say eleven o'clock? You are to call – with George Harrowby.'

'Eleven it is,' said Trimmer. They had reached a little park by the harbor's edge. Trimmer looked at his watch. 'And that being all settled, I'll run back to the theater.'

'I myself have advised Harrowby to surrender –' Minot began.

'Wise boy. Goodnight,' said Trimmer, moving away.

'Not that I have been particularly impressed by your standing as a publicity man,' continued Minot.

Mr Trimmer stopped in his tracks.

'As a matter of fact,' went on Minot, 'I never heard of you or any of the things you claim to have advertised, until I came to San Marco.'

Mr Trimmer came slowly back up the gravel walk.

'In just what inland hamlet, untouched by telegraph, telephone, newspaper and railroad,' he asked, 'have you been living?'

Minot dropped to a handy bench, and smiled up into Mr Trimmer's thin face.

'New York City,' he replied.

Mr Trimmer glanced back at the lights of San Marco, hesitatingly. Then – it was really a cruel temptation – he sat down beside Minot on the bench.

'Do you mean to tell me,' he inquired, 'that you lived in New York two years ago and didn't hear of Cotrell's Ink Eraser?'

'Such was my unhappy fate,' smiled Minot.

'Then you were in Ludlow Street jail, that's all I've got to say,' Trimmer replied. 'Why, man – what I did for that eraser is famous. I rigged up a big electric sign in Times Square and all night long I had an electric Cotrell's erasing indiscreet sentences – the kind of things people write when they get foolish with their fountain pens – for instance – "I hereby deed to Tottie Footlights all my real and personal property" – and the like. It took the town by storm. Theatrical managers complained that people preferred to stand and look at my sign rather than visit the shows. Can you look me in the eye and say that you never saw that sign?'

'Well,' Minot answered, 'I begin to remember a little about it now.'

'Of course you do.' Mr Trimmer gave him a congratulatory slap on the knee. 'And if you think hard, probably you can recall my neat little stunt of the prima donna and the cough drops. I want to tell you about that –'

He spoke with fervor. The story of his brave deeds rose high to shatter the stars apart. A half-hour passed while his picturesque reminiscences flowed on. Mr Minot sat enraptured, his eyes on the harbor where the *Lileth*, like a painted ship, graced a painted ocean.

'My boy,' Trimmer was saying, 'I have made the public stop, look and listen. When I get my last publicity in the shape of an "In Memoriam" let them run that tag on my headstone. And the story of me that I guess will be told longest after I am gone, is the one about the grape juice that I –'

He paused. His audience was not listening; he felt it intuitively. Mr Minot sat with his eyes on the *Lileth*. In the bow of that handsome boat a red light had been waved three times.

'Mr Trimmer,' Minot said, 'your tales are more interesting than the classics.' He stood. 'Some other time I hope to hear a continuation of them. Just at present Lord Harrowby – or Mr if you prefer – is waiting to hear what arrangement I have made with you – You must pardon me.'

'I can talk as we walk along,' said Trimmer, and proved it. In the middle of the deserted plaza they separated. At the dark stage door of the opera house Trimmer sought his proposition.

'Who d'yer mean?' asked the lone stagehand there.

'George, Lord Harrowby,' insisted Mr Trimmer.

'Oh – that bum actor. Seen him going away a while back with two men that called for him.'

'Bum actor!' cried Trimmer indignantly. He stopped. 'Two men – who were they?'

The stagehand asked profanely how he could know that, and Mr Trimmer hurriedly departed for the side-street boarding house where he and his fallen nobleman shared a suite.

About the same time Dick Minot blithely entered Lord Harrowby's apartments in the Hotel de la Pax.

'Well,' he announced, 'you can cheer up. Little George is painlessly removed. He sleeps tonight aboard the good ship *Lileth*, thanks to the efforts of Martin Wall, assisted by yours truly.' He stopped, and stared in awe at his lordship. 'What's the matter with you?' he inquired.

Harrowby waved a hopeless hand.

'Minot,' he said, 'it was good of you. But while you have been assisting me so kindly in that quarter, another – and a greater – blow has fallen.'

'Good lord – what?' cried Minot.

'It is no fault of mine –' Harrowby began.

'On which I would have gambled my immortal soul,' Minot said.

'I thought it was all over and done with – five years ago. I was young – sentimental – calcium light and grease paint and that sort of thing hit me hard. I saw her from the stalls – fell desperately in love – stayed so for six months – wrote letters – burning letters – and now –'

'Yes – and now?'

'Now she's here. Gabrielle Rose is here. She's here – with the letters.'

'Oh, for a Cotrell's Ink Eraser,' Minot groaned.

'My man saw her downstairs,' went on Harrowby, mopping his damp forehead. 'Fifty thousand she wants for the letters or she gives them to a newspaper and begins to sue – at once – tomorrow.'

'I suppose,' said Minot, 'she is the usual Gaiety girl.'

'Not the usual, old chap. Quite a remarkable woman. She'll do what she promises – trust her. And I haven't a farthing. Minot – it's all up now. There's no way out of this.'

Minot sat thinking. The telephone rang.

'I won't talk to her,' cried Harrowby in a panic. 'I won't have anything to do with her. Minot, old chap – as a favor to me –'

'The old family solicitor,' smiled Minot. 'That's me.'

He took down the receiver. But no voice that had charmed thousands at the Gaiety answered his. Instead there came over the wire, heated, raging, the tones of Mr Henry Trimmer.

'Hello – I want Allan Harrowby – ah, that's Minot talking, isn't it? Yes. Good. I want a word with you. Do you know what I think of your methods? Well, you won't now – telephone rules in the way. Think you're going to get ahead of Trimmer, do you? Think you've put one over, eh? Well – let me tell you, you're wrong. You're in for it now. You've played into my hands. Steal Lord Harrowby, will you? Do you know what that means? Publicity. Do you know what I'll do tomorrow? I'll start a cyclone in this town that –'

'Goodnight,' said Minot, and hung up.

'Who was it?' Harrowby wanted to know.

'Our friend Trimmer, on the warpath,' Minot replied. 'It seems he's missed his vaudeville partner.' He sat down. 'See here, Harrowby,' he said – it was the first time he had dropped the prefix, 'it occurs to me that an unholy lot of things are happening to spoil this wedding. So I'm going to ask you a question.'

'Yes.'

'Harrowby' – Minot looked straight into the weak, but noble eyes – 'are you on the level?'

'Really – I'm not very expert in your astounding language –'

'Are you straight – honest – do you want to be married yourself?'

'Why, Minot, my dear chap! I've told you a thousand times – I want nothing more – I never shall want anything more –'

'All right,' said Minot, rising. 'Then go to bed and sleep the sleep of the innocent.'

'But where are you going? What are you going to do?'

'I'm going to try and do the same.'

And as he went out, Minot slammed the door on a peer.

Sticking above the knob of the door of 389 he found a telegram. Turning on his lights, he sank wearily down on the bed and tore it open.

'It rained in torrents,' said the telegram, 'at the dowager duchess's garden party. You know what that means.'

It was signed 'John Thacker'.

'Isn't that a devil of a night-cap?' muttered Minot gloomily.

Chapter X
Two Birds of Passage

On the same busy night when the *Lileth* flashed her red signal and Miss Gabrielle Rose arrived with a package of letters that screamed for a Cotrell, two strangers invaded San Marco by means of the eight-nineteen freight south. Frayed, fatigued and famished as they were, it would hardly have been kind to study them as they strolled up San Sebastian Avenue toward the plaza. But had you been so unkind, you would never have guessed that frequently, in various corners of the little round globe, they had known prosperity, the weekly pay envelope, and the buyer's crook of the finger summoning a waiter.

One of the strangers was short, with flaming red hair and in his eye the twinkle without which the collected works of Bernard Shaw are as sounding brass. He twinkled about him as he walked – at the bright lights and spurious gaiety under the spell of which San Marco sought to forget the rates per day with bath.

'The French,' he mused, 'are a volatile people, fond of light wines and dancing. So, it would seem, are the inhabitants of San Marco. White flannels, Harry, white flannels. They should encase that leaning tower of Pisa you call your manly form.'

The other – long, cadaverous, immersed in a gentle melancholy – groaned.

'Another tourist hothouse! Packed with innocents abroad, and everybody bleeding 'em but us. Everything here but a real home, with chintz table-covers and a cold roast of beef in the ice chest. What are we doing here? We should have gone north.'

'Ah, Harry, chide me no more,' pleaded the little man. 'I was weak, I know, but all the freights seemed to be coming south, and I have always longed for a winter amid the sunshine and flowers. Look at this fat old duffer coming! Alms! For the love of Allah, alms!'

'Shut up!' growled the thin one. 'Save your breath till we stand hat in hand in the office of the local newspaper. A job! Two jobs! Good lord, there aren't two newspaper jobs in the entire South. Well – we can only be kicked out into the night again. And perhaps staked to a meal, in the name of the guild in which we have served so long and liquidly.'

'Some day,' said the short man dreamily, 'when I am back in the haunts of civilization again, I am going to start something. A Society for Melting the Stone Hearts of Editors. Motto: 'Have a heart – have a heart!' Emblem, a roast beef sandwich rampant, on a cloth of linen. Ah, well – the day will come.'

They halted in the plaza. In the round stone tub provided, the town alligator dozed. Above him hung a warning sign:

Do not feed or otherwise annoy the alligator.

The short man read, and drew back with a tragic groan.

'Feed or otherwise annoy!' he cried. 'Heavens, Harry, is that the way they look at it here? This is no place for us. We'd better be moving on to the next town.'

But the lean stranger gave no heed. Instead he stepped over and entered into earnest converse with a citizen of San Marco. In a moment he returned to his companion's side.

'One newspaper,' he announced. '*The Evening Chronicle.* Suppose the office is locked for the night – but come along, let's try.'

'Feed or otherwise annoy,' muttered the little man blankly. 'For the love of Allah – alms!'

They traversed several side streets, and came at last to the office of the *Chronicle.* It was a modest structure, verging on decay. One man sat alone in the dim interior, reading exchanges under an electric lamp.

'Good evening,' said the short man genially. 'Are you the editor?'

'Uh, huh,' responded the *Chronicle* man without enthusiasm, from under his green eye-shade.

'Glad to know you. We just dropped in – a couple of newspaper men, you know. This is Mr Harry Howe, until recently managing editor of the Mobile Press. My own name is Robert O'Neill – a humble editorial writer on the same sheet.'

'Uh, huh. If you had jobs for God's sake why did you leave them?'

'Ah, you may well ask,' The red-haired one dropped, uninvited, into a chair. 'Old man, it's a dramatic story. The chief of police of Mobile happened to be a crook and a grafter, and we happened to mention it in the Press. Night before last twenty-five armed cops invaded the peace and sanctity of our sanctum. Harry and I – pure accident – landed in the same general heap at the foot of the fire escape out back. And here we are! Here we are!'

'My newspaper instinct,' said the *Chronicle* man, 'had already enabled me to gather that last.'

Sarcasm. It was a bad sign. But blithely Bob O'Neill continued.

'Here we are,' he said, 'two experienced newspaper men, down and out. We thought there might possibly be a vacancy or two on the staff of your paper –'

The editor threw off his eye-shade, revealing a cynical face.

'Boys,' he said, 'I thank you, from the bottom of my heart. I've been running this alleged newspaper for two long dreary years, and this laugh you've just handed me is the first I've had during that time. Vacancies! There is one – a big one. See my pocket for particulars. Two years, boys. And all the time hoping – praying – that some day I'd make two dollars and sixty cents, which is the railroad fare to the next town.'

Howe and O'Neill listened with faces that steadily grew more sorrowful.

'I'd like to stake you to a meal,' the editor went on. 'But a man's first duty is to his family. Any burglar will tell you that.'

'I suppose,' ventured O'Neill, most of the flash gone from his manner, 'there is no other newspaper here?'

'No, there isn't. There's a weird thing here called the *San Marco Mail* – a morning outrage. It's making money, but by different methods than I'd care to use. You might try there. You look unlucky. Perhaps they'd take you on.'

He rose from his chair, and gave them directions for reaching the *Mail* office.

'Good night, boys,' he said. 'Thank you for calling. You're the first newspaper men I've seen in two years, except when I've looked in the glass. And the other day I broke my looking glass. Goodnight, and bad luck go with you to the extent of jobs on the *Mail*.'

'Cynic,' breathed O'Neill in the street. 'A bitter tongue makcth a sour face. I liked him not. A morning outrage called the *Mail*. Sounds promising – like smallpox in the next county.'

'We shall see,' said Howe, 'that which meets our vision. Forward, march!'

'The alligator and I,' muttered O'Neill, 'famished, perishing. For the love of Allah, as I remarked before, alms!'

In the dark second-floor hallway where the *Mail* office was suspected of being, they groped about determinedly. No sign of any nature proclaimed San Marco's only morning paper. A solitary light, shining through a transom, beckoned. Boldly O'Neill pushed open the door.

To the knowing nostrils of the two birds of passage was wafted the odor they loved, the unique inky odor of a newspaper shop. Their eyes beheld a rather bare room, a typewriter or two, a desk. In the center of the room was a small table under an electric lamp. On this table was a bottle and glasses, and at it two silent men played poker. One of the men was burly and bearded; the other was slight, pale, nervous. From an inner room came the click of linotypes – lonesome linotypes that seemed to have strayed far from their native haunts.

The two men finished playing the hand, and looked up.

'Good evening,' said O'Neill, with a smile that had drawn news as a magnet draws steel in many odd corners. 'Gentlemen, four newspaper men meet in a strange land. I perceive you have on the table a greeting unquestionably suitable.'

The bearded man laughed, rose and discovered two extra glasses on a nearby shelf.

'Draw up,' he said heartily. 'The place is yours. You're as welcome as pay-day.'

'Thanks.' O'Neill reached for a glass. 'Let me introduce ourselves.' And he mentioned his own name and Howe's.

'Call me Mears,' said the bearded one. 'I'm managing editor of the *Mail*. And this is my city editor, Mr Elliott.'

'Delighted,' breathed O'Neill. 'A pleasant little haven you have found here. And your staff – I don't see the members of your staff running in and out?'

'Mr O'Neill,' said Mears impressively, 'you have drunk with the staff of the Mail!'

'You two?' O'Neill's face shone with joy. 'Glory be – do you hear that, Harry? These gentlemen all alone on the premises.' He leaned over, and poured out eloquently the story of the tragic flight from Mobile. 'I call this luck,' he finished. 'Here we are, broke, eager for work. And we find you minus a –'

O'Neill stopped. For he had seen a sickly smile of derision float across the face of the weary city editor. And he saw the bearded man shaking his great head violently.

'Nothing doing,' said the bearded man firmly. 'Sorry to dash your hopes – always ready to pour another drink. But – there are no vacancies here. No, sir. Two of us are plenty and running over, eh, Bill?'

'Plenty and running over,' agreed the city editor warmly.

Into their boots tumbled the hearts of the two strangers in a strange land. Gloom and hunger engulfed them. But the managing editor of the *Mail* was continuing – and what was this he was saying?

'No, boys – we don't need a staff. Have just as much use for a manicure set. But – you come at an opportune time. Wanderlust – it tickles the soles of four feet tonight, and those four feet are editorial feet on the *Mail*. Something tells us that we are going away from here. Boys – how would you like our jobs?'

He stared placidly at the two strangers. O'Neill put one hand to his head.

'See me safely to my park bench, Harry,' he said. 'It was that drink on an empty stomach. I'm all in a daze. I hear strange things.'

'I hear 'em, too,' said Howe. 'See here' – he turned to Mears – 'are you offering to resign in our favor?'

'The minute you say the word.'

'Both of you?'

'Believe me,' said the city editor, 'you can't say the word too soon.'

'Well,' said Howe, 'I don't know what's the matter with the place, but you can consider the deal closed.'

'Spoken like a sport!' The bearded man stood up. 'You can draw lots to determine who is to be managing editor and who city editor. It's an excellent scheme – I attained my proud position that way. One condition I attach. Ask no questions. Let us go out into the night unburdened with your interrogation points.'

Elliott, too, stood. The bearded man indicated the bottle. 'Fill up, boys. I propose a toast. To the new editors of the *Mail*. May Heaven bless them and bring them safely back to the North when Florida's fitful fever is past.'

Dizzily, uncertainly, Howe and O'Neill drank.

Mr Mears reached out a great red hand toward the bottle.

'Pardon me – private property,' he said. He pocketed it. 'We bid you goodbye and good luck. Think of us on the choo-choo, please. Riding far – riding far.'

'But – see here –' cried O'Neill.

'But me no buts,' said Mears again. 'Nary a question, I beg of you. Take our jobs, and if you think of us at all, think of gleaming rails and a speeding train. Once more – goodbye.'

The door slammed. O'Neill looked at Howe.

'Fairies,' he muttered, 'or the D.T.s. What is this – a comic opera or a town? You are managing editor, Harry. I shall be city editor. Is there a city to edit? No matter.'

'No,' said Howe. He reached for the greasy pack of cards. 'We draw for it. Come on. High wins.'

'Jack,' announced Mr O'Neill.

'Deuce,' smiled Howe. 'What are your orders, sir?'

O'Neill passed one hand before his eyes.

'A steak,' he muttered. 'Well done. Mushroom sauce. French fried potatoes. I've always dreamed of running a paper some day. Hurry up with that steak.'

'Forget your stomach,' said Howe. 'If a subordinate may make a suggestion, we must get out a newspaper. Ah, whom have we here?'

A stocky, red-faced man appeared from the inner room and stood regarding them.

'Where's Mears and Elliott?' he demanded.

'On a train, riding far,' said O'Neill. 'I am the new managing editor. What can I do for you?'

'You can give me four columns of copy for the last page of tomorrow's *Mail*,' said the stocky man calmly. 'I'm foreman of something in there we call a composing-room. Glad to meet you.'

'Four columns,' mused O'Neill. 'Four columns of what?'

The foreman pointed to a row of battered books on a shelf.

'It's been the custom,' he said, 'to fill up with stuff out of that encyclopedia there.'

'Thanks,' O'Neill answered. He took down a book. 'We'll fix you up in ten minutes. Mr Howe, will you please do me two columns on – er – mulligatawny – murder – mushrooms. That's it. On mushrooms. The life story of the humble little mushroom. I myself will dash off a column or so on the climate of Algeria.'

The foreman withdrew, and Howe and O'Neill stood looking at each other.

'Once,' said O'Neill, 'I ran an editorial page in Boston, where you can always fill space by printing letters from citizens who wish to rewrite Lincoln's Gettysburg Address, and do it right. But I never struck anything like this before.'

'Me either,' said Howe. 'Mushrooms, did you say?'

They sat down before typewriters.

'One thing worries me,' remarked O'Neill. 'If we'd asked the president of the First National Bank for jobs, do you suppose we'd be in charge there now?'

'Write, man, write,' said Howe. The clatter of their fingers on the keys filled the room.

They looked up suddenly ten minutes later to find a man standing between them. He was a little man, clad all in white, suit, shoes, stockings. His sly old face was a lemon yellow, and his eyes suggested lights flaming in the dark woods at night.

'Beg pardon,' said the little man.

'Ah, and what can we do for you?' inquired O'Neill.

'Nothing. Mr Mears? Mr Elliott?'

'Gone. Vamosed. You are now speaking to the managing editor of the Mail.'

'Ah. Indeed?'

'We are very busy. If you'll just tell me what you want –'

'I merely dropped in. I am Manuel Gonzale, owner of the *Mail*.'

'Good lord!' cried O'Neill.

'Do not be disturbed. I take it you gentlemen have replaced Mears and Elliott. I am glad. Let them go. You look like bright young men to me – quite bright enough. I employ you.'

'Thanks,' stammered the managing editor.

'Don't mention it. Here is Madame On Dit's column for tomorrow. It runs on the first page. As for the rest of the paper, suit yourselves.'

O'Neill took the copy, and glanced through it.

'Are there no libel laws down here?' he asked.

'The material in that column,' said the little man, his eyes narrowing, 'concerns only me. You must understand that at once.'

'The Madame writes hot stuff,' ventured O'Neill.

'I am the Madame,' said the owner of the *Mail* with dignity.

He removed the copy from O'Neill's hand, and glided with it into the other room. Scarcely had he disappeared when the door was opened furiously and a panting man stood inside. Mr Henry Trimmer's keen eye surveyed the scene.

'Where's Mears – Elliott?' he cried.

'You're not the cashier, are you?' asked O'Neill with interest.

'Don't try to be funny,' roared Trimmer. 'I'm looking for the editor of this paper.'

'Your search is ended,' O'Neill replied. 'What is it?'

'You mean you – Say! I've got a front-page story for tomorrow's issue that will upset the town.'

'Come to my arms,' cried O'Neill. 'What is it?'

'The real Lord Harrowby has been kidnaped.'

O'Neill stared at him sorrowfully.

'Have you been reading the Duchess again? he asked. 'Who the hell is Lord Harrowby?'

'Do you mean to say you don't know? Where have you been buried alive?'

Out of the inner room glided Manuel Gonzale, and recognizing him, Mr Trimmer poured into his ear the story of George's disappearance. Mr Gonzale rubbed his hands.

'A good story,' he said. 'A very good story. Thank you, a thousand times. I myself will write it.'

With a scornful glance at the two strangers, Mr Trimmer went out, and Manuel Gonzale sat down at his desk. O'Neill and Howe returned to their encyclopedic despatches.

'There you are,' said Gonzale at last, standing. 'Put an eight column head on that, please, and run it on the front page. A very fine story. The paper must go to press' – he looked at a diamond studded watch – 'in an hour. Only four pages. Please see to the make-up. My circulation manager will assist you with the distribution.' At the door he paused. 'It occurs to me that your exchequer may be low. Seventy-five dollars a week for the managing editor. Fifty for the city editor. Allow me – ten dollars each in advance. If you need more, pray remind me.'

Into their hands he put crinkling bills. And then, gliding still like the fox he looked, he went out into the night.

'Sister,' cried O'Neill weakly, 'the fairies are abroad tonight. I hear the rustle of their feet over the grass.'

'Fairies,' sneered Howe. 'I could find another and a harsher name for them.'

'Don't,' pleaded O'Neill. 'Don't look a gift bill in the treasury number. Don't try to penetrate behind the beyond. Say nothing and let us eat. How are you coming with the mushroom serial?'

An hour later they sent the paper to press, and sought the grill room of the Hotel Alameda. As they came happily away from that pleasant spot, O'Neill spied a fruit-stand. He stopped and made a few purchases.

'Now,' said Howe, 'let us go over and meet the circulation manager. Here – where are you going, Bob?'

'Just a minute,' O'Neill shouted back. 'Come along, Harry. I'm going over to the plaza! I'm going over to feed that alligator!'

Chapter XI
Tears from The Gaiety

Friday morning found Mr Minot ready for whatever diplomacy the day might demand of him. He had a feeling that the demand would be great. The unheralded arrival of Miss Gabrielle Rose and her packet of letters presented no slight complication. Whatever the outcome of any suit she might start against Harrowby, Minot was sure that the mere announcement of it would be sufficient to blast Jephson's hopes for all time. Old Spencer Meyrick, already inflamed by the episode of the elder brother, was not likely to take coolly the publication of Harrowby's incriminating letters.

After an early breakfast, Minot sent a cable to Jephson telling of Miss Rose's arrival and asking for information about her. Next he sought an interview with the Gaiety lady.

An hour later, in a pink and gold parlor of the Hotel de la Pax, he stood gazing into the china-blue eyes of Miss Gabrielle Rose. It goes without saying that Miss Rose was pretty; innocent she seemed, too, with a baby stare that said as plainly as words: 'Please don't harm me, will you?' But – ah, well, Lord Harrowby was not the first to learn that a business woman may lurk back of a baby stare.

'You come from Lord Harrowby?' And the smile that had decorated ten million postcards throughout the United Kingdom flashed on Mr Minot. 'Won't you sit down?'

'Thanks.' Minot fidgeted. He had no idea what to say. Time – it was time he must fight for, as he was fighting with Trimmer. 'Er – Miss Rose,' he began, 'when I started out on this errand I had misgivings. But now that I have seen you, they are gone. Everything will be all right, I know. I have come to ask that you show Lord Harrowby some leniency.'

The china-blue eyes hardened.

'You have come on a hopeless errand, Mr – er – Minot. Why should I show Harrowby any consideration? Did he show me any – when he broke his word to me and made me the laughing stock of the town?'

'But that all happened five years ago –'

'Yes, but it is as vivid as though it were yesterday. I have always intended to demand some redress from his lordship. But my art – Mr – Mr Minot – you have no idea how exacting art can be. Not until now have I been in a position to do so.'

'And the fact that not until now has his lordship proposed to marry someone else – that of course has nothing to do with it?'

'Mr Minot!' A delightful pout. 'If you knew me better you could not possibly ask that.'

'Miss Rose, you're a clever woman –'

'Oh, please don't. I hate clever women, and I'm sure you do, too. I'm not a bit clever, and I'm proud of it. On the contrary, I'm rather weak – rather easily got round. But when I think of the position Allan put me in – even a weak woman can be firm in the circumstances.'

'Have it your own way,' said Minot, bowing. 'But you are at least clever enough to understand the futility of demanding financial redress from a man who is flat broke. I assure you Lord Harrowby hasn't a shilling.'

'I don't believe it. He can get money somehow. He always could. The courts can force him to. I shall tell my lawyer to go ahead with the suit.'

'If you would only delay – a week –'

'Impossible.' Miss Rose spoke with haughty languor. 'I begin rehearsals in New York in a week. No, I shall start suit today. You may tell Lord Harrowby so.'

Poor Jephson! Minot had a mental picture of the little bald man writing at that very moment a terribly large check for the Dowager Duchess of Tremayne – paying for the rain that had fallen in torrents. He must at least hold this woman off until Jephson answered his cable.

'Miss Rose,' he pleaded, 'grant us one favor. Do not make public your suit against Harrowby until I have seen you again – say, at four o'clock this afternoon.'

Coldly she shook her head.

'But you have already waited five years. Surely you can wait another five hours – as a very great favor to me?'

'I should like to – since you put it that way – but it's impossible. I'm sorry.' The great beauty and business woman leaned closer. 'Mr Minot, you can hardly realize what Allan's unkindness cost me – in bitter tears. I loved him – once. And – I believe he loved me.'

'There can not be any question about that.'

'Ah – flattery –'

'No – spoken from the heart.'

'Really!'

'My dear lady – I should like to be your press agent. I could write the most gorgeous things about you – and no one could say I lied.'

'You men are so nice,' she gurgled, 'when you want to be.' Ah, yes, Gabrielle Rose had always found them so, and had yet to meet one not worth her while to capture. She turned the baby stare full on Minot. Even to a beauty of the theater he was an ingratiating picture. She rose and strolled to a piano in one corner of the room. Minot followed.

'When Harrowby first met me,' she said, her fingers on the keys, 'I was singing *Just a Little*. My first dear song – ah, Mr Minot, I was happy then.'

In another minute she began to sing – softly – a plaintive little love song, and in spite of himself Minot felt his heart beat faster.

'How it brings back the old days,' she whispered. 'The lights, and the friendly faces – Harrowby in the stalls. And the little suppers after the show –'

She leaned forward and sang at Minot as she had sung at Harrowby five years before:

You could love me just a little – if you tried –
You could feel your heart go pit-a-pat inside –

Really, she had a way with her!

Dear, it's easy if you try;
Cross your heart and hope to die –
Don't you love me just a little – now?

That baby stare in all its pathos, all its appealing helplessness, was focused full on Minot.

He gripped the arms of his chair. Gabrielle Rose saw. Had she made another captive? So it seemed. She felt very kindly toward the world.

'Promise.' Minot leaned over. His voice was hoarse. 'You'll meet me here at four. Quite aside from my errand – quite aside from everything – I want to see you again.'

'Do you really?' She continued to hum beneath her breath. 'Very well – here at four.'

'And –' he hesitated, fearing to break the spell. 'In the meantime –'

'In the meantime,' she said, 'I'll think only of – four o'clock.'

Minot left that pink and gold parlor at sea in several respects. The theory was that he had played with this famous actress – wound her round his finger – cajoled a delay. But somehow he didn't feel exactly as one who has mastered a delicate situation should. Instead he felt dazed by the beauty of her.

Still more was he at sea as to what he was going to do at four o'clock. Of what good was the delay if he could not make use of it? And at the moment he hadn't the slightest notion of what he could do to prepare himself for the afternoon interview. He must wait for Jephson's cable – perhaps that would give him an idea.

Minot was walking blankly down the street in the direction of his morning paper when a poster in a deserted store window caught his eye. It was an atrocious poster – red letters on a yellow background. It announced that five hundred dollars reward would be paid by Mr Henry Trimmer for information that would disclose the present whereabouts of the real Lord Harrowby.

As Minot stood reading it, a heavy hand was laid upon his shoulder. Turning, he looked into the lean and hostile face of Henry Trimmer himself.

'Good morning,' said Mr Trimmer.

'Good morning,' replied Minot.

'Glad to number you among my readers,' sneered Trimmer. 'What do you think – reward large enough?'

'Looks about the right size to me,' Minot answered.

'Me, too. Ought to bring results pretty quick. By the way, you were complaining last night that you never heard of me until you came here. I've been thinking that over, and I've decided to make up to you in the next few days for all those lonely years –'

But the morning had been too much for Minot. Worried, distressed, he lost for the moment his usual smiling urbanity.

'Oh, go to the devil!' he said, and walked away.

Lunchtime came – two o'clock. At half past two, out of London, Jephson spoke. Said his cable:

Know nothing of G. R. except that she's been married frequently. Do best you can.

And what help was this, pray? Disgustedly Minot read the cable again. Four o'clock was coming on apace, and with every tick of the clock his feeling of helplessness grew. He mentally berated Thacker and Jephson. They left him alone to grapple with wild problems, offering no help and asking miracles. Confound them both!

Three o'clock came. What – what was he to say? Lord Harrowby, interrogated, was merely useless and frantic. He couldn't raise a shilling.

He couldn't offer a suggestion. 'Dear old chap,' he moaned, 'I depend on you.'

Three-thirty! Well, Thacker and Jephson had asked the impossible, that was all. Minot felt he had done his best. No man could do more. He was very sorry for Jephson, but – golden before him opened the possibility of Miss Cynthia Meyrick free to be wooed.

Yet he must be faithful to the last. At a quarter to four he read Jephson's cablegram again. As he read, a plan ridiculous in its ineffectiveness occurred to him. And since no other came in the interval before four, he walked into Miss Rose's presence determined to try out his weak little bluff.

The Gaiety lady was playing on the piano – a whispering, seductive little tune. As Minot stepped to her side she glanced up at him with a coy inviting smile. But she drew back a little at his determined glare.

'Miss Rose,' he said sharply, 'I have discovered that you can not sue Lord Harrowby for breach of contract to marry you,'

'Why – why not?'

'Because,' said Minot, with a triumphant smile – though it was a shot in the dark – 'you already had a husband when those letters were written to you.'

Well, he had done his best. A rather childish effort, but what else was there to attempt? Poor old Jephson!

'Nonsense,' said the Gaiety lady, and continued to play.

'Nothing of the sort,' Minot replied. 'Why, I can produce the man himself.'

Might as well go the limit while he was about it. That should be his consolation when Jephson lost. Might as well – but what was this?

Gabrielle Rose had turned livid with anger. Her lips twitched, her china-blue eyes flashed fire. If only her lawyer had been by her side then! But he wasn't. And so she cried hotly:

'He's told! The little brute's told!'

Good lord! Minot felt his knees weaken. A shot in the dark – had it hit the target after all?

'If you refer to your husband,' said Minot, 'he has done just that.'

'He's not my husband,' she snapped.

Oh, what was the use? Providence was with Jephson.

'No, of course not – not since the divorce,' Minot answered. 'But he was when those letters were written.'

The Gaiety lady's chin began to tremble.

'And he promised me, on his word of honor, that he wouldn't tell. But I suppose you found him easy. What honor could one expect in a Persian carpet dealer?'

A Persian carpet dealer? Into Minot's mind floated a scrap of conversation heard at Mrs Bruce's table.

'But you must remember,' he ventured, 'that he is also a prince.'

'Yes,' said the woman, 'that's what I thought when I married him. He's the prince of liars – that's as far as his royal blood goes.'

A silence, while Miss Gabrielle Rose felt in her sleeve for her handkerchief.

'I suppose,' Minot suggested, 'you will abandon the suit –'

She looked at him. Oh, the pathos of that baby stare!

'You are acting in this matter simply as Harrowby's friend?' she asked.

'Simply as his friend.'

'And – so far — only you know of my – er – ex–husband?'

'Only I know of him,' smiled Minot. The smile died from his face. For he saw bright tears on the long lashes of the Gaiety lady. She leaned close.

'Mr Minot,' she said, 'it is I who need a friend. Not Harrowby. I am here in a strange country – without funds – alone. Helpless. Mr Minot. You could not be so cruel.'

'I – I – I'm sorry,' said Minot uncomfortably.

The lady was an actress, and she acted now, beautifully.

'I – I feel so desolate,' she moaned, dabbing daintily at her eyes. 'You will help me. It can not be I am mistaken in you. I thought – did I imagine it – this morning when I sang for you – you liked me – just a little?'

Nervously Minot rose from his chair and stood looking down at her. He tried to answer, but his voice seemed lost.

'Just a very little?' She, too, rose and placed her butterfly hands on his shoulders. 'You do like me – just a little, don't you?'

Her pleading eyes gazed into his. It was a touching scene. To be besought thus tenderly by a famous beauty in the secluded parlor of a southern hotel! The touch of her hands on his shoulders thrilled him. The odor of Jockey Club –

It was at this instant that Mr Minot, looking past the Gaiety lady's beautiful golden coiffure, beheld Miss Cynthia Meyrick standing in the doorway of that parlor, a smile on her face. She disappeared on the instant, but Gabrielle Rose's 'big scene' was ruined beyond repair.

'My dear lady' – gently Minot slipped from beneath her lovely hands – 'I assure you I do like you – more than a little. But unfortunately my loyalty to Harrowby – no, I won't say that – circumstances are such that I can not be your friend in this instance. Though, if I could serve you in any other way –'

Gabrielle Rose snapped her fingers.

'Very well.' Her voice had a metallic ring now. 'We shall see what we shall see.'

'Undoubtedly. I bid you good day.'

As Minot, somewhat dazed, walked along the veranda of the De la Pax he met Miss Meyrick. There was a mischievous gleam in her eye.

'Really, it was so tactless of me, Mr Minot,' she said. 'A thousand apologies.'

He pretended not to understand.

'My untimely descent on the parlor.' She beamed on him. 'I presume it happened because romance draws me – like a magnet. Even other people's.'

Minot smiled wanly, and for once sought to end their talk.

'Oh, do sit down just a moment,' she pleaded. 'I want to thank you for the great service you did Harrowby and me – last night.'

'Wha – what service?' asked Minot, sinking into a chair.

She leaned close, and spoke in a whisper.

'Your part in the kidnaping. Harrowby has told me. It was sweet of you – so unselfish.'

'Damn!' thought Minot. And then he thought two more.

'To put yourself out that our wedding may be a success!' Was this sarcasm, Minot wondered. 'I'm so glad to know about it, Mr Minot. It shows me at last – just what you think is' – she looked away – 'best for me.'

'Best for you? What do you mean?'

'Can't you understand? From some things you've said I have thought – perhaps – you didn't just approve of my – marriage. And now I see I misconstrued you – utterly. You want me to marry Harrowby. You're working for it. I shouldn't be surprised if you were on that train last Monday just to make sure that – I'd – get here – safely.'

Really, it was inhuman. Did she realize how inhuman it was? One glance at Minot might have told her. But she was still looking away.

'So I want to thank you, Mr Minot,' she went on. 'I shall always remember your – kindness. I couldn't understand at first, but now – I wonder? You know, it's an old theory that as soon as one has one's own affair of the heart arranged, one begins to plan for others?'

Minot made a little whistling sound through his clenched teeth. The girl stood up.

'Your thoughtfulness has made me very happy,' she laughed. 'It shows that perhaps you care for me – just a little too.'

She was gone! Minot sat swearing softly to himself, banging the arm of his chair with his fist. He raged at Thacker, Jephson, the solar system. Gradually his anger cooled. Underneath the raillery in Cynthia Meyrick's tone he had thought he detected something of a serious note – as though she were a little wistful – a little hurt.

Did she care? Bittersweet thought! In the midst of all this farce and melodrama, had she come to care? – just a little? –

Just a little! Bah!

Minot rose and went out on the avenue.

Prince Navin Bey Imno was accustomed to give lectures twice daily on the textures of his precious rugs, at his shop in the Alameda courtyard. His afternoon lecture was just finished as Mr Minot stepped into the shop. A dozen awed housewives from the Middle West were hurrying away to write home on the hotel stationery that they had met a prince. When the last one had gone out Minot stepped forward.

'Prince – I've dropped in to warn you. A very angry woman will be here shortly to see you.'

The handsome young Persian shrugged his shoulders, and took off the jacket of the native uniform with which he embellished his talks.

'Why is she angry? All my rugs – they are what I say they are. In this town are many liars selling oriental rugs. Oriental! Ugh! In New Jersey they were made. But not my rugs. See! Only in my native country, where I was a prince of the –'

'Yes, yes. But this lady is not coming about rugs. I refer to your ex-wife.'

'Ah. You are mistaken. I have never married.'

'Oh, yes, you have. I know all about it. There's no need to lie. The whole story is out, and the lady's game in San Marco is queered. She thinks you told. That's why she'll be here for a chat.'

'But I did not tell. Only this morning did I see her first. I could not tell – so soon. Who could I tell – so soon?'

'I know you didn't tell. But can you prove it to an agitated lady? No. You'd better close up for the evening.'

'Ah, yes – you are right. I am innocent – but what does Gabrielle care for innocence? We are no longer married – still I should not want to meet her now. I will close. But first – my friend – my benefactor – could I interest you in this rug? See! Only in my native country, where –'

'Prince,' said Minot, 'I couldn't use a rug if you gave me one.'

'That is exactly what I would do. You are my friend. You serve me. I give you this. Fifty dollars. That is giving it to you. Note the weave. Only in my –'

'Good night,' interrupted Minot. 'And take my advice. Hurry!'

Gloomy, discouraged, he turned back toward his own hotel. It was true, Gabrielle Rose's husband at the time of the letters was in San Marco. The emissary of Jephson was serving a cause that could not lose. That afternoon he had hoped. Was there anything dishonorable in that? Jephson and Thacker could command his service, they could not command his heart. He had hoped – and now –

At a corner a negro gave him a handbill. He read:

WHO HAS KIDNAPED

THE REAL

LORD HARROWBY?

AT THE OPERA HOUSE TONIGHT!!

Mr Henry Trimmer Will Appear in Place of His Unfortunate
Friend, Lord Harrowby, and Will Make a Few

WARM AND SIZZLING

REMARKS.

NO ADVANCE IN PRICES.

Mr Minot tossed the bill into the street. Into his eyes came the
ghostlike semblance of a smile. After all, the famous Harrowby
wedding had not yet taken place.

Chapter XII
Exit a Lady, Laughingly

After dinner Minot lighted a cigar and descended into the hotel gardens for a stroll.

Farther and farther he strayed down the shadowy gravel paths, until only the faint far suggestion of music at his back recalled the hotel's lights and gaiety. It was a deserted land he penetrated; just one figure did he encounter in a fifteen minutes' walk – a little man clad all in white scurrying like a wraith in the black shade of the royal palms.

At a distant corner of the grounds near the tennis courts was a summerhouse in which tea was served of an afternoon. Into this Minot strolled, to finish his cigar and ponder the day's developments in the drama he was playing. As he drew a comfortable chair from moonlight into shadow he heard a little gasp at his elbow, and turning, beheld a beautiful vision.

Gabrielle Rose was made for the spotlight, and that being absent, moonlight served as well. Under its soft merciful rays she stood revealed – the beauty thousands of playgoers knew and worshiped. Dick Minot gazed at her in awe. He was surprised that she held out her hand to him, a smile of the utmost friendliness on her face.

'How fortunate,' she said, as though speaking the cue for a lovely song. 'I stand here, the wonder of this old Spanish night getting into my very blood – and the only thing lacking in the picture is – a man. And then, you come.'

'I'm glad to be of service,' said Minot, tossing away his cigar.

'What an unromantic way to put it! Really, this chance meeting – it was a chance meeting, I suppose? –'

'A lucky chance,' he agreed.

She pouted.

'Then you did not follow? Unromantic to the last! But as I was saying, this chance meeting is splendid. My train goes in an hour – and I wanted so very much to see you – once again.'

'You flatter me.'

'Ah – you don't understand.' She dropped into a chair. 'I wanted to see you – to put your conscience at rest. You were so sorry when you had to be – cruel – to me today. You will be so glad to know that it has all turned out happily, after all.'

'What do you mean?' asked Minot, new apprehensions rising in his mind.

'Alas, if I could only tell you.' She was laughing at him now – an experience he did not relish. 'But – my lips are sealed, as we say on the stage. I can only give you the hint. You thought you left me a broken vanquished woman. How the thought did pain you! Well, your victory was not absolute. Let that thought console you.'

'You are too kind,' Minot answered.

'And – you are glad I am not leaving San Marco quite beaten?'

'Oh, yes – I'm wild with pleasure.'

'Really – that is sweet of you. I am so sorry we must part. The moonlight, the palms, the distant music – all so romantic. But – we shall meet again?'

'I don't know.'

'Don't know? How unkind – when it all depends on you. You will look me up in New York, won't you? New York is not so romantic – but I shall try to make it up to you. I shall sing for you. *Just a Little*.'

She stood up, and held out a slim white hand.

'Goodbye, Mr Minot.' Still she laughed. 'It has been so good to know you.'

'Er – goodbye,' said Minot. He took the hand. He heard her humming beneath her breath – humming *Just a Little*. 'I've enjoyed your singing immensely.'

She laughed outright now – a silvery joyous laugh. And, refusing the baffled Minot's offer to take her back to the hotel, she fled away from him down the dark path.

He fell back into his chair, and lighted another cigar. Exit the Gaicty lady, laughing merrily. What was the meaning of that? What new complication must he meet and solve?

For his answer, he had only to return to the hotel. On the steps he was met by Lord Harrowby's man, agitated, puffing.

'Been looking all about for you, sir,' he announced. ''Is lordship wishes to see you at once – most h'important.'

'More trouble, Minot,' was Lord Harrowby's gloomy greeting. 'Sit down, old chap. Just had a very nasty visitor.'

'Sorry to hear it.'

'Little brown monkey of a man – Manuel Gonzale, proprietor of the *San Marco Mail*. I say, old boy, there's a syllable missing in the name of that paper. Do you get me?'

'You mean it should be the *San Marco Blackmail*? Pretty good, Harrowby, pretty good.'

And Minot added to himself 'for you'.

'That's exactly what I do mean. Gabrielle has sold out her bunch of letters to Mr Gonzale. And it appears from the chap's sly hints that unless I pay him ten thousand dollars before midnight, the best of those letters will be in tomorrow's *Mail*.'

'He's got his nerve – working a game like that,' said Minot.

'Nerve – not at all,' replied Harrowby. 'He's as safe as a child in its own nursery. He knows as well as anybody that the last thing I'd do would be to appeal to the police. Too much publicity down that road. Well?'

'His price is a bit cheaper than Gabrielle's.'

'Yes, but not cheap enough. I'm broke, old boy. The governor and I are on very poor terms. Shouldn't think of appealing to him.'

'We might pawn Chain Lightning's Collar,' Minot suggested.

'Never! There must be some way – only three days before the wedding. We mustn't lose on the stretch, old boy.' A pause.

Minot sat glumly. 'Have you no suggestion?' Harrowby asked anxiously.

'I have not,' said Minot, rising. 'But I perceive clearly that it now devolves on little Dicky Minot to up and don his fighting armor once more.'

'Really, old boy, I'm sorry,' said Harrowby. 'I'm hoping things may quiet down a bit after a time.'

'So am I,' replied Minot with feeling. 'If they don't I can see nervous prostration and a hospital cot ahead for me. You stay here and study the marriage service – I'm going out on the broad highway again.'

He went down into the lobby and tore Jack Paddock away from the side of one of the Omaha beauties. Mr Paddock was resplendent in evening clothes, and thoughtful, for on the morrow Mrs Bruce was to give an important luncheon.

'Jack,' Minot said, 'I'm going to confide in you. I'm going to tell you why I am in San Marco.'

'Unbare your secrets,' Paddock answered.

Crossing the quiet plaza Minot explained to his friend the matter of the insurance policy written by the romantic Jephson in New York. He told of how he had come south with the promise to his employer that Miss Cynthia Meyrick would change her mind only over his dead body. Incredulous exclamations broke from the flippant Paddock as he listened.

'Knowing your love of humor,' Minot said, 'I hasten to add the crowning touch. The moment I saw Cynthia Meyrick I realized that if I couldn't marry her myself life would be an uninteresting blank forever after. Every time I've seen her since I've been surer of it. What's the answer. Jack?'

Paddock whistled.

'Delicious,' he cried. 'Pardon me – I'm speaking as a rank outsider. She is a charming girl. And you adore her! Bless my soul, how the plot does thicken! Why don't you resign, you idiot?'

'My first idea. Tried it, and it wouldn't work. Besides, if I did resign, I couldn't stick around and queer Jephson's chances – even supposing she'd listen to my pleading, which she wouldn't.'

'Children, see the very Christian martyr! If it was me I'd chuck the job and elope with – oh, no, you couldn't do that, of course. It would be a low trick. You are in a hole, aren't you?'

'Five million fathoms deep. There's nothing to do but see the wedding through. And you're going to help me. Just now, Mr Manuel Gonzale has a packet of love letters written by Harrowby in his salad days, which he proposes to print on the morrow unless he is paid not to tonight. You and I are on our way to take 'em away from him.'

'Um – but if I help you in this I'll be doing you a mean trick. Can't quite make out, old boy, whether to stand by you in a business or a personal way.'

'You're going to stand by me in a business way. I want you along tonight to lend your moral support while I throttle that little blackmailer.'

'Ay, ay, sir. I've been hearing some things about Gonzale myself. Go to it!'

They groped about in a dark hallway hunting the *Mail* office.

'Shady are the ways of journalism,' commented Paddock. 'By the way, I've just thought of one for Mrs Bruce to spring tomorrow. In case we fail and the affinity letters are published, she might say that Harrowby's epistles got into the *Mail* once too often. It's only a rough idea – ah – I see you don't like it. Well, here's success to our expedition.'

They opened the door of the *Mail* office. Mr O'Neill sat behind a desk, the encyclopedia before him, seeking lively material for the morrow's issue. Mr Howe hammered at a typewriter. Both of the newspaper men looked up at the intrusion.

'Ah, gentlemen,' said O'Neill, coming forward. 'What can I do for you?'

'Who are you?' Minot asked.

'What? Can it be? Is my name not a household word in San Marco? I am managing editor of the *Mail*.' His eyes lighted on Mr Paddock's giddy attire. 'We can't possibly let you give a ball here tonight, if that's what you want.'

'Very humorous,' said Minot. 'But our wants are far different. I won't beat around the bush. You have some letters here written by a friend of mine to a lady he adored – at the moment. You are going to print them in tomorrow's *Mail* unless my friend is easy enough to pay you ten thousand dollars. He isn't going to pay you anything. We've come for those letters – and we'll get them or run you and your boss out of town in twenty-four hours – you raw little blackmailers!'

'Blackmailers!' Mr O'Neill's eyes seemed to catch fire from his hair. His face paled. 'I've been in the newspaper business seventeen years, and nobody ever called me a blackmailer and got away with it. I'm in a generous mood. I'll give you one chance to take that back –'

'Nonsense. It happens to be true –' put in Paddock.

'I'm talking to your friend here.' O'Neill's breath came fast. 'I'll attend to you, you lily of the field, in a minute. You – you liar – are you going to take that back?'

'No,' cried Minot.

He saw a wild Irishman coming for him, breathing fire. He squared himself to meet the attack. But the man at the typewriter leaped up and seized O'Neill from behind.

'Steady, Bob,' he shouted. 'How do you know this fellow isn't right?'

Unaccountably the warlike one collapsed into a chair.

'Damn it, I know he's right,' he groaned. 'That's what makes me rave. Why didn't you let me punch him? It would have been some satisfaction. Of course he's right. I had a hunch this was a blackmailing sheet from the moment my hot fingers closed on Gonzale's money. But so long as nobody told us, we were all right.'

He glared angrily at Minot.

'You – you killjoy,' he cried. 'You skeleton at the feast. You've put us in a lovely fix.'

'Well, I'm sorry,' said Minot, 'but I don't understand these heroics.'

'It's all up now, Harry,' moaned O'Neill. 'The free trial is over and we've got to send the mattress back to the factory. Here in this hollow lotus land, ever to live and lie reclined – I was putting welcome on the mat for a fate like that. Back to the road for us. That human fish over in the *Chronicle* office was a prophet – "You look unlucky – maybe they'll give you jobs on the *Mail*." Remember.'

'Cool off, Bob,' Howe said. He turned to Minot and Paddock. 'Of course you don't understand. You see, we're strangers here. Drifted in last night broke and hungry, looking for jobs. We got them – under rather unusual circumstances. Things looked suspicious – the proprietor parted with money without screaming for help, and no regular newspaper is run like that. But – when you're down and out, you know –'

'I understand,' said Minot, smiling. 'And I'm sorry I called you what I did. I apologize. And I hate to be a – er – a killjoy. But as a matter of fact, your employer is a blackmailer, and it's best you should know it.'

'Yes,' put in Paddock. 'Do you gentlemen happen to have heard where the editor of Mr Gonzale's late newspaper, published in Havana, is now?'

'We do not,' said O'Neill, 'but maybe you'll tell us.'

'I will. He's in prison, doing ten years for blackmail. I understand that Mr Gonzale prefers to involve his editors, rather than himself.'

O'Neill came over and held out his hand to Minot.

'Shake, son,' he said. 'Thank God I didn't waste my strength on you. Gonzale will be in here in a minute –'

'About those letters?' Howe inquired.

'Yes,' said Minot. 'They were written to a Gaiety actress by a man who is in San Marco for his wedding next Tuesday – Lord Harrowby.'

'His ludship again,' O'Neill remarked. 'Say, I always thought the South was democratic.'

'Well,' said Howe, 'we owe you fellows something for putting us wise. We've stood for a good deal, but never for blackmailing. As a matter of fact, Gonzale hasn't brought the letters in yet, but he's due at any minute. When he comes – take the letters away from him. I shan't interfere. How about you, Bob?'

'I'll interfere,' said O'Neill, 'and I'll interfere strong – if I think you fellows ain't leaving enough of little Manuel for me to caress –'

The door opened, and the immaculate proprietor of the *Mail* came noiselessly into the room. His eyes narrowed when they fell on the strangers there.

'Are you Manuel Gonzale?' Minot demanded.

'I – I am.' The sly little eyes darted everywhere.

'Proprietor of the *Mail*?'

'Yes.'

'The gentleman who visited Lord Harrowby an hour back?'

'Man! Man! You're wasting time,' O'Neill cried.

'Excuse me,' smiled Minot. 'Unintentional, I assure you.' He seized the little Spaniard suddenly by the collar. 'We're here for Lord Harrowby's letters,' he said. His other hand began a rapid search of Manuel Gonzale's pockets.

'Let me go, you thief,' screamed the proprietor of the *Mail*. He squirmed and fought. 'Let me go!' He writhed about to face his editors. 'You fools! What are you doing, standing there? Help me – help –'

'We're waiting,' said O'Neill. 'Waiting for our turn. Remember your promise, son. Enough of him left for me.'

Minot and his captive slid back and forth across the floor. The three others watched, O'Neill in high glee.

'Go to it!' he cried. 'That's Madame On Dit you're waltzing with. I speak for the next dance, Madame.'

Mr Minot's eager hand came away from the Spaniard's inner waistcoat pocket, and in it was a packet of perfumed letters, tied with a cute blue ribbon. He released his victim.

'Sorry to be so impolite,' he said. 'But I had to have these tonight.'

Gonzale turned on him with an evil glare.

'Thief!' he cried. 'I'll have the law on you for this.'

'I doubt that,' smiled Minot. 'I guess that about concludes our business with the *Mail*.' He turned to Howe and O'Neill. 'You boys look me up at the De la Pax, I want to wish you bon voyage when you start north. For the present – goodbye.'

And he and Paddock departed.

'You're a fine pair,' snarled Gonzale, when the door had closed. 'A fine pair to take my salary money, and then stand by and see me strangled.'

'You're not strangled yet,' said O'Neill. He came slowly toward his employer, like a cat stalking a bird. 'Did you get my emphasis on the word yet?'

Gonzale paled beneath his lemon skin, and got behind a desk.

'Now, boys,' he pleaded, 'I didn't mean anything, I'll be frank with you – I have been a little indiscreet here. But that's all over now. It would be dangerous to try any more – er – deals at present. And I want you to stay on here until I can get new men in your places.'

'Save your breath,' said O'Neill through his teeth.

'Your work has been excellent – excellent,' went on Gonzale hastily. 'I feel I am not paying you enough. Stay on with me until your week is up. I will give you a hundred each when you go – and I give you my word I'll attempt nothing dangerous while you are here.'

He retreated farther from O'Neill.

'Wait a minute, Bob,' said Howe. 'No blackmailing stunts while we stay?'

'Well – I shouldn't call them that –'

'No blackmailing stunts?'

'No – I promise.'

'Harry,' wailed the militant O'Neill. 'What's the matter with you? We ought to thrash him – now – and –'

'Go back on the road?' Howe inquired. 'A hundred dollars each. Bob. It means New York in a parlor car.'

'Then you will stay?' cried Gonzale.

'Yes – we'll stay,' said Howe firmly.

'See here –' pleaded O'Neill. 'Oh, what's the use? This *dolce far niente* has got us.'

'We stay only on the terms you name,' stipulated Howe.

'It is agreed,' said Gonzale, smiling wanly. 'The loss of those letters cost me a thousand dollars – and you stood by. However, let us forgive and forget. Here – Madame On Dit's copy for tomorrow.' Timidly he held out a roll of paper toward O'Neill.

'All right.' O'Neill snatched it. 'But I'm going to edit it from now on. For instance, there's a comma I don't like. And I'm going to keep an eye on you, my hearty.'

'As you wish,' said Gonzale humbly. 'I – I am going out for a moment.' The door closed noiselessly behind him.

Howe and O'Neill stood looking at each other.

'Well – you had your way,' said O'Neill, shamefacedly. 'I don't seem to be the man I was. It must be the sunshine and the posies. And the thought of the road again.'

'A hundred each,' said Howe grimly. 'We had to have it, Bob. It means New York.'

'Yes.' O'Neill pondered. 'But – that good-looking young fellow, Harry – the one who apologized to us for calling us blackmailers –'

'Yes?'

'I'd hate to meet him on the street tomorrow. Five days. A lot could happen in five days –'

'What are your orders. Chief?' asked Howe.

At that moment Minot, followed by Paddock was rushing triumphantly into the Harrowby suite. He threw down on the table a package of letters.

'There they are!' he cried. 'I –'

He stopped.

'Thanks,' said Lord Harrowby wildly. 'Thanks a thousand times. My dear Minot – we need you. My man has been to the theater – Trimmer is organizing a mob to board the *Lileth*.'

'Yes – to search for that creature who calls himself Lord Harrowby.'

'Come on, Jack,' Minot said to Paddock. They ran down several flights of stairs, through the lobby, and out into the street.

'Where to?' panted Paddock.

'The harbor!' Minot cried.

As they passed the opera house they saw a crowd forming and heard the buzz of many voices.

Chapter XIII
'And on The Ships at Sea'

Mr Paddock knew of a man on the waterfront who had a gasoline launch to rent, and fortunately it happened to be in commission. The two young men leaped into it, Paddock started the engine, and they zipped with reassuring speed over the dark waters toward the lights of the *Lileth*.

The accommodation ladder of the yacht was down, and leaving a member of the crew to make fast the launch, Minot and Paddock climbed hurriedly to the deck. Mr Martin Wall was at the moment in the main cabin engaged in a game of German whist, and his opponent was no less a person than George Harrowby of the peerage. Upon this quiet game the two young men rushed in.

'Unexpected visitors,' said Wall. 'Why – what's the matter, boys?'

'Come out on deck a minute,' said Minot rapidly. Wall threw down his cards and followed. Once outside, Minot went on: 'No time to waste words. Trimmer is collecting a mob in front of the opera house, and they are coming out here to search this boat. You know who they're looking for.'

With exaggerated calmness Wall took out a cigar and lighted it.

'Indeed?' he remarked. 'I told you it might be advisable to look up the penalty for kidnaping. But you knew best. Ah, the impetuosity of youth!'

'Well – this is no time to discuss that,' replied Minot. 'We've got to act, and act quickly!'

'Yes?' Mr Wall drawled. 'What would you suggest? Shall we drown him? I've come to like George mighty well, but if you say the word –'

'My plan is this,' said Minot, annoyed by Wall's pleasantries. 'Turn George over to us. We'll bundle him into our launch and run off out of sight behind Tarragona Island. Then, let Trimmer search to his heart's content. When he gets tired and quits, signal us by hanging a red lantern in the bow.'

Martin Wall smiled broadly.

'Not bad for an amateur kidnaper,' he said.

'Will I turn George over to you? Will a duck swim? A good idea.'

'For God's sake, hurry!' cried Minot.

'Look!'

He pointed to the largest of San Marco's piers. The moon was lost under clouds now, but the electric lights on the waterfront revealed a swarming shouting crowd of people. Martin Wall stepped to the door of the main cabin.

'Lord Harrowby!' he cried. He turned to Minot and Paddock. 'I call him that to cheer him in captivity,' he explained. The tall weary Englishman strode out upon the deck.

'Lord Harrowby,' said Wall, 'these two gentlemen have come to take you for a boat ride. Will you be kind enough to step into that launch?'

Poor old George pulled himself together.

'If you'll pardon my language, I'll be damned if I do,' he said. 'I take it Mr Trimmer is on his way here. Well, gentlemen, the first to grasp his hand when he boards the boat will be the chap who now addresses you.'

They stood gazing doubtfully at George in revolt. Then Minot turned, and saw a rowboat putting off from the pier.

'Come on,' he cried, and leaped on the shoulders of the aspirant to the title. Paddock and Wall followed. Despite his discouraged appearance, George put up a lively fight. For a time the four men struggled back and forth across the deck, now in moonlight, now in shadow. Once George slipped and fell, his three captors on top of him, and at that moment Mr Minot felt a terrific tugging at his coat. But the odds were three to one against George Harrowby, and finally he was dragged and pushed into the launch. Again Paddock started the engine, and that odd boat load drew away from the *Lileth*.

They had gone about ten feet when poor old George slipped out from under Minot and leaped to his feet.

'Hi – Trimmer – it's me – it's George –' he thundered in a startlingly loud tone. Minot put his hand over George's lips, and they locked in conflict. The small launch danced wildly on the waters. And fortunately for Minot's plans the moon still hid behind the clouds.

With a stretch of Tarragona's rank vegetation between them and the *Lileth*, Mr Paddock stopped the engine and they stood still on the dark waters. Paddock lighted a cigarette, utilizing the same match to consult his watch.

'Ten o'clock,' he said. 'Can't say this is the jolliest little party I was ever on.'

'Never mind,' replied Minot cheerfully. 'It won't take Trimmer fifteen minutes to find that his proposition isn't on board. In twenty minutes we'll slip back and look for the signal.'

The 'proposition' in question sat up and straightened his collar.

'The pater and I split,' he said, 'over the matter of my going to Oxford. The old boy knew best. I wish now I'd gone. Then I might have words to tell you chaps what I think of this damnable outrage.'

Minot and Paddock sat in silence.

'I've been in America twenty odd years,' the proposition went on. 'Seen all sorts of injustice and wrong – but I've lived to experience the climax myself.'

Still silence from his captors, while the black waters swished about the launch.

'I take it you chaps believe me to be an impostor, just as Allan does. Well, I'm not. And I'm going to give you my little talk on the old days at Rakedale Hall. When I've finished –'

'No, you're not,' said Minot. 'I've heard all that once.'

'And you weren't convinced? Why, everybody in San Marco is convinced. The mayor, the chief of police, the –'

'My dear George,' said Minot with feeling. 'It doesn't make the slightest difference who you are. You and Trimmer stay separated until after next Tuesday.'

'Yes. And rank injustice it is, too. We'll have the law on you for this. We'll send you all to prison.'

'Pleasant thought,' commented Paddock. 'Mrs Bruce would have to develop lockjaw at the height of the social season. Oh, the devil – I'd better be thinking about that luncheon.'

All thought. All sat there silent. The black waters became a little rougher. On their surface small flecks of white began to appear. Minot looked up at the dark sky.

'Twenty-two after,' said Paddock finally, and turned toward the engine. 'Heaven grant that red light is on view. This is getting on my nerves.'

Slyly the little launch poked its nose around the corner of the island and peeped at the majestic *Lileth*. Paddock snorted.

'Not a trace of it.'

'I must have underestimated the time,' said Minot. 'Wha– what's that?'

'That? That's only thunder. Oh, this is going to be a pretty party!'

Suddenly the heavens blazed with lightning. The swell of the waters increased. Hastily Paddock backed the boat from the range of the *Lileth*'s vision.

'Trimmer must go soon,' cried Minot.

Fifteen minutes passed in eloquent silence. The lightning and the thunder continued.

'Try it again,' Minot suggested. Again they peeped. And still no red light on the *Lileth*.

And even as they looked, out of the black heavens swept a sheet of stinging rain. It lashed down on that frail tossing boat with cruel force; it obscured the *Lileth*, the island, everything but the fact of its own damp existence. In two seconds the men unprotected in that tiny launch were pitiful dripping figures, and the glory of Mr Paddock's evening clothes departed never to return.

'A fortune-teller in Albuquerque,' said poor old George, 'told me I was to die of pneumonia. It'll be murder, gentlemen – plain murder.'

'It's suicide, too, isn't it?' snarled Paddock. 'That ought to satisfy you.'

'I'm sorry,' said Minot through chattering teeth.

No answer. The downfall continued.

'The rain is raining everywhere,' quoted Paddock gloomily. 'It falls on the umbrellas here and on the ships at sea. Damn the ships at sea.'

'Here, here,' said poor old George.

A damp doleful pause.

'Greater love hath no man than this, that he lay down his life for a friend,' continued Paddock presently.

'A thousand apologies,' Minot said. 'But I'm running the same chances, Jack.'

'Yes – but it's your party – your happy little party,' replied Paddock. 'Not mine.'

Minot did not answer. He was as miserable as the others, and he could scarcely blame his friend for losing temporarily his good nature.

'It's after eleven,' said Paddock, after another long pause.

'Put in closer to the *Lileth*,' suggested Minot.

Mr Paddock fumbled about beneath the canvas cover of the engine, and they put in. But still no red light aboard the yacht.

'I'd give a thousand dollars,' said Paddock, 'to know what's going on aboard that boat.'

The knowledge would hardly have been worth the price he offered. Aboard the *Lileth*, on the forward deck under a protecting awning, Mr Trimmer sat firmly planted in a chair.

Beside him, in other chairs, sat three prominent citizens of San Marco – one of them the chief of police. Mr Martin Wall was madly walking the deck near by.

'Going to stay here all night?' he demanded at last.

'All night, and all day tomorrow,' replied Mr Trimmer, 'if necessary. We're going to stay here until that boat that's carrying Lord Harrowby comes back. You can't fool Henry Trimmer.'

'There isn't any such boat!' flared Martin Wall.

'Tell it to the marines,' remarked Trimmer, lighting a fresh cigar.

Just as well that the three shivering figures huddled in the launch on the heaving bosom of the waters could not see this picture. Mr Wall looked out at the rain, and shivered himself.

Eleven-thirty came. And twelve. Two matches from Mr Paddock's store went to the discovery of these sad facts. Soaked to the skin, glum, silent, the three on the waters sat staring at the unresponsive *Lileth*. The rain was falling now in a fine drizzle.

'I suppose,' Paddock remarked, 'we stay here until morning?'

'We might try landing on Tarragona,' said Minot.

'We might try jumping into the ocean, too,' responded Paddock, through chattering teeth.

'Murder,' droned poor old George. 'That's what it'll be.'

At one o'clock the three wet watchers beheld unusual things. Smoke began to belch from the *Lileth*'s funnels. Her siren sounded.

'She's steaming out!' cried Minot. 'She's steaming out to sea!'

And sure enough, the graceful yacht began to move – out past Tarragona Island – out toward the open sea.

Once more Paddock started his faithful engine, and, hallooing madly, the three set out in pursuit. Not yet had the *Lileth* struck its gait, and in fifteen minutes they were alongside. Martin Wall, beholding them from the deck, had a rather unexpected attack of pity, and stopped his engines. The three limp watchers were taken aboard.

'What – what does this mean?' chattered Minot.

'You poor devils,' said Martin Wall. 'Come and have a drink. Mean?' He poured. 'It means that the only way I could get rid of our friend Trimmer was to set out for New York.'

'For New York?' cried Minot, standing glass in hand.

'Yes. Came on board, Trimmer did, searched the boat, and then declared I'd shipped George away until his visit should be over. So he and his friends – one of them the chief of police, by the way – sat down to wait for your return. Gad – I thought of you out in that rain. Sat and sat and sat. What could I do?'

'To Trimmer, the brute,' said Paddock, raising his glass.

'Finally I had an idea. I had the boys pull up anchor and start the engines. Trimmer wanted to know the answer. "Leaving for New York tonight," I said. "Want to come along?" He wasn't sure whether he would go or not, but his friends were sure they wouldn't. Put up an awful howl, and just before we got under way Mr Trimmer and party crawled into their rowboat and splashed back to San Marco.'

'Well – what now?' asked Minot.

'I've made up my mind,' said Wall. 'Been intending to go back north for some time, and now that I've started, I guess I'll keep on going.'

'Splendid,' cried Minot. 'And you'll take Mr George Harrowby with you?'

Mr Wall seemed in excellent spirits. He slapped Minot on the back.

'If you say so, of course. Don't know exactly what they can do to us – but I think George needs the sea air. How about it, your lordship?'

Poor old George, drooping as he had never drooped before, looked wearily into Wall's eyes.

'What's the use?' he said. 'Fight's all gone out of me. Losing interest in what's next. Three hours on that blooming ocean with the rain soaking in – I'm going to bed. I don't care what becomes of me.'

And he sloshed away to his cabin.

'Well, boys, I'm afraid we'll have to put you off,' said Martin Wall. 'Glad to have met both of you. Sometime in New York we may run into each other again.'

He shook hands genially, and the two young men dropped once more into that unhappy launch. As they sped toward the shore the *Lileth*, behind them, was heading for the open sea.

'Sorry if I've seemed to have a grouch tonight,' said Paddock, as they walked up the deserted avenue toward the hotel. 'But these Florida rainstorms aren't the pleasantest things to wear next to one's skin. I apologize, Dick.'

'Nonsense,' Minot answered. 'Old Job himself would have frowned a bit if he'd been through what you have tonight. It was my fault for getting you into it –'

'Forget it,' Paddock said. 'Well, it looks like a wedding, old man. The letters home again, and George Harrowby headed for New York – a three days' trip. Nothing to hinder now. Have you thought of that?'

'I don't want to think,' said Minot gloomily. 'Good night, old man.'

Paddock sped up the stairs to his room, which was on the second floor, and Minot turned toward the elevator. At that moment he saw approaching him through the deserted lobby Mr Jim O'Malley, the house detective of the De la Pax.

'Can we see you a minute in the office, Mr Minot?' he asked.

'Certainly,' Minot answered. 'But – I'm soaked through – was out in all that rain –'

'Too bad,' said O'Malley, with a sympathetic glance. 'We won't keep you but a minute –'

He led the way, and wondering, Minot followed. In the tiny office of the hotel manager a bullet-headed man stood waiting.

'My friend, Mr Huntley, of the Secret Service,' O'Malley explained. 'Awful sorry that this should happen, Mr Minot, but – we got to search you.'

'Search me – for what?' Minot cried.

And in a flash, he knew. Through that wild night he had not once thought of it. But it was still in his inside coat pocket, of course. Chain Lightning's Collar!

'What does this mean?' he asked.

'That's what they all say,' grunted Huntley. 'Come here, my boy. Say, you're pretty wet. And shivering! Better have a warm bath and a drink. Turn around, please. Ah –'

With practised fingers the detective explored rapidly Mr Minot's person and pockets. The victim of the search stood limp, helpless. What could he do? There was no escape. It was all up now – for whatever reason they desired Chain Lightning's Collar, they could not fail to have it in another minute.

Side pockets – trousers pockets – now! The inner coat pocket! Its contents were in the detective's hand. Minot stared down. A little gasp escaped him.

The envelope that held Chain Lightning's Collar was not among them!

Two minutes longer Huntley pursued, then with an oath of disappointment he turned to O'Malley.

'Hasn't got it!' he announced.

Minot swept aside the profuse apologies of the hotel detective, and somehow got out of the room. In a daze, he sought 389. He didn't have it! Didn't have Chain Lightning's Collar! Who did?

It was while he sat steaming in a hot bath that an idea came to him. The struggle on the deck of the *Lileth*, with Martin Wall panting at his side! The tug on his coat as they all went down together. The genial spirits of Wall thereafter. The sudden start for New York.

No question about it – Chain Lightning's Collar was well out at sea now.

And yet – why had Wall stopped to take the occupants of the launch aboard?

After his bath, Minot donned pajamas and a dressing gown and ventured out to find Lord Harrowby's suite. With difficulty he succeeded in arousing the sleeping peer. Harrowby let him in, and then sat down on his bed and stared at him.

'What is it?' he inquired sleepily.

Briefly Minot told him of the circumstances preceding the start of the *Lileth* for New York, of his return to the hotel, and the search party he encountered there. Harrowby was very wide awake by this time.

'That finishes us,' he groaned.

'Wait a minute,' Minot said. 'They didn't find the necklace. I didn't have it. I'd lost it.'

'Lost it?'

'Yes. And if you want my opinion, I think Martin Wall stole it from me on the *Lileth* and is now on his way –'

Harrowby leaped from bed, and seized Minot gleefully by the hand.

'Dear old chap. What the deuce do I care who took it. It's gone. Thank God – it's gone.'

'But – I don't understand –'

'No. But you can understand this much. Everything's all right. Nothing in the way of the wedding now. It's splendid! Splendid!'

'But – the necklace was stolen –'

'Yes. Good! Very good! My dear Minot, the luckiest thing that can happen to us will be – never, never to see Chain Lightning's Collar again!'

As completely at sea as he had been that night – which was more or less at sea – Minot returned to his room. It was after three o'clock. He turned out his lights and sought his bed. Many wild conjectures kept him awake at first, but this had been the busiest day of his life. Soon he slept, and dreamed thrilling dreams.

The sun was bright outside his windows when he was aroused by a knock.

'What is it?' he cried.

'A package for you, sir,' said a bellboy voice.

He slipped one arm outside his door to receive it – a neat little bundle, securely tied, with his name written on the wrappings. Sleepily he undid the cord, and took out – an envelope.

He was no longer sleepy. He held the envelope open over his bed. Chain Lightning's Collar tumbled, gleaming, upon the white sheet!

Also in the package was a note, which Minot read breathlessly.

Dear Mr Minot:

I have decided not to go north after all, and am back in the harbor with the Lileth. *As I expect Trimmer at any moment I have sent George over to Tarragona Island in charge of two sailormen for the day.*

Cordially,

Martin Wall.

P.S. You dropped the enclosed in the scuffle on the boat last night.

Chapter XIV
Jersey City Interferes

At ten o'clock that Saturday morning Lord Harrowby was engrossed in the ceremony of breakfast in his rooms. For the occasion he wore an orange and purple dressing gown with a floral design no botanist could have sanctioned – the sort of dressing gown that Arnold Bennett, had he seen it, would have made a leading character in a novel. He was cheerful, was Harrowby, and as he glanced through an old copy of the London *Times* he made strange noises in his throat, under the impression that he was humming a musical comedy chorus.

There was a knock, and Harrowby cried: 'Come in.' Mr Minot, fresh as the morning and nowhere near so hot, entered.

'Feeling pretty satisfied with life, I'll wager,' Minot suggested.

'My dear chap, gay as – as – a robin,' Harrowby replied.

'Snatch your last giggle,' said Minot. 'Have one final laugh, and make it a good one. Then wake up!'

'Wake up? Why, I am awake –'

'Oh, no – you're dreaming on a bed of roses. Listen! Martin Wall didn't go north with the impostor after all. Changed his mind. Look!'

And Minot tossed something on the table, just abaft his lordship's eggs.

'The devil! Chain Lightning's Collar,' cried Harrowby.

'Back to its original storage,' said Minot. 'What is this, Harrowby? A Drury Lane melodrama?'

'My word. I can't make it out.'

'Can't you? Got the necklace back with a note from Martin Wall, saying I dropped it last night in the scrap on the deck of the *Lileth*.'

'Confound the thing!' sighed Harrowby, staring morosely at the diamonds.

'My first impulse,' said Minot, 'is to hand the necklace back to you and gracefully withdraw. But of course I'm here to look after Jephson's interests –'

'Naturally,' put in Harrowby quickly. 'And let me tell you that should this necklace be found before the wedding, Jephson is practically certain to pay that policy. I think you'd better keep it. They're not likely to search you again. If I took it – dear old chap – they search me every little while.'

'You didn't steal this, did you?' Minot asked.

'Of course not.' Harrowby flushed a delicate pink. 'It belongs in our family – has for years. Everybody knows that.'

'Well, what is the trouble?'

'I'll explain it all later. There's really nothing dishonorable – as men of the world look at such things. I give you my word that you can serve Mr Jephson best by keeping the necklace for the present – and seeing to it that it does not fall into the hands of the men who are looking for it.'

Minot sat staring gloomily ahead of him. Then he reached out, took up the necklace, and restored it to his pocket.

'By the way,' Harrowby remarked, 'I'm giving a little dinner tonight – at the Manhattan Club. May I count on you?'

'Surely,' Minot smiled. 'I'll be there, wearing our necklace!'

'My dear fellow – ah, I see you mean it pleasantly. Wear it, by all means.'

Minot passed from the eccentric blooms of that dressing gown to the more authentic flowers of the Florida outdoors. In the plaza he met Cynthia Meyrick, rival candidate to the morning in its glory.

'Matrimony,' she said, 'is more trouble than it seems on a moonlit night under the palms. I've never been so busy in my life. By the way, two of my bridesmaids arrived from New York last night. Lovely girls – both of them. But I forget!'

'Forget what?'

'Your young heart is already ensnared, isn't it?'

'Yes,' replied Minot fervently. 'It is. But no matter. Tell me about your preparations for the wedding. I should like to enjoy the thrill of it – by proxy.'

'How like a man – wants all the thrill and none of the bother. It's dreadfully hard staging a wedding, way down here a thousand miles from everything. But – my gown came last night from Paris. Can you imagine the thrill of that!'

'Only faintly.'

'How stupid being a man must be.'

'And how glorious being a girl, with man only an afterthought – even at wedding time.'

'Poor Harrowby! He keeps in the limelight fairly well, however.' They walked along a moment in silence. 'I've wondered,' she said at length. 'Why *did* you kidnap – Mr Trimmer's – friend?'

'Because –'

'Yes?' – eagerly.

Minot looked at her, and something rose in his throat to choke him.

'I can't tell you,' he said. 'It is the fault of – the Master of the Show. I'm only the pawn – the baffled, raging, unhappy little pawn. That's all I can tell you. You – you were speaking of your wedding gown?'

'A present from Aunt Mary,' she answered, a strange tenderness in her tone. 'For a good little girl who's caught a lord.'

'A charming little girl,' said Minot softly. 'May I say that?'

'Yes –' Her brown eyes glowed. 'I'm – glad – to have you – say it. I go in here. Goodbye Mr Kidnaper.'

She disappeared into a shop, and Minot walked slowly down the street. Girls from Peoria and Paris, from Boise City and London, passed by. Girls chaperoned and girls alone – tourist girls in swarms. And not a few of them wondered why such a good-looking young man should appear to be so sorry for himself.

Returning to the hotel at noon, Minot met Martin Wall on the veranda.

'Lucky I put old George on Tarragona for the day,' Wall confided.

'As I expected, Trimmer was out to call early this morning. Searched the ship from stem to stern. I rather think we have Mr Trimmer up a tree. He went away not quite so sure of himself.'

'Good,' Minot answered. 'So you changed your mind about going north?'

'Yes. Think I'll stay over for the wedding. By the way, wasn't that Chain Lightning's Collar you left behind you last night?'

'Y-yes.'

'Thought so. You ought to be more careful. People might suspect you of being the thief at Mrs Bruce's.'

'If you think that, I wish you'd speak to his lordship.'

'I have. Your innocence is established. And I've promised Harrowby to keep his little mystery dark.'

'You're very kind,' said Minot, and went on into the hotel.

The remainder of the day passed lazily. Dick Minot felt lost indeed, for seemingly there were no more doughty deeds to be done in the name of Jephson. The Gaiety lady was gone; her letters were in the hands of the man who had written them. The claimant to the title languished among the alligators of Tarragona, a prisoner. Trimmer appeared to be baffled. Bridesmaids arrived. The wedding gown appeared. It looked like smooth sailing now.

Jack Paddock, met for a moment late in the afternoon, announced airily:

'By the way, the Duke and Duchess of Lismore have come. You know – the sausage lady and her captive. My word – you should see her! A wardrobe to draw tears of envy from a theatrical star. Fifty costly necklaces – and only one neck!'

'Tragic,' smiled Minot.

'Funny thing's happened,' Paddock whispered. 'I met the duchess once abroad. She sent for me this noon and almost bowled me over. Seems she's heard of Mrs Bruce as the wittiest woman in San Marco. And she's jealous. "You're a clever boy," says her ladyship to me. "Coach me up so I can outshine Mrs Bruce. What do you know?"'

'Ah – but you were the pioneer,' Minot reminded him.

'Well, I was, for that matter,' said Mr Paddock. 'But I know now it wasn't a clever idea, if this woman can think of it, too.'

'What did you tell her?'

'I was shocked. I showed it. It seemed deception to me. Still – she made me an offer that – well, I told her I'd think it over.'

'Good heavens, Jack! You wouldn't try to sell 'em both dialogue?'

'Why not? Play one against the other – make 'em keener for my goods. I've got a notion to clean up here quick and then go back to the real stuff. That little girl from the Middle West – I've forgot all about her, of course. But speaking of cleaning up – I'm thinking of it, Dick, my boy. Yes, I believe I'll take them both on – secretly, of course. It means hard work for me, but when one loves one's art, no service seems too tough.'

'You're hopeless,' Minot groaned.

'Say not so,' laughed Paddock, and went away humming a frivolous tune.

At a quarter before seven, for the first time, Minot entered Mr Tom Stacy's Manhattan Club and Grill. To anyone who crossed Mr Stacy's threshold with the expectation of immediately encountering lights and gaiety, the first view of the interior came as a distinct shock. The main dining room of the Manhattan Club was dim with the holy dimness of a cathedral. Its lamps, hung high, were buried in oriental trappings, and shone half-heartedly. Faintly through the gloom could be discerned white tablecloths, gleaming silver. The scene demanded voices, noiseless footsteps. It got both.

The main dining room was hollowed out of the center of the great stone building, and its roof was off in the dark three stories above, side of the entrance, stairways led to second and third-floor balconies which stretched around the room on three sides. From these balconies doors opened into innumerable rooms – rooms where lights shone brighter, and from which the chief of police, when he came to make certain financial arrangements with Mr Stacy, heard frequently a gentle click-click.

It may have been that the furnishing of the main dining room and the balconies were there before Mr Stacy's coming, or again they may have set forth his own idea of suitable decoration. Looking about him, Mr Minot was reminded of a play like *Sumurun* after three hard seasons on the road. Moth-eaten rugs and musty tapestries hung everywhere. Here and there an atrocious cozy corner belied its name. Iron lanterns gave parsimonious light. Aged sofa-pillows lay limply. 'Oriental,' Mr Stacy would have called the effect. Here in this dim, but scarcely religious light, the patrons of his 'grill' ate their food, being not without misgivings as they stared through the gloom at their plates.

The long tables for the Harrowby dinner were already set, and about them hovered waiters of a color to match the room. Most of the guests had arrived. Mr Paddock made it a point to introduce Mr Minot at once to the Duchess of Lismore. This noble lady with the packing-house past was making a commendable effort to lighten the Manhattan Club by a wonderful display of jewels.

'Then felt I like some watcher of the skies, when a new planet swims into his ken!' whispered Minot, as the duchess moved away.

Paddock laughed.

'A dowdy little woman by day, but a pillar of fire by night,' he agreed. 'By the way, I'm foreman of her composing room, beginning tomorrow.'

'Be careful, Jack,' Minot warned.

'A double life from now on,' Paddock replied, 'but I think I can get away with it. Say for ways that are dark this man Stacy hold a better hand than the heathen Chinee.'

In one corner the portly Spencer Meyrick was orating to a circle of young people on the evils of gambling. Minot turned away, smiling cynically. Meyrick, as everybody knew, had made a large part of his fortune in Wall Street.

The dinner was much larger than Mrs Bruce's. Minot met a number of new people – the anaemic husband of the jewels, smug in his dukedom, and several very attractive girls thrilled at being present in Mr Stacy's sinful lair. He bestowed a smile upon Aunt Mary, serene among the best people, and discussed with Mrs Bruce – who wasted no boughten wit on him – the Florida climate. Also, he asked the elder of the Omaha girls if she had heard of Mr Nat Goodwin's latest wife.

For once the dinner itself was a minor event. It sped rapidly there in the gloom, and few so much as listened to the flashes of Mrs Bruce's wit – save perhaps the duchess, enviously. It was after the dinner, when Harrowby led his guests to the entertainment above, that interest grew tense.

No gloom in that bright room overhead. A cluster of electric lights shed their brilliance on Mr Stacy's pet roulette tables, set amid parlor furnishings of atrocious plush. From one corner a faro layout that had once flourished on Fifty-eighth Street, New York, beckoned. And on each side, through open doors, might be seen rooms furnished for the game of poker.

Mr Stacy's assistant, a polished gentleman with a face like aged ivory, presided over the roulette table. He swung the wheel a few times, an inviting smile on his face. Harrowby, his eyes bright, laid a sum of money beside a row of innocent figures. He won. He tried again, and won. Some of the young women pushed close to the table, visibly affected. Others pretended this sort of thing was an old story to them.

A few of the more adventurous women borrowed coins from the men, and joined in the play. Arguments and misunderstanding arose, which Mr Stacy's assistant urbanely settled. More of the men – Paddock among them – laid money on the table.

A buzz of excited conversation, punctuated now and then by a deathly silence as the wheel spun and the little ball hovered heart-breakingly, filled the room. Cheeks glowed red, eyes sparkled, the crush about the table increased. Spencer Meyrick himself risked from his endless store. Mr Tom Stacy's place was in full swing.

Dick Minot caught Cynthia Meyrick as she stood close beside Lord Harrowby. She seemed another girl tonight, grave rather than gay, her great brown eyes apparently looking into the future, wondering, fearing. As for Harrowby, he was a man transformed. Not for nothing was he the son of the sporting Earl of Raybrook – the peer who never failed to take a risk. The excitement of the game was reflected in his tall tense figure, his flaming cheeks. This was the Harrowby who had made Jephson that gambling proposition on a seventeenth floor in New York.

And Harrowby won consistently. Won, until a fatal choice of numbers with an overwhelming stake left him poor again, and he saw all his winnings swept to swell Tom Stacy's store. Quickly he wormed his way out of the crowd and sought Minot.

'May I see you a moment?' he asked. 'Out here.' And he led the way to the gloom of the balcony.

'If I only had the cash,' Harrowby whispered excitedly, 'I could break Stacy tonight. And I'm going to get it. Will you give me the necklace, please.'

'You forget,' Minot objected, 'that the necklace is supposed to have been stolen.'

'No. No. That's no matter. I'll arrange that. Hurry –'

'You forget, too, that you told me this morning that should this necklace be found now –'

'Mr Minot – the necklace belongs to me. Will you kindly let me have it.'

'Certainly,' said Minot coldly. And, much annoyed, he returned to the room amid the buzz and the thrill of gambling.

Harrowby ran quickly down the stairs. In the office of the club he found Tom Stacy in amiable converse with Martin Wall. He threw Chain Lightning's Collar on the manager's desk.

'How much can you loan on me on that?' he demanded.

With a grunt of surprise, Mr Stacy took up the famous collar in his thick fingers. He gazed at it for a moment. Then he looked up, and caught Martin Wall's crafty eye over Harrowby's shoulder.

'Not a cent,' said Mr Stacy firmly.

'What! I don't understand.' Harrowby gazed at him blankly. 'It's worth –'

'Not a cent,' Stacy repeated. 'That's final.'

Harrowby turned appealingly to Martin Wall. 'You –' he pleaded.

'I'm not investing,' Wall replied, with a queer smile.

Lord Harrowby restored the necklace to his pocket and, crestfallen, gloomy, went back to the room above.

'Wouldn't loan me anything on it,' he whispered to Minot. 'I don't understand, really.'

Thereafter Harrowby suffered the pain of watching others play. And while he watched, in the little office downstairs, a scene of vital bearing on his future was enacted.

A short stocky man with a bullet-shaped head had pushed open the door on Messrs Stacy and Wall. He stood, looking about him with a cynical smile.

'Hello, Tom,' he said.

'Old Bill Huntley!' cried Stacy. 'By gad, you gave me a turn. I forgot for a minute that you can't raid me down here.'

'Them happy days is past,' returned Mr Huntley dryly. 'I'm working for Uncle Sam, now, Tom. Got new fish to fry. Used to have some gay times in New York, didn't we? Oh, hello, Craig!'

'My name is Martin Wall,' said that gentleman stiffly.

'Ain't he got lovely manners,' said Huntley, pretending admiration. 'Always did have, too. And the swell friends. Still going round in the caviar crowd, I hear. What if I was to tell your friends here who you are?'

'You won't do that,' said Wall unshaken, but his breath came faster.

'Oh – you're sure of that, are you?'

'Yes. Who I am isn't one of your worries in your new line of business. And you're going to keep still because I can do you a favour – and I will.'

'Thanks, Craig. Excuse me – Martin Wall. Sort of a strain keeping track of your names, you know.'

'Forget that. I say I can do you a favour – if you'll promise not to mix in my affairs.'

'Well – what is it?'

'You're down here looking for a diamond necklace known as Chain Lightning Collar.'

'Great little guesser, you are. Well – what about it?'

'Promise?'

'You deliver the good, and I'll see.'

'All right. You'll find that necklace in Lord Harrowby's pocket right now. And you'll find Lord Harrowby in a room upstairs.'

Mr Huntley stood for a moment staring at the man he called Craig. Then with a grunt he turned away.

Two minutes later, in the bright room above, that same rather vulgar grunt sounded in Lord Harrowby's patrician ear. He turned, and his face paled. Hopelessly he looked toward Minot. Then without a word he followed Huntley from the room.

Only two of that excited crowd about the wheel noticed. And these two fled simultaneously to the balcony. There, half hidden behind an ancient musty rug, Cynthia Meyrick and Minot watched together.

Harrowby and Huntley descended the soft stairs. At the bottom, Martin Wall and Stacy were waiting. The sound of voices pitched low could be heard on the balcony, but though they strained to hear, the pair above could not. However, they could see the plebeian hand of Mr Huntley held out to Lord Harrowby. They could see Harrowby reach into his pocket, and bring forth a white envelope. Next they beheld Chain Lightning's Collar gleam in the dusk as Huntley held it up. A few low words, and Harrowby went out with the detective.

Martin Wall ascended the stair. On the dim balcony he was confronted by a white-faced girl whose wonderful copper hair had once held Chain Lightning's Collar.

'What does it mean?' she asked, her voice low and tense.

'Mean?' Martin Wall laughed. 'It means that Lord Harrowby must go north and face a United States Commissioner in Jersey City. It seems that when he brought that necklace over he quite forgot to tell the customs officials about it.'

'Go north! When?'

'Tonight. On the midnight train. North to Jersey City.'

Mr Wall went into the bright room where the excitement buzzed on, oblivious. Cynthia Meyrick turned to Minot.

'But he can't possibly get back –' she cried.

'No. He can't get back. I'm sorry.'

'And my wedding dress – came last night.'

She stood clutching a moth-eaten tapestry in her slim white hand. In the gloom of that dull old balcony her eyes shone strangely.

'Some things aren't to be,' she whispered. 'And' – very faintly – 'others are.'

A thrill shot through Minot, sharp as a pain, but glorious. What did she mean by that? What indeed but the one thing that must not happen – the thing he wanted most of all things in the world to happen – the thing he had come to San Marco to prevent. He came closer to her – and closer – the blood was pounding in his brain. Dazed, exulting, he held out his arms.

'Cynthia!' he cried.

And then suddenly behind her, on the stairs, he caught sight of a great bald head ascending through the dusk. It was an ordinary bald head, the property of Mr Stacy in fact, but to Minot a certain Jephson seemed to be moving beneath it. He remembered. His arms fell to his sides. He turned away.

'We must see what can be done,' he said mechanically.

'Yes,' Cynthia Meyrick agreed in tone, 'we must see what can be done.'

And a tear, unnoticed, fell on Mr Stacy's oriental tapestry.

Chapter XV
A Bit of a Blow

Miss Meyrick turned back toward the room of chance to find her father. Minot, meanwhile, ran down the steps, obtained his hat and coat, and hurried across the street to the hotel. He went at once to Harrowby's rooms.

There he encountered a scene of wild disorder. The round-faced valet was packing trunks against time, and his time-keeper, Mr Bill Huntley, sat in a corner, grim and silent, watch in hand. Lord Harrowby paced the floor madly. When he saw Minot he held out his long, lean, helpless hands.

'You've heard, old boy?' he said.

'Yes, I've heard,' said Minot sharply. 'A fine fix, Harrowby. Why the deuce didn't you pay the duty on that necklace?'

'Dear boy! Was saving every cent I had for – you know what. Besides, I heard of such a clever scheme for slipping it in –'

'Never mind that! Mr Huntley, this gentleman was to have been married on Tuesday. Can't you hold off until then?'

'Nothing doing,' said Mr Huntley firmly. 'I got to get back to New York. He'll postpone his wedding. Ought to have thought of these things before he pulled off his little stunt.'

'It's no use, Minot,' said Harrowby hopelessly. 'I've gone all over it with this chap. He won't listen to reason. What the deuce am I to do?'

A knock sounded on the door and Spencer Meyrick, red-faced, flirting with apoplexy, strode into the room.

'Lord Harrowby,' he announced, 'I desire to see you alone.'

'Er – step into the bedroom,' Harrowby suggested.

Mr Huntley rose promptly to his feet.

'Nix,' he said. 'There's a door out of that room leading into the hall. If you go in there, I go, too.'

Mr Meyrick glared. Harrowby stood embarrassed.

'Very well,' said Meyrick through his teeth. 'We'll stay here. It doesn't matter to me. I simply want to say, Lord Harrowby, that when you get to Jersey City you needn't trouble to come back, as far as my family is concerned.'

A look of pain came into Harrowby's thin face.

'Not come back,' he said. 'My dear sir –'

'That's what I said. I'm a plain man, Harrowby. A plain American. It doesn't seem to me that marrying into the British nobility is worth all the trouble it's costing us –'

'But really –'

'It may be, but it doesn't look that way to me. I prefer a simple wedding to a series of vaudeville acts. If you think I'm going to stand for the publicity of this latest affair, you're mistaken. I've talked matters over with Cynthia – the marriage is off – for good!'

'But my dear sir, Cynthia and I are very fond of each other –'

'I don't give a damn if you are!' Meyrick fumed. 'This is the last straw. I'm through with you. Goodnight, and goodbye.'

He stamped out as he had come and Lord Harrowby fell limply into a chair.

'All over, and all done,' he moaned.

'And Jephson loses,' said Minot with mixed emotions.

'Yes – I'm sorry.' Harrowby shook his head tragically. 'Sorrier than you are, old chap. I love Cynthia Meyrick – really I do. This is a bit of a blow.'

'Come, come!' cried Mr Huntley, 'I'm not going to miss that train while you play act. We've only got half an hour, now.'

Harrowby rose unhappily and went into the inner room, Huntley at his heels. Minot sat, his unseeing eyes gazing down at the old copy of the London *Times* which Harrowby had been reading that morning at breakfast.

Gradually, despite his preoccupation, a name in a headline forced itself to his attention. Courtney Giles. Where had he heard that name before? He picked up the *Times* from the table on which it was lying. He read:

The 'Ardent Lover', the new romantic comedy in which Courtney Giles has appeared briefly at the West End Road Theater, will be removed from the boards tonight. The public has not been appreciative. If truth must be told – and bitter truth it is – the once beloved matinee idol has become too fat to hold his old admirers, and they have drifted steadily to other, slimmer gods. Mr Giles' early retirement from the stage is rumored.

Minot threw down the paper. Poor old Jephson! First the rain on the dowager duchess then an actor's expanding waist – and tomorrow the news that Harrowby's wedding was not to be. Why, it would ruin the man! Minot stepped to the door of the inner room.

'I'm going out to think,' he announced. 'I'll see you in the lobby before you leave.'

Two minutes later, in the summerhouse where he had bid goodbye to the sparkling Gaiety lady, he sat puffing furiously at a cigar. Back into the past as it concerned Chain Lightning's Collar he went. That night when Cynthia Meyrick had worn it in her hair, and Harrowby, hearing of the search for it – had snatched it in the dark. His own guardianship of the valuable trinket – Martin Wall's invasion of his rooms – the dropping of the jewels on shipboard, and the return of them by Mr Wall next morning. And last, but not least, Mr Stacy's firm refusal to loan money on the necklace that very night.

All these things Minot pondered.

Meanwhile Harrowby, having finished his packing, descended to the lobby of the De la Pax. In a certain pink parlor he found Cynthia Meyrick, and stood gazing helplessly into her eyes. 'Cynthia – your father said – is it true?'

'It's true, Allan.'

'You too wish the wedding – indefinitely postponed?'

'Father thinks it best –'

'But you?' He came closer. 'You, Cynthia?'

'I – I don't know. There has been so much trouble, Allan –'

'I know. And I'm fearfully sorry about this latest. But, Cynthia – you mustn't send me away – I love you. Do you doubt that?'

'No, Allan.'

'You're the most wonderful girl who has ever come into my life – I want you in it always – beside me –'

'At any rate, Allan, a wedding next Tuesday is impossible now.'

'Yes, I'm afraid it is. And after that –'

'After that – I don't know, Allan.'

Aunt Mary came into the room, distress written plainly in her plump face. No misstep of the peerage was beyond Aunt Mary's forgiveness. She took Harrowby's hand.

'I'm so sorry, your lordship,' she said. 'Most unfortunate. But I'm sure it will all be cleared away in time –'

Mr Huntley made it a point to interrupt. He stood at the door, watch in hand.

'Come on,' he said. 'We've got to start.'

Harrowby followed the ladies from the room.

In the lobby Spencer Meyrick joined them. His lordship shook hands with Aunt Mary, with Mr Meyrick – then he turned to the girl.

'Goodbye, Cynthia,' he said unhappily. He took her slim white hand in his. Then he turned quickly and started with Huntley for the door.

It was at this point that Mr Minot, his cigar and his cogitations finished, entered upon the scene.

'Just a minute,' he said to Mr Huntley.

'Not another minute!' remarked Huntley with decision. 'Not for the King of England himself. We got just fifteen of 'em left to catch that train, and if I know San Marco hackmen –'

'You've got time to answer our questions.' Impressed by Minot's tone, the Meyrick family moved nearer. 'There's no doubt, is there, Mr Huntley, that the necklace you have in your pocket is the one Lord Harrowby brought from England?'

'Of course not. Now get out of the way –'

'Are you a good judge of jewels, Mr Huntley?'

'Well, I've got a little reputation in that line. But say –'

'Then I suggest,' said Minot impressively, 'that you examine Chain Lightning's Collar closely.'

'Thanks for the suggestion,' sneered Mr Huntley. 'I'll follow it – when I get time. Just now I've got to –'

'You'd better follow it now – before you catch a train. Otherwise you may be so unfortunate as to make a fool of yourself.'

Mr Huntley stood, hesitating. There was something in Minot's tone that rang true. The detective again looked at his watch. Then, with one of his celebrated grunts, he pulled out the necklace, and stood staring at it with a new expression.

He grunted again, and stepped to a near-by writing desk, above which hung a powerful electric light. The others followed. Mr Huntley laid the necklace on the desk, and took out a small microscope which was attached to one end of his watch-chain. With rapt gaze he stared at the largest of the diamonds. He went the length of the string, examining each stone in turn. The expression on Mr Huntley's face would have made him a star in the "movies".'

'Hell!' he cried, and threw Chain Lightning's Collar down on the desk.

'What's the matter?' Mr Minot smiled.

'Glass,' snarled Huntley. 'Fine old bottle glass. What do you know about that?'

'But really – it can't be –' put in Harrowby.

'Well it is,' Mr Huntley glared at him. 'The inspector might have known you moth-eaten noblemen ain't got any of the real stuff left.

'I won't believe it –' Harrowby began, but caught Minot's eye.

'It's true, just the same,' Minot said. 'By the way, Mr Huntley, how much is that little ornament worth?'

'About nine dollars and twenty-five cents.' Mr Huntley still glared angrily.

'Well – you can't take Lord Harrowby back for not declaring that, can you?'

'No,' snorted Huntley. 'But I can go back myself, and I'm going – that midnight train. Goodbye.'

Minot followed him to the door.

'Aren't you going to thank me?' he asked. 'You know, I saved you –'

'Thank you! Hell!' said Huntley, and disappeared into the dark.

When Minot returned he found Harrowby standing facing the Meyricks, and holding the necklace in his hand as though it were a bomb on the point of exploding.

'I say, I feel rather low,' he was saying, 'when I remember that I made you a present of this thing, Cynthia. But on my honor, I didn't know. And I can scarcely believe it now. I know the governor has been financially embarrassed – but I never suspected him of this – the associations were so dear – really –'

'It may not have been your father who duplicated Chain Lightning's Collar with a fake,' Minot suggested.

'My word, old boy, who then?'

'You remember,' said Minot, addressing the Meyricks, 'that the necklace was stolen recently. Well – it was returned to Lord Harrowby under unusual circumstances. At least, this collection of glass was returned. My theory is that the thief had a duplicate made – an old trick.'

'The very idea,' Harrowby cried. 'I say, Minot, you are clever. I should never have thought of that.'

'Thanks,' said Minot dryly. He sought to avoid Miss Cynthia Meyrick's eyes.

'Er – by the way,' said Harrowby, looking at Spencer Meyrick. 'There is nothing to prevent the wedding now.'

The old man shrugged his shoulders.

'I leave that to my daughter,' he said, and turned away.

'Cynthia?' Harrowby pleaded.

Miss Meyrick cast a strange look at Minot, standing forlorn before her. And then she smiled – not very happily.

'There seems to be no reason for changing our plans,' she said slowly. 'It would be a great disappointment to so many people. Goodnight.'

Minot followed her to the elevator.

'It's as I told you this morning,' he said miserably, 'I'm just one of the pawns in the hands of the Master of the Show. I can't explain –'

'What is there to explain?' the girl asked coldly. 'I congratulate you on a highly successful evening.'

The elevator door banged shut between them.

Turning, Minot encountered Aunt Mary.

'You clever boy,' she cried. 'We are all so very grateful to you. You have saved us from a very embarrassing situation.'

'Please don't mention it,' Minot replied, and he meant it.

He sat down beside the dazed Harrowby on one of the lobby sofas.

'I'm all at sea, really, old chap,' Harrowby confessed. 'But I must say – I admire you tremendously. How the devil did you know the necklace was a fraud?'

'I didn't know – I guessed,' said Minot. 'And the thing that led me to make that happy guess was Tom Stacy's refusal to loan you money on it tonight. Mr Stacy is no fool.'

'And you think that Martin Wall has the real Chain Lightning's Collar?'

'It looks that way to me. There's only one thing against my theory. He didn't clear out when he had the chance. But he may be staying on to avert suspicion. We haven't any evidence to arrest him on – and if we did there'd be the customs people to deal with. If I were you I'd hire a private detective to watch Wall, and try to get the real necklace back without enlisting the arm of the law.'

'Really,' said Harrowby, 'things happening so swiftly I'm at a loss to follow them. I am, old boy. First one obstacle and then another. You've been splendid, Minot, splendid. I want to thank you for all you have done. I thought tonight the wedding had gone glimmering. And I'm fond of Miss Meyrick. Tremendously.'

'Don't thank me,' Minot replied. 'I'm not doing it for you – we both know that. I'm protecting Jephson's money. In a few days, wedding bells. And then me back to New York, shouting never again on the Cupid act. If I'm ever roped into another job like this –'

'It has been a trying position for you,' Harrowby said sympathetically. 'And you've done nobly. I'm sure your troubles are all out of the way now. With the necklace worry gone –'

He paused. For across the lobby toward them walked Henry Trimmer, and his walk was that of a man who is going somewhere.

'Ah – Mister Harrowby,' he boomed, 'and Mr Minot. I've been looking for you both. It will interest you to know that I had a wireless message from Lord Harrowby this noon.'

'A wireless?' cried Minot.

'Yes.' Trimmer laughed. 'Not such a fool as you think him, Lord Harrowby isn't. Managed to send me a wireless from Tarragona despite the attentions of your friends. So I went out there this afternoon and brought George back with me.'

Silently Minot and Harrowby stared at each other.

'Yes,' Mr Trimmer went on, 'George is back again – back under the direction of little me, a publicity man with no grass under the feet. I've come to give you gentlemen your choice. You either see Lord Harrowby tomorrow morning at ten o'clock and recognize his claims, or I'll have you both thrown into jail for kidnaping.'

'Tomorrow morning at ten,' Harrowby repeated gloomily.

'That's what I said,' replied Mr Trimmer blithely. 'How about it, little brother?'

'Minot – what would you advise?'

'See him,' sighed Minot.

'Very well.' Harrowby's tone was resigned. 'I presume I'd better.'

'Ah – coming to your senses, aren't you?' said Trimmer. 'I hope we aren't spoiling the joyous wedding day. But then, what I say is, if the girl's marrying you just for the title –'

Harrowby leaped to his feet. 'You haven't been asked for an opinion,' he said.

'No, of course not. Don't get excited. I'll see you both in the morning at ten.' And Mr Trimmer strolled elegantly away.

Harrowby turned hopefully to Minot.

'At ten in the morning,' he repeated. 'Old chap, what are we going to do at ten in the morning?'

'I don't know,' smiled Minot. 'But if past performances mean anything, we'll win.'

Chapter XVI
Who's Who in England

'What's the matter with you?'

Seated in the lobby of the De la Pax on Sunday morning, Mr Trimmer turned a disapproving eye upon the lank Englishman at his side as he made this query. And his question was not without good foundation. For the aspirant to the title of Lord Harrowby was at the moment a jelly quaking with fear.

'Fawncy meeting you after all these years,' said poor old George in an uncertain treble.

'Come, come,' cried Mr Trimmer, 'put a little more authority into your voice. You can't walk up and claim your rights with your knees dancing the tango. This is the moment we've been looking forward to. Act determined. Walk into that room upstairs as though you were walking into Rakedale Hall to take charge of it.'

'Allan, don't you know me – I'm your brother George,' went on the Englishman, intent on rehearsing.

'More like it,' said Trimmer. 'Put the fire into it. You're not expecting a thrashing, you know. You're expecting the title and recognition that belongs to you. I wish I was the real Lord Harrowby. I guess I'd show 'em a thing or two.'

'I wish you was,' agreed poor old George sadly. 'Somehow, I don't seem to have the spirit I used to have.'

'A good point,' commented Trimmer. 'Years of wrong and suffering have made you timid. I'll call that to their attention. Five minutes of ten, your lordship.'

His lordship groaned.

'All right, I'm ready,' he said. 'What is it I say as I go in? Oh, yes –' He stepped into the elevator – 'Fawncy seeing you after all these years.'

The negro elevator boy was somewhat startled at this greeting, but regained his composure and started the car. Mr Trimmer and his 'proposition' shot up toward their great opportunity.

In Lord Harrowby's suite that gentleman sat in considerable nervousness, awaiting the undesired encounter. With him sat Miss Meyrick and her father, whom he had thought it necessary to invite to witness the ordeal. Mr Richard Minot uneasily paced the floor, avoiding as much as possible the glances of Miss Meyrick's brown eyes. Ten o'clock was upon him, and Mr Minot was no nearer a plan of action than he had been the preceding night.

Every good press agent is not without a live theatrical sense, and Mr Trimmer was no exception. He left his trembling claimant in the entrance hall and strode into the room.

'Good morning,' he said brightly. 'Here we are, on time to the minute. Ah – I beg your pardon.'

Lord Harrowby performed brief introductions which Mr Trimmer effusively acknowledged. Then he turned dramatically toward his lordship.

'Out here in the hallway stands a poor broken creature,' he began. 'Your own flesh and blood, Allan Harrowby.' Obviously Mr Trimmer had prepared speeches for himself as well as for poor old George. 'For twenty years,' he went on, 'this man has been denied his just heritage. We are here this morning to perform a duty –'

'My dear fellow,' broke in Harrowby wearily, 'why should you inflict oratory upon us? Bring in this – er – gentleman.'

'That I will,' replied Trimmer heartily. 'And when you have heard his story, digested his evidence, I am sure –'

'Yes, yes. Bring him in.'

Mr Trimmer stepped to the door. He beckoned. A very reluctant figure shuffled in.

George's face was green with fright. His knees rattled together. He made, altogether, a ludicrous picture, and Mr Trimmer himself noted this with sinking heart.

'Allow me,' said Trimmer theatrically. 'George, Lord Harrowby.'

George cleared his throat, but did not succeed in dislodging his heart, which was there at the moment.

'Fancy seeing you after all these years,' he mumbled weakly, to no one in particular.

'Speak up,' said Spencer Meyrick sharply. 'Who is it you're talking to?'

'To him,' explained George, nodding toward Lord Harrowby. 'To my brother Allan. Don't you know me, Allan? Don't you know –'

He stopped. An expression of surprise and relief swept over his worried face. He turned triumphantly to Trimmer.

'I don't have to prove who I am to him,' he announced.

'Why don't you?' demanded Trimmer in alarm.

'Because he can't, I fancy,' put in Harrowby.

'No,' said George slowly, 'because I never saw him before in all my life.'

'Ah – you admit it,' cried Allan Harrowby with relief.

'Of course I do,' replied George, 'I never saw you before in my life.'

'And you've never been at Rakedale Hall, have you?' Lord Harrowby demanded.

'Here – wait a minute –' shouted Trimmer, in a panic.

'Oh, yes – I've been at Rakedale Hall,' said the claimant firmly. 'I spent my boyhood there. But you've never been there.'

'I – what –'

'You've never been at Rakedale Hall. Why? Because you're not Allan Harrowby! That's why.'

A deathly silence fell. Only a little traveling clock on the mantel was articulate.

'Absurd – ridiculous –' cried Lord Harrowby.

'Talk about impostors,' cried George, his spirit and his courage sweeping back. 'You're one yourself. I wish I'd got a good look

169

at you sooner, I'd have put a stop to all this. Allan Harrowby, eh? I guess not. I guess I'd know my own brother if I saw him. I guess I know the Harrowby features. I give you twenty-four hours to get out of town – you blooming fraud.'

'The man's crazy,' Allan Harrowby cried. 'Raving mad. He's an impostor – this is a trick of his –' He looked helplessly around the circle. In every face he saw doubt, questioning. 'Good heavens – you're not going to listen to him? He's come here to prove that he's George Harrowby. Why doesn't he do it?'

'I'll do it,' said George sweetly, 'when I meet a real Harrowby. In the meantime, I give you twenty-four hours to get out of town. You'd better go.'

Victorious, George turned toward the door. Trimmer, lost between admiration and doubt, turned also.

'Take my advice,' George proclaimed. 'Make him prove who he is. That's the important point now. What does it matter to you who I am? Nothing. But it matters a lot about him. Make him prove that he's Allan Harrowby.'

And, with the imperious manner that he should have adopted on entering the room, George Harrowby left it. Mr Trimmer, eclipsed for once, trotted at his side.

'Say,' cried Trimmer in the hall, 'is that on the level? Isn't he Allan Harrowby?'

'I should say not,' said George grandly. 'Doesn't look any-thing like Allan.'

Trimmer chortled in glee.

'Great stuff,' he cried. 'I guess we tossed a bomb, eh? Now we'll run him out of town.'

'Oh, no,' said George, 'we've done our work here. Let's go over to London now and see the pater.'

'That we will,' cried Trimmer. 'That we will. By gad, I'm proud of you today, Lord Harrowby.'

Inside Allan Harrowby's suite three pairs of questioning eyes were turned on that harassed nobleman. He fidgeted in his chair.

'I say,' he pleaded. 'It's all his bluff, you know.'

'Maybe,' said old Spencer Meyrick, rising. 'But Harrowby – or whatever your name is – there's altogether too much three-ring circus about this wedding to suit me. My patience is exhausted, sir – clean exhausted. Things look queer to me – have right along. I'm more than inclined to believe what that fellow said.'

'But my dear sir – that chap is a rank impostor. There wasn't a word of truth in what he said. Cynthia – you understand –'

'Why, yes – I suppose so,' the girl replied. 'You are Allan Harrowby, aren't you?'

'My dear girl – of course I am.'

'Nevertheless,' said Spencer Meyrick with decision, 'I'm going to call the wedding off again. Some of your actions haven't made much of a hit with me. I'm going to call it off until you come to me and prove you're Allan Harrowby – a lord in good and regular standing, with all dues paid.'

'But – confound it, sir – a gentleman's word –'

'Mr Meyrick,' put in Minot, 'may I be allowed to say that I consider your action hasty –'

'And may I be allowed to ask what affair this is of yours?' demanded Mr Meyrick hotly.

'Father!' cried Miss Meyrick. 'Please don't be harsh with Mr Minot. His heart is set on my marriage with Lord Harrowby! Naturally he feels very badly over all this.'

Minot winced.

'Come, Cynthia,' said Meyrick, moving toward the door. 'I've had enough of acting. Remember, sir – the wedding is off – absolutely off – until you are able to establish your identity beyond question.'

And he and his daughter went out.

Minot stood for a long time staring at Lord Harrowby. Finally he spoke.

'Say, Harrowby,' he inquired, 'who the devil are you?'

His lordship sadly shook his head.

'You, too, Brutus,' he sighed. 'Haven't I one friend left? I'm Allan Harrowby. Ask Jephson. If I weren't, that policy that's causing you so much trouble wouldn't be worth the paper it's written on.'

'That's right, too. Well, admitting you're Harrowby, how are you going to prove it?'

'I've an idea,' Harrowby replied.

'Everything comes to him who waits. What is it?'

'A very good friend of mine – an old Oxford friend – is attached to our embassy at Washington. He was planning to come down for the wedding. I'll telegraph him to board the next train.'

'Good boy,' said Minot. 'That's a regular idea. Better send the wire at once.'

Harrowby promised, and they parted. In the lobby below Mr Minot met Jack Paddock. Paddock looked drawn and worried.

'Working on my stuff for the dinner tomorrow night,' he confided. 'Say, it's no cinch to do two of them. Can't you suggest a topc that's liable to come up?'

'Yes,' replied Minot. 'I can suggest one. Fake noblemen.' And he related to Mr Paddock the astounding events of the morning.

That Sunday that had begun so startlingly progressed as a Sunday should, in peace. Early in the afternoon Harrowby hunted Minot up and announced that his friend would arrive at noon, and that the Meyricks had agreed no definite step pending his arrival.

Shortly after six o'clock a delayed telegram was delivered to Mr Minot. It was from Mr Thacker, and it read:

Have located the owner of the yacht Lileth *its real name the* Lady Evelyn *stolen from owner in North River he is on his way south will look you up on arrival*

Minot whistled. Here was a new twist for the drama to take.

At about the same time that Minot received his message, a similar slip of yellow paper was put into the hands of Lord Harrowby. Three times he read it, his eyes staring, his cheeks flushed.

Then he fled to his rooms. The elevator was not quick enough; he sped up the stairs. Once in his suite he dragged out the nearest traveling bag and began to pack like a mad man.

Mr Minot was finishing a leisurely and lonely dinner about an hour later when Jack Paddock ran up to his table. Mr Paddock's usual calm was sadly ruffled.

'Heck,' he cried, 'here's news for you. I met Lord Harrowby sliding out a side door with a suitcase just now.'

Minot leaped to his feet.

'What does that mean?' he wondered aloud.

'Mean?' answered Mr Paddock. 'It means just one thing. Old George had the right dope. Harrowby is a fake. He's making his getaway.'

Minot threw down his napkin.

'Oh, he is, is he?' he cried. 'Well, I guess not. Come on, Jack.'

'What are you going to do?'

'I'm going down to the station and stop him. He's caused me too much trouble to let him slide out like this. A fake, eh? Well, I'll have him behind bars tonight.'

A cab driver was, by superhuman efforts, roused to hasty action. He rattled the two young men wildly down the silent street to the railway station. They dashed into the drab little waiting room just as a voice called:

'Train for the north! Jacksonville! Washington! New York!'

'There he is!' Paddock cried, and pointed at the lean figure of Lord Harrowby slipping out the door nearest the train shed.

Paddock and Minot ran across the waiting room and out into the open. In the distance they saw Harrowby passing through the gate and on to the tracks. They ran up just in time to have the gate banged shut in their face.

'Where's your ticket?' demanded the great stone face on guard.

'I haven't got one, but –'

'Too late anyhow,' said the face. 'The train's started.'

Through the wooden pickets Minot saw the long yellow string of coaches slipping by. He turned to Paddock.

'Oh, very well,' he cried, exulting. 'Let him go. Come on!'

He dashed back to the carriage that had brought them from the hotel, the driver of which sat in a stupor trying to regain his wits and nonchalance.

'What now?' Paddock wanted to know.

'Get in!' commanded Minot. He pushed his friend on to the musty seat, and followed.

'To the De la Pax,' he cried, 'as fast as you can go.'

'But what the devil's the need of hurrying now?' demanded Paddock.

'All the need in the world,' replied Minot joyously. 'I'm going to have a talk with Cynthia Meyrick. A little talk – alone.'

Chapter XVII
The Shortest Way Home

The moon was shining in that city of the picturesque past. Its light fell silvery on the narrow streets, the old adobe houses, the listless palms. In every shadow seemed to lurk the memory of a love long dead – a love of the old passionate Spanish days. A soft breeze came whispering from the very sea Ponce de Leon had sailed. It was as if at a signal – a bugle call, a rose thrown from a window, the boom of a cannon at the water's edge – the forgotten past of hot hearts, of arms equally ready for cutlass or slender waist, could live again.

And Minot was as one who had heard such a signal. He loved. The obstacle that had confronted him, wrung his heart, left him helpless, was swept away. He was like a man who, released from prison, sees the sky, the green trees, the hills again. He loved! The moon was shining!

He stood amid the colorful blooms of the hotel courtyard and looked up at her window, with its white curtain waving gently in the breeze. He called out, softly. And then he saw her face, peering out as some senorita of the old days from her lattice –

'I've news – very important news,' he said. 'May I see you a moment?'

Far better this than the telephone of the bellboy. Far more in keeping with the magic of the night. She came, dressed in the white that set off so well her hair of gleaming copper. Minot met on the veranda. She smiled into his eyes inquiringly.

'Do you mind – a little walk?'

'Where to?'

'Say to the fort – the longest way.'

She glanced back toward the hotel.

'I'm not sure that I ought –'

'But that will only make it more exciting. Please. And I've news – real news.'

She nodded her head, and they crossed the courtyard to the avenue. From this bright thoroughfare they turned in a moment into a dark and unkempt street.

'See,' said Minot suddenly, 'the old Spanish churchyard. They built cities around churches in the old days. The world do move. It's railroad stations now.'

They stood peering through the gloom at a small chapel dim amid the trees, and aged stones leaning tipsily among the weeds.

'At the altar of that chapel,' Minot said, 'a priest fell – shot in the back by an Indian's arrow. Sounds unreal, doesn't it? And when you think that under these musty stones lies the dust of folks who walked this very ground, and loved, and hated, like you and –'

'Yes – but isn't it all rather gloomy?' Cynthia Meyrick shuddered.

They went on, to pass shortly through the crumbling remains of the city gates. There at the water's edge the great gray fort loomed in the moonlight like a historical novelist's dream. Its huge iron-bound doors were locked for the night; its custodian home in the bosom of his family. Only its lower ramparts were left for the feet of romantic youth to tread.

Along the ramparts, close to the shimmering sea, Miss Meyrick and Minot walked. Truth to tell, it was not so very difficult to keep one's footing – but once the girl was forced to hold out an appealing hand.

'French heels are treacherous,' she explained.

Minot took her hand, and for the first time knew the thrill that, encountered often on the printed page, he had mentally classed as 'rubbish!' Wisely she interrupted it:

'You said you had news?'

He had, but it was not so easy to impart as he had expected.

'Tell me,' he said, 'if it should turn out that what poor old George said this morning was fact – that Allan Harrowby was an impostor – would you feel so very badly?'

She withdrew her hand.

'You have no right to ask that,' she replied.

'Forgive me. Indeed I haven't. But I was moved to ask it for the reason that – what George said was evidently true. Allan Harrowby left suddenly for the north an hour ago.'

The girl stood still, looking with wide eyes out over the sea.

'Left – for the north,' she repeated. There was a long silence. At length she turned to Minot, a queer light in her eyes. 'Of course, you'll go after him and bring him back?' she asked.

'No.' Minot bowed his head. 'I know I must have looked rather silly of late. But if you think I did the things I've done because I chose to – you're wrong. If you think I did them because I didn't love you – you're wrong, too. Oh, I –'

'Mr Minot!'

'I can't help it. I know it's indecently soon – I've got to tell you just the same. There's been so much in the way – I'm wild to say it now. I love you.'

The water breaking on the ancient stones below seemed to be repeating 'Sh – sh,' but Minot paid no heed to the warning.

'I've cared for you,' he went on, 'ever since that morning on the train when we raced the razorbacks – ever since that wonderful ride over that god forsaken road that looked like Heaven to me. And every time since that I've seen you I've known that I'd come to care more –'

The girl stood and stared thoughtfully out at the soft blue sea. Minot moved closer, over those perilous slippery rocks.

'I know it's an old story to you,' he went on, 'and that I'd be a fool to hope that I could possibly be anything but just another man who adores you. But – because I love you so much –'

She turned and looked at him.

'And in spite of all this,' she said slowly, 'from the first you have done everything in your power to prevent the breaking off of my engagement to Harrowby.'

'Yes, but –'

'Weren't you overly chivalrous to a rival? Wouldn't what – what you are saying be more convincing if you had remained neutral?'

'I know. I can't explain it to you now. It's all over, anyway. It was horrible while it lasted – but it's over now. I'm never going to work again for your marriage to anybody – except one man. The man who is standing before you – who loves you – loves you –'

He stopped, for the girl was smiling. And it was not the sort of smile that his words were entitled to.

'I'm sorry, really,' she said. 'But I can't help it. All I can see now is your triumphant entrance last night – your masterly exposure of that silly necklace – your clever destruction of every obstacle in order that Harrowby and I might be married on Tuesday. In the light of all that has happened – how can you expect to appear other than –'

'Foolish? You're right. And you couldn't possibly care – just a little –'

He stopped, embarrassed. Poorly chosen words, those last. He saw the light of recollection in her eye.

'I should say,' he went on hastily, 'isn't there just a faint gleam of hope – for me –'

'If we were back on the train,' she said, 'and all that followed could be different – and Harrowby had never been – I might –'

'You might – yes?'

'I might not say what I'm going to say now. Which is – hadn't we better return to the hotel?'

'I'm sorry,' remarked Minot. 'Sorry I had the bad taste to say what I have at this time – but if you knew and could understand – which you can't of course – Yes, let's go back to the hotel – the shortest way.'

He turned, and looked toward the tower of the De la Pax rising to meet the sky – seemingly a million miles away. So Peary might have gazed to the north, setting out for the Pole.

They went back along the ramparts, over the dry moat, through the crumbling gates. Conversation languished. Then the ancient graveyard, ghastly in the gloom. After that the long lighted street of humble shops. And the shortest way home seemed a million times longer than the longest way there.

'Considering what you have told me of – Harrowby,' she said, 'I shall be leaving for the north soon. Will you look me up in New York?'

'Thank you,' Minot said. 'It will be a very great privilege.'

Cynthia Meyrick entered the elevator and out of sight in that gilded cage she smiled a twisted little smile.

Mr Minot beheld Mr Trimmer and his 'proposition' basking in the limelight of the De la Pax, and feeling in no mood to listen to the publicity man's triumphant cackle, he hurried to the veranda. There he found a bellboy calling his name.

'Gen'lemun to see you,' the boy explained. He led the way back into the lobby and up to a tall athletic-looking man with a ruddy, frank, attractive face.

The stranger held out his hand.

'Mr Minot, of Lloyds?' he asked. 'How do you do, sir? I'm very glad to know you. Promised Thacker I'd look you up at once. Let's adjourn to the grill–room.'

Minot followed in the wake of the tall breezy one. Already he liked the man immensely.

'Well,' said the stranger, over a table in the grill, 'what'll you have? Waiter? Perhaps you heard I was coming. I happen to be the owner of the yacht in the harbor, which somebody has christened the *Lileth*.'

'Yes, I thought so,' Minot replied. 'I'm mighty glad you've come. As Mr Martin Wall is posing as the owner just at present.'

'So I learned from Thacker. Nervy lad, this Wall. I live in Chicago myself – left my boat – Lady Evelyn, I called her – in the North River for the winter in charge of a caretaker. This Wall, it seems, needed a boat for a month and took a fancy to mine. And since my caretaker was evidently a crook, it was a simple matter to rent it. Never would have found it out except for you people. Too busy. Really ought not to have taken this trip – business needs me every minute – but I've got sort of a hankering to meet Mr Martin Wall.'

'Shall we go out to the boat right away?'

'No need of that. We'll run out in the morning with the proper authorities.' The stranger leaned across the table, and something in his eyes startled Minot 'In the meantime,' he said, 'I happen to be interested in another matter. What's all this talk about George Harrowby coming back to life?'

'Well, there's a chap here,' Minot explained, 'who claims to be the elder brother of Allan Harrowby. His cause is in the hands of an advertising expert named Trimmer.'

'Yes. I saw a story in a Washington paper.'

'This morning George Harrowby, so-called, confronted Allan Harrowby and denounced Allan himself as a fraud.'

The man from Chicago threw back his head, and a roar of unexpected laughter smote on Minot's hearing.

'Good joke,' said the stranger.

'No joke at all. George was right – at least, so it seems. Allan Harrowby cleared out this evening.'

'Yes. So I was told by the clerk in there. Do you happen to know – er – Allan?'

'Yes. Very well indeed.'

'But you don't know the reason he left?'

'Why,' answered Minot, 'I suppose because George Harrowby gave him twenty-four hours to get out of town.'

Again the Chicago man laughed.

'That can't have been the reason,' he said. 'I happen to know.'

'Just how,' inquired Minot, 'do you happen to know?'

Leaning far back in his chair, the westerner smiled at Minot with a broad engaging smile.

'I fancy I neglected to introduce myself,' he said. 'I make automobiles in Chicago – and my name's George Harrowby.'

'You – you –' Minot's head went round dizzily. 'Oh, no,' he said firmly. 'I don't believe it.'

The other's smile grew even broader.

'Don't blame you a bit, my boy,' he said. 'Must have been a bit of a mix-up down here. Then, too, I don't look like an Englishman. Don't want to. I'm an American now, and I like it.'

'You mean you're the real Lord Harrowby?'

'That's what I mean – take it slowly, Mr Minot. I'm George, and if Allan ever gets his eyes on me, I won't have to prove who I am. He'll know, the kid will. But by the way – what I want now is to meet this chap who claims to be me – also his friend, Mr Trimmer.'

'Of course you do. I saw them out in the lobby a minute ago.' Minot rose. 'I'll bring them in. But – but –'

'What is it?'

'Oh, never mind. I believe you.'

Trimmer and his proposition still adorned the lobby, puffed with pride and pompousness. Briefly Minot explained that a gentleman in the grill-room desired to be introduced, and graciously the two followed after. The Chicago George Harrowby rose as he saw the group approach his table. Suddenly behind him Minot heard a voice:

'My God!' And the limp Englishman of the sandwich boards made a long lean streak toward the door. Minot leaped after him, and dragged him back.

'Here, Trimmer,' he said, 'your proposition has chilblains.'

'What's the trouble?' Mr Trimmer glared about him.

'Allow me,' said Minot. 'Sir – our leading vaudeville actor and his manager. Gentlemen – Mr George Harrowby, of Chicago!'

'Sit down, boys,' said Mr Harrowby genially.

He indicated a chair to Mr Trimmer, but that gentleman stood, his eyes frozen to the face of his proposition. The Chicago man turned to that same proposition. 'Brace up, Jenkins. 'Nobody will hurt you.'

But Jenkins could not brace. He allowed Minot to deposit his limp body in a chair.

'I thought you was dead, sir,' he mumbled.

'A common mistake,' smiled Harrowby. 'My family has thought the same, and I've been too busy making automobiles to tell them differently. Mr Trimmer, will you have a – what's the matter, man?'

For Mr Trimmer was standing, purple, over his proposition.

'I want to get this straight,' he said with assumed calm. 'See here, you cringing cur – what does this mean?'

'I thought he was dead,' murmured Jenkins in terror.

'You'll think the same about yourself in a minute – and you'll be right,' Trimmer predicted.

'Come, come,' said George Harrowby pacifically. 'Sit down, Mr Trimmer. Sit down and have a drink. Do you mean to say you didn't know Jenkins here was faking?'

'Of course I didn't,' said Trimmer. He sat down on the extreme edge of a chair, as one who proposed to rise soon. 'All this has got me going. I never went round in royal circles before, and I'm dizzy. I suppose you're the real Lord Harrowby?'

'To be quite correct, I am. Don't you believe it?'

'I can believe anything – when I look at him,' said Trimmer, indicating the pitiable ex-claimant to the title. 'Say, who is this Jenkins we hear so much about?'

'Jenkins was the son of my father's valet,' George Harrowby explained. 'He came to America with me. We parted suddenly on a ranch in southern Arizona.'

'Everybody said you was dead,' persisted Jenkins, as one who could not lose sight of that fact.

'Yes? And they gave you my letters and belongings, eh? So you thought you'd pose as me?'

'Yes, sir,' confessed Jenkins humbly.

Mr Trimmer slid farther back into his chair.

Well,' he said, 'it's unbelievable, but Henry Trimmer has been buncoed. I met this able liar in a boarding house in New York, and he convinced me he was Lord Harrowby. It was between jobs for me, and I had a bright idea. If I brought this guy down to the wedding, established him as the real lord, and raised Cain generally, I figured my stock as a publicity man would rise a hundred per cent. I'd be turning down fifty-thousand-dollar jobs right and left. I suppose I was easy, but I'd never mixed up with such things before, and all the dope he had impressed me – the family coat of arms, and the motto –'

The Chicago man laughed softly.

'Credo Harrowby,' he said.

'That was it – trust Harrowby,' said Trimmer bitterly. 'Lord, what a fool I've been. And it's ruined my career. I'll be the laughing-stock –'

'Oh, cheer up, Mr Trimmer,' smiled George Harrowby. 'I'm sure you're unduly pessimistic about your career. I'll have something to say to you on that score later. For the present –'

'For the present,' broke in Trimmer with fervor, 'iron bars for Jenkins here. I'll swear out the warrant myself –'

'Nonsense,' said Harrowby, 'Jenkins is the most harmless creature in the world. Led astray by ambition, that's all. With anyone but Allan his claims wouldn't have lasted five minutes. Poor Allan always was a helpless youngster.'

'Oh – Jenkins,' broke in Minot suddenly. 'What was the idea this morning? I mean your calling Allan Harrowby an impostor?'

Jenkins hung his head.

'I was rattled,' he admitted. 'I couldn't keep it up before all those people. So it came to me in a flash – if I said Allan was a fraud maybe I wouldn't have to be cross-examined myself.'

'And that was really Allan Harrowby?'

'Yes – that was Allan, right enough.'

Mr Minot sat studying the wall in front of him. He was recalling a walk through the moonlight to the fort. Jephson and Thacker pointed accusing fingers at him over the oceans and lands between.

'I say – let Jenkins go,' continued the genial western Harrowby, 'provided he returns my property and clears out for good. After all his father was a faithful servant if he is not.'

'But,' objected Trimmer, 'he's wasted my time. He's put a crimp in the career of the best publicity man in America it'll take years to straighten out –'

'Not necessarily,' said Harrowby. 'I was coming to that. I've been watching your work for the last week, and I like it. It's alive – progressive. We're putting out a new car this spring – an inexpensive little car bound to make a hit. I need a man like you to convince the public –'

Mr Trimmer's eyes opened wide. They shone. He turned and regarded the unhappy Jenkins.

'Clear out,' he commanded. 'If I ever see you again I'll wring your neck. Now, Mr Harrowby, you were saying –'

'Just a minute,' said Harrowby. 'This man has certain letters and papers of mine –'

'No, he hasn't,' Trimmer replied. 'I got 'em. Right here in my pocket.' He slid a packet of papers across the table. 'They're yours. Now, about –'

Jenkins was slipping silently away. Like a frightened wraith he flitted gratefully through the swinging doors.

'A middle-class car,' explained Harrowby, 'and I want a live man to boost it –'

'Beg pardon,' interrupted Minot, rising, 'I'll say goodnight. We'll get together about that other matter in the morning. By the way, Mr Harrowby, have you any idea what has become of Allan?'

'No, I haven't. I sent him a telegram this afternoon saying that I was on my way here. Must have run off on business. Of course, he'll be back for his wedding.'

'Oh, yes – of course,' Minot agreed sadly, 'he'll be back for his wedding. Good night, gentlemen.'

A few minutes later he stood at the window of 389, gazing out at the narrow street, at the stately Manhattan Club, and the old Spanish houses on either side.

'And she refused me!' he muttered. 'To think that should be the biggest piece of luck that's come to me since I hit this accursed town!'

Chapter XVIII
A Rotten Bad Fit

Minot rose early on Monday morning and went for a walk along the beach. He had awakened to black despair, but the sun and the matutinal breeze elevated his spirits considerably. Where was Allan Harrowby? Gone, with his wedding little more than twenty-four hours away. If he should not return – golden thought. By his own act he would forfeit his claim on Jephson, and Minot would be free to – To what? Before him in the morning glow the great gray fort rose to crush his hopes. There on those slanting ramparts she had smiled at his declaration. Smiled, and labeled him foolish. Well, foolish he must have seemed. But there was still hope. If only Allan Harrowby did not return.

Mr Trimmer, his head down, breathing hard, marched along the beach like a man with a destination. Seeing Minot, he stopped suddenly.

'Good morning,' he said, holding out his hand, with a smile. 'No reason why we shouldn't be friends, eh? None whatever. You're out early. So am I. Thinking up ideas for the automobile campaign.'

Minot laughed.

'You leap from one proposition to another with wonderful aplomb,' he said.

'The agile mountain goat hopping from peak to peak,' Trimmer replied. 'That's me. Oh, I'm the goat all right. Sad old Jenkins put it all over me, didn't he?'

'I'm afraid he did. Where is he?'

'Ask of the railway folder. He lit out in the night. Say – he did have a convincing way with him – you know it.'

'He surely did.'

'Well, the best of us make mistakes,' admitted Mr Trimmer. 'The trouble with me is I'm too enthusiastic. Once I get an idea,

I see rosy for miles ahead. As I look back I realize that I actually helped Jenkins prove to me that he was Lord Harrowby. I was so anxious for him to do it – the chance seemed so gorgeous. And if I'd put it over – but there. The automobile business looks mighty good to me now. Watch the papers for details. And when you get back to Broadway, keep a lookout for the hand of Trimmer writing in fire on the sky.'

'I will,' promised Minot, laughing. He turned back to the hotel shortly after. His meeting with Trimmer had cheered him mightily. With a hopeful eye worthy of Trimmer himself, he looked toward the future. Twenty-four hours would decide it. If only Allan failed to return!

The first man Minot saw when he entered the lobby of the De la Pax was Allan Harrowby, his eyes tired with travel, handing over a suitcase to an eager black boy.

What was the use? Listlessly Minot relinquished his last hope. He followed Harrowby, and touched his arm.

'Good morning,' he said drearily. 'You gave us all quite a turn last night. We thought you'd taken the advice you got in the morning, and cleared out for good.'

'Well, hardly,' Harrowby replied. 'Come up to the room, old man. I'll explain there.'

'Before we go up,' replied Minot, 'I want you to get Miss Meyrick on the phone and tell her you've returned. Yes – right away. You see – last night I rather misunderstood – I thought you weren't Allan Harrowby after all – and I am afraid I gave Miss Meyrick a wrong impression.'

'By gad – I should have told her I was going,' Harrowby replied. 'But I was so rattled, you know –'

He went into a booth. His brief talk ended, he and Minot entered the elevator. Once in his suite, Harrowby dropped wearily into a chair.

'Confound your stupid trains. I've been traveling for ages. Now, Minot, I'll tell you what carried me off. Yesterday afternoon I got a message from my brother George saying he was on his way here.'

'Yes?'

'Seems he's alive and in business in Chicago. The news excited me a bit, old boy. I pictured George rushing in here, and the word spreading that I was not to be the Earl of Raybrook, after all. I'm frightfully fond of Miss Meyrick, and I want that wedding to take place tomorrow. Then, too, there's Jephson. Understand me – Cynthia is not marrying me for my title. I'd stake my life on that. But there's the father and Aunt Mary – and considering the number of times the old gentleman has forbidden the wedding already –'

'You saw it was up to you, for once.'

'Exactly. So for my own sake – and Jephson's – I boarded a train for Jacksonville with the idea of meeting George's train there and coming on here with him. I was going to ask George not to make himself known for a couple of days. Then I proposed to tell Cynthia, and Cynthia only, of his existence. If she objected, all very well – but I'm sure she wouldn't. And I'm sure, too, that George would have done what I asked – he always was a bully chap. But – I missed him. These confounded trains – always late. Except when you want them to be. I dare say George is here by this time?'

'He is,' Minot replied. 'Came a few hours after you left. And by the way, I arranged a meeting for him with Trimmer and his proposition. The proposition fled into the night. It seems he was the son of an old servant of your father's – Jenkins by name.'

'Surely! Surely that was Jenkins! I thought I'd seen the chap somewhere – couldn't quite recall – Well, at any rate, he's out of the way. Now the thing to do is to see good old George at once –'

He went to the telephone, and got his brother's room.

'George!' A surprising note of affection crept into his lord-ship's voice. 'George, old boy – this is Allan. I'm waiting for you in my rooms.'

'Dear old chap,' said his lordship, turning away from the tele-phone. 'Twenty-three years since he has seen one of his own flesh and blood! Twenty-three years of wandering in this Godforsaken country – I beg your pardon, Minot. I wonder what he'll say to me. I wonder what George will say after all those years.'

Nervously Allan Harrowby walked the floor. In a moment the door opened, and the tall, blond Chicago man stood in the doorway. His blue eyes glowed. Without a word he came into the room, and gripped the hand of his brother, then stood gazing as if he would never get enough.

And then George Harrowby spoke.

'Is that a ready-made suit you have on, Allan?' he asked huskily.

'Why – why – yes, George.'

'I thought so. It's a rotten bad fit, Allan. A rotten bad fit.'

Thus did George Harrowby greet the first of his kin he had seen in a quarter of a century. Thus did he give the lie to fiction, and to Trimmer, writer of 'fancy seeing you after all these years' speeches.

He dropped his younger brother's hand and strode to the window. He looked out. The courtyard of the De la Pax was strangely misty even in the morning sunlight. Then he turned, smiling.

'How's the old boy?' he asked.

'He's well, George. Speaks of you – now and then. Think he'd like to see you. Why not run over and look him up?'

'I will,' George Harrowby turned again to the window. 'Ought to have buried the hatchet long ago. Been so busy – but I'll change all that. I'll run over and see him first chance I get – and I'll write to him today.'

'Good. Great to see you again, George. Heard you'd shuffled off.'

'Not much. Alive and well in Chicago. Great to see you.'

'Suppose you know about the wedding?'

'Yes. Fine girl, too. Had a waiter point her out to me at breakfast – rather rude, but I was in a hurry to see her. Er – pretty far gone and all that, Allan?'

'Pretty far gone.'

'That's the eye. I was afraid it might be a financial proposition until I saw the girl.'

Allan shifted nervously.

'Ah – er – of course, you're Lord Harrowby,' he said.

George Harrowby threw back his head and laughed his hearty pleasant laugh.

'Sit down, kid,' he said. And the scion of nobility, thus informally addressed, sat.

'I thought you'd come at me with the title!' said George Harrowby, also dropping into a chair. 'Don't go, Mr Minot – no secrets here. Allan, you and your wife must come out and see us. Got a wife myself – fine girl – she's from Marion, Indiana. And I've got two of the liveliest little Americans you ever saw. Live in a little Chicago suburb – homey house, shady street, neighbors all from down country way. Gibson's drawings on the walls, George Ade's books on the tables, phonograph in the corner with all of George M. Cohan's songs. Whole family wakes in the morning ready for a McCutcheon cartoon. My boys talk about nothing but Cubs and White Sox all summer. They're going to a western university in a few years. We raised 'em on James Whitcomb Riley's poems. Well, Allan –'

'Well, George –'

'Say, what do you imagine would happen if I went back to a home like that with the news that I was Lord Harrowby, in line to become the Earl of Raybrook. There'd be a riot. Wife would be startled out of her wits. Children would hate me. Be an outcast in my own family. Neighbors would turn up their noses when they went by our house. Fellows at the club would guy me. Lord Harrowby, eh! Take off your hats to his ludship, boys. Business would fall off.'

Smilingly George Harrowby took a cigar and lighted it.

'No, Allan,' he finished, 'a lord wouldn't make a hell of a hit anywhere in America, but in Chicago, in the automobile business – say, I'd be as lonesome and deserted as the reading room of an Elks' Club.'

'I don't quite understand,' Allan began.

'No,' said George, turning to meet Minot's smile, 'but this gentleman does. It all means, Allan, that there's nothing doing. You are Lord Harrowby, the next Earl of Raybrook. Take the title, and God bless you.'

'But, George,' Allan objected, 'legally you can't.'

'Don't worry, Allan,' said the man from Chicago, 'there's nothing we can't do in America, and do legally. How's this? I've always been intending to take out naturalization papers. I'll do it the minute I get back to Chicago – and then the title *is* yours. In the meantime, when you introduce me to your friends here, we'll just pretend I've taken them out already.'

Allan Harrowby got up and laid his hand affectionately on his brother's shoulder.

'You're a brick, old boy,' he said. 'You always were. I'm glad you're to be here for the wedding. How did you happen to come?'

'That's right – you don't know, do you? I came in response to a telegram from Lloyds, of New York.'

'From – er – Lloyds?' asked Allan blankly.

'Yes, Allan. That yacht you came down here on didn't belong to Martin Wall. It belonged to me. He made away with it from North River because he happened to need it. Wall's a crook, my boy.'

'The *Lileth* your ship! My word!'

'It is. I called it the *Lady Evelyn*, Allan. Lloyds found out that it had been stolen and sent me a wire. So here I am.'

'Lloyds found out through me,' Minot explained to the dazed Allan.

'Oh – I'm beginning to see,' said Allan slowly. 'By the way, George, we've another score to settle with Wall.'

He explained briefly how Wall had acquired Chain Lightning's Collar, and returned a duplicate of paste in its place. The elder Harrowby listened with serious face.

'It's no doubt the Collar he was trailing you for, Allan,' he said. 'And that's how he came to need the yacht. But when finally he got his eager fingers on those diamonds, poor old Wall must have had the shock of his life.'

'How's that?'

'It wasn't Wall who had the duplicate made. It was – father – years ago, when I was still at home. He wanted money to bet, as usual – had the duplicate made – risked and lost.'

'But,' Allan objected, 'he gave it to me to give to Miss Meyrick. Surely he wouldn't have done that.'

'How old is he now? Eighty-two? Allan, the old boy must be a little childish by now – he forgot. I'm sure he forgot. That's the only view to take of it.'

A silence fell. In a moment the elder brother said:

'Allan, I want you to assure me again that you're marrying because you love the girl – and for no other reason.'

'Straight, George,' Allan answered, and looked his brother in the eye.

'Good kid. There's nothing in the other kind of marriage – all unhappiness – all wrong. I was sure you must be on the level – but, you see, after Mr Thacker – the insurance chap in New York – knew who I was and that I wouldn't take the title, he told me about that fool policy you took out.'

'No? Did he?'

'All about it. Sort of knocked me silly for a minute. But I remembered the Harrowby gambling streak – and if you love the girl, and really want to marry her, I can't see any harm in the idea. However, I hope you lose out on the policy. Everything OK now? Nothing in the way?'

'Not a thing,' Lord Harrowby replied. 'Minot here has been a bully help – worked like mad to put the wedding through. I owe everything to him.'

'Insuring a woman's mind,' reflected George Harrowby. 'Not a bad idea, Allan. Almost worthy of an American. Still – I could have insured you myself after a fashion – promised you a good job as manager of our new London branch in case the marriage fell through. However, your method is more original.'

Allan Harrowby was slowly pacing the room. Suddenly he turned, and despite the fact that all obstacles were removed, he seemed a very worried young man.

'George – Mr Minot,' he began, 'I've a confession to make. It's about that policy.' He stopped. 'The old family trouble, George. We're gamblers to the bone – all of us. Last Friday night – at the Manhattan Club – I turned over that policy to Martin Wall to hold a five thousand dollar loan.'

'Why the devil did you do that?' Minot cried.

'Well,' and Allan Harrowby was in his old state of helplessness again. 'I wanted to save the day. Gonzale was hounding us for money – I thought I saw a chance to win.'

'But Wall! Wall of all people!'

'I know. I oughtn't to have done it. Knew Wall wasn't altogether straight. But nobody else was about – I got excited – borrowed – lost the whole of it, too. Wha – what are we going to do?'

He looked appealingly at Minot. But for once it was not on Minot's shoulders that the responsibility for action fell. George Harrowby cheerfully took charge.

'I was just on the point of going out to the yacht, with an officer,' he said. 'Suppose we three run out alone and talk business with Martin Wall.'

Fifteen minutes later the two Harrowbys and Minot boarded the yacht which Martin Wall had christened the *Lileth*. George Harrowby looked about him with interest.

'He's taken very good care of it – I'll say that for him,' he remarked.

Martin Wall came suavely forward.

'Mr Wall,' said Minot pleasantly, 'allow me to present Mr George Harrowby, the owner of the boat on which we now stand.'

'I beg your pardon,' said Wall, without a quiver of an eyelash. 'So careless of me. Don't stand, gentlemen. Have chairs – all of you.'

And he stared George Harrowby calmly in the eye.

'You're flippant this morning,' said the elder Harrowby. 'We'll be glad to sit, thank you. And may I repeat what Mr Minot has told you – I own this yacht.'

'Indeed?' Mr Wall's face beamed. 'You bought it from Wilson, I presume.'

'Just who is Wilson?'

'Why – he's the man I rented it from in New York.'

'So that's your tale, is it?' Allan Harrowby put in.

'You wound me,' protested Mr Wall. 'That is my tale, as you call it. I rented this boat in New York from a man named Albert Wilson. I have the lease to show you, also my receipt for one month's rent.'

'I'll bet you have,' commented Minot.

'Bet anything you like. You come from a betting institution, I believe.'

'No, Mr Wall, I did not buy the yacht from Wilson,' said George Harrowby. 'I've owned it for several years.'

'How do I know that?' asked Martin Wall.

'Glance over that,' said the elder Harrowby, taking a paper from his pocket. 'A precaution you failed to take with Albert Wilson.'

'Dear, dear.' Mr Wall looked over the paper and handed it back. 'Can it be that Wilson was a fraud? I suggest the police, Mr Harrowby. I shall be very glad to testify.'

'I suggest the police, too,' said Minot hotly, 'for Mr Martin Wall. If you thought you had a right on this boat, Wall, why did you throw me overboard into the North River when I mentioned the name of Lloyds?'

Mr Wall regarded him with pained surprise.

'I threw you overboard because I didn't want you on my boat,' he said. 'I thought you understood that fully.'

'Nonsense,' Minot cried. 'You stole this boat by bribing the caretaker, and when I mentioned Lloyds, famous the world over as a marine insurance firm, you thought I was after you, and threw me over the rail. I see it all very clearly now.'

'You're a wise young man –'

'Mr Wall,' George Harrowby broke in, 'it may interest you to know that we don't believe a word of the Wilson story. But it may also interest you to know that I am willing to let the whole matter drop – on one condition.'

'What's that?'

'My brother Allan here borrowed five thousand dollars from you the other night, and gave you as security a bit of paper quite worthless to anyone save himself. Accept my thousand and hand him back the paper.'

Mr Wall smiled. He reached into his inner coat pocket.

'With the greatest pleasure,' he said. 'Here is the – er – the document.' He laughed. Then noting the checkbook on the elder Harrowby's knee, he added: 'There was a little matter of interest.'

'Not at all!' George Harrowby looked up. 'The interest is forfeited to pay wear and tear on this yacht.'

For a moment Wall showed fight, but he did not much care for the light he saw in the elder Harrowby's eyes. He recognized a vast difference in brothers.

'Oh – very well,' he said. The check was written, and the exchange made.

'Since you are convinced I am the owner of the yacht,' said George Harrowby, rising, 'I take it you will leave it at once?'

'As soon as I can remove my belongings,' Wall said. 'A most unfortunate affair all round.'

'A fortunate one for you,' commented Mr Minot.

Wall glared.

'My boy,' he said angrily, 'did anyone ever tell you you were a bad-luck jinx?'

'Never,' smiled Minot.

'You look like one to me,' growled Martin Wall.

George Harrowby arranged to keep the crew Wall had engaged, in order to get the *Lady Evelyn* back to New York. It was thought best for the owner to stay aboard until Wall had gathered his property and departed, so Allan Harowby and Minot alone returned to San Marco. As they crossed the plaza Allan said:

'By gad – everything looks lovely now. Jenkins out of the way, good old George side-stepping the title, the policy safe in my pocket. Not a thing in the way!'

'It's almost too good to be true,' replied Minot, with a very mirthless smile.

'It must be a great relief to you, old boy. You have worked hard. Must feel perfectly jolly over all this?'

'Me?' said Minot. 'Oh, I can hardly contain myself for joy. I feel like twining orange blossoms in my hair.'

He walked on, kicking the gravel savagely at each step. Not a thing in the way now. Not a single, solitary, hopeful, little thing.

Chapter XIX
Mr Minot Goes Through Fire

The Duchess of Lismore elected to give her dinner and dance in Miss Meyrick's honor as near to the bright Florida stars as she could. On the top floor of the De la Pax was a private dining room, only partially enclosed, with a picturesque view of the palm-dotted courtyard below. Adjacent to this was a sun-room with a removable glass roof, and this the duchess had ordered transformed into a ballroom. There in the open the newest society dances should rise to offend the soft southern sky.

Being a good general, the hostess was early on the scene, marshaling her forces. To her there came Cynthia Meyrick, radiant and lovely and wide-eyed on the eve of her wedding.

'How sweet you look, Cynthia,' said the duchess graciously. 'But then, you long ago solved the problem of what becomes you.'

'I have to look as sweet as I can,' replied the girl wearily. 'All the rest of my life I shall have to try to live up to nobility.'

She sighed.

'To think,' remarked the duchess, busy over a great bowl of flowers, 'that tomorrow night this time little Cynthia will be Lady Harrowby. I suppose you'll go to Rakedale Hall for part of the year at least?'

'I suppose so.'

'I, too, have had my Rakedale Hall. Formal, Cynthia dear, formal. Nothing but silly little hunts, silly little shoots – American men would die there. As for American women – nothing ever happens – the hedges bloom in neat little rows – the trees blossom – they're bare again – Cynthia, sometimes I've been in a state where I'd give ten years of my life just to hear the rattle of an elevated train!'

She stood looking down at the girl, an all too evident pity in her eyes.

'It isn't all it might be, I fancy marrying into the peerage,' Cynthia said.

'My dear,' replied the duchess, 'I've nearly died at times. I never was exactly what you'd call a patriot, but – often I've waked in the night and thought of Detroit. My little car rattling over the cobblestones – a new gown tried on at Madame Harbier's – a matinee – and chocolate afterward at that little place – you remember it. And our house on Woodward Avenue – the good times there. On the veranda in the evening, and Jack Little just back from college in the east running across the lawns to see me. What became of Jack, dear?'

'He married Elise Perkins.'

'Ah – I know – and they live near our old house – have a box when the opera comes – entertain the Yale glee club every Christmas – oh, Cynthia, maybe it's crude, maybe it's middle-class in English eyes – but it's home! When you introduced that brother of Lord Harrowby's this afternoon – that big splendid chap who said America looked better than a title to him – I could have thrown my arms about his neck and kissed him!' She came closer to the girl, and stood looking down at her with infinite tenderness in her washed-out eyes.

'Wasn't there an American boy, my dear?' she asked.

'I – I – hundreds of them,' answered Cynthia Meyrick, trying to laugh.

The duchess turned away.

'It's wrong of me to discourage you like that,' she said. 'Marrying into the peerage is something, after all. You must come home every year – insist on it. Johnson – are these the best caviar bowls the hotel can furnish?'

And the Duchess of Lismore, late of Detroit, drifted off into a bitter argument with the humble Johnson.

Miss Meyrick strolled away, out upon a little balcony opening off the dining room. She stood gazing down at the waving fronds in the courtyard six stories below. If only that fountain down there were Ponce de Leon's! But it wasn't. Tomorrow she must put youth behind. She must go far from the country she loved – did she care enough for that? Strangely enough, burning tears filled her eyes. Hot revolt surged into her heart. She stood looking down.

Meanwhile the party were gathering with tender solicitude about their hostess in the ballroom beyond. Dick Minot, hopeless, glum, stalked moodily among them. Into the crowd drifted Jack Paddock, his sprightly air noticeably lacking, his eyes worried, dreadful.

'For the love of heaven,' Minot asked, as they stepped together into a secluded corner, 'what ails you?'

'Be gentle with me, boy,' said Paddock unhappily. 'I'm in a horrible mess. The graft, Dick – the good old graft. It's over and done with now.'

'What do you mean?'

'It happened last night after our wild chase of Harrowby – I – was fussed – excited. I prepared two sets of repartee for my two customers to use tonight.'

'Yes?'

'I always make carbon copies to refer to myself just before the stuff is to be used. A few minutes ago I took out my copies. Dick! I sent the same repartee to both of them!'

'Good lord!'

'Good lord is meek and futile. So is dammit. Put on your little rubber coat, my boy. I predict a hurricane.'

In spite of his own troubles, Minot laughed.

'Mirth, eh?' said Paddock grimly, 'I can't see it that way. I'll be as popular as a Republican in Texas before this evening is over. Got a couple of hasty rapid-fire resignations ready. Thought at first I wouldn't come – but that seemed cowardly. Anyway, this is my last appearance on any stage as a librettist. Kindly omit flowers.'

And Mr Paddock drifted gloomily away.

While the servants were passing cocktails on gleaming trays, Minot found the balcony and stepped outside. A white wraith flitted from the shadows to his side.

'Mr Minot,' said a soft, scared voice.

'Ah – Miss Meyrick,' he cried.

Merciful fate this, that they met for the time since that incident on the rampart in kindly darkness.

'Miss Meyrick,' began Minot hurriedly, 'I'm very glad to have a moment alone with you. I want to apologize – for last night – I was mad – I did Harrowby a very palpable wrong. I'm very ashamed of myself as I look back. Can I hope that you will – forget – all I said?'

She did not reply, but stood looking down at the palms far below.

'Can I hope that you will forget – and forgive?'

She glanced up at him, and her eyes shone in the dusk.

'I can forgive,' she said softly. 'But I can't forget. Mr – Mr Minot –'

'Yes?'

'What – what – is – woman's greatest privilege?'

Something in the tone of her voice sent a cold chill sweeping through Minot's very soul. He clutched the rail for support.

'If – if you'd answer,' said the girl, 'it would make it easier for –'

Aunt Mary's generous form appeared in the doorway.

'Oh, there you are, Cynthia! You are keeping the duchess' dinner waiting.'

Cynthia Meyrick joined her aunt. Minot stayed behind a moment. Below him Florida swam in the azure night. What had the girl been about to say?

Pulling himself together, he learned that he was to take into dinner a glorious blond bridesmaid. When they were seated, he found that Miss Meyrick's face was hidden from him by a profusion of Florida blossoms. He was glad of that. He wanted to think – think.

A few others were thinking at that table, Mrs Bruce and the duchess among them. Mrs Bruce was mentally rehearsing. The duchess glanced at her.

'The wittiest woman in San Marco,' thought the hostess. 'Bah!'

Mr Paddock, meanwhile, was toying unhappily with his food. He had little to say. The attractive young lady he had taken in had already classified him as a bore. Most unjust of the attractive young lady.

'It's lamentable, really.' Mrs Bruce was speaking. 'Even in our best society conversation has given way to the turkey trot. Our wits are in our feet. Where once people talked art, music, literature – now they tango madly. It really seems –'

'Everything you say is true,' interrupted the duchess blandly. 'I sometimes think the race of the future will be – a trotting race.'

Mrs Bruce started perceptibly. Her eyes lighted with fire. She had been working up to this line herself, and the coincidence was passing strange. She glared at the hostess. Mr Paddock studied his plate intently.

'I for one,' went on the Duchess of Lismore, 'do not dance the tango or the turkey trot. Nor am I willing to take the necessary steps to learn them.'

A little ripple ran round the table – the ripple that up to now had been the exclusive privilege of Mrs Bruce. That lady paled visibly. She realized that there was no coincidence here.

'It seems too bad, too,' she said, fixing the hostess firmly with an angry eye. 'Because women could have the world at their feet – if they'd only keep their feet still long enough.'

It was the turn of the duchess to start, and start she did. As one who could not believe her ears, she stared at Mrs Bruce. The wittiest hostess in San Marco was militantly under way.

'Women are not what they used to be,' she continued. 'Either they are mad about clothes, or they go to the other extreme and harbor strange ideas about the vote, eugenics, what not. In fact, the sex reminds me of the type of shop that abounds in a small town – its speciality is goods and notions.'

The duchess pushed away a plate which had only that moment been set before her. She regarded Mrs Bruce with the eye of Mrs Pankhurst face to face with a prime minister.

'We are hardly kind to our sex,' she said, 'but I must say I agree with you. And the extravagance of women! Half the women of my acquaintance wear gorgeous rings on their fingers – while their husbands wear blue rings about their eyes.'

Mrs Bruce's face was livid.

'Madam!' she said through her teeth.

'What is it?' asked the duchess sweetly.

They sat glaring at each other. Then with one accord they turned – to glare at Mr Jack Paddock.

Mr Paddock, prince of assurance, was blushing furiously. He stood the combined glare as long as he could – then he looked up into the night.

'How – how close the stars seem,' he murmured faintly.

It was noted afterward that Mrs Bruce maintained a vivid silence during the remainder of that dinner. The duchess, on the contrary, wrung from her purchased lines every possibility they held.

And in that embattled setting Mr Minot sat, deaf to the delicious lisp of the debutante at his side. What was woman's greatest privilege? Wasn't it –

His forehead grew damp. His knees trembled beneath the table. 'Jephson – Thacker, Jephson – Thacker,' he said over and over to himself.

After dinner, when the added guests invited by the duchess for the dance crowded the ballroom, Minot encountered Jack Paddock. Mr Paddock was limp and pitiable.

'Ever apologize to an angry woman?' he asked. 'Ever try to expostulate with a storm at sea? I've had it out with Mrs Bruce – offered to do anything to atone – she said the best thing I could

204

do would be to disappear from San Marco. She's right. I'm going. This is my exit from the butterfly life. And I don't intend to say goodbye to the duchess, either.'

'I wish I could go with you,' said Minot sadly.

'Well – come along.'

'No. I – I'll stick it out. See you later.'

Mr Paddock slipped unostentatiously away in the direction of the elevator. On a dais hidden by palms the orchestra began to play softly.

'You haven't asked to see my card,' said Cynthia Meyrick at Minot's side.

He smiled a wan smile, and wrote his name opposite number five. She drifted away. The music became louder, rising to the bright stars themselves. The dances that had furnished so much bitter conversation at table began to break out. Minot hunted up the balcony and stood gazing miserably down at fairy-land below.

There Miss Meyrick found him when the fifth dance was imminent.

'Is it customary for girls to pursue their partners?' she inquired.

'I'm sorry,' he said weakly. 'Shall we go in?'

'It's so – so glorious out here.'

He sighed – a sigh of resignation. He turned to her.

'You asked me – what is woman's greatest privilege,' he said.

'Yes.'

'Is it – to change her mind?'

She looked timidly into his eyes.

'It – is,' she whispered faintly.

The most miserably happy man in history, he gasped.

'Cynthia! It's too late – you're to be married tomorrow. Do you mean – you'd call it all off now – at the last minute?'

She nodded her head, her eyes on the ground.

'My God!' he moaned, and turned away.

'It would be all wrong – to marry Harrowby,' she said faintly. 'Because I've come to – I – oh, Dick, can't you see?'

'See! Of course I see!' He clenched his fists. 'Cynthia, my dearest –'

Below him stretched six stories of open space. In his agony he thought of leaping over the rail – of letting that be his answer. But no – it would disarrange things so – it might even postpone the wedding!

'Cynthia,' he groaned, 'you can't understand. It mustn't be – I've given my word. I can't explain. I can never explain. But Cynthia – Cynthia.'

Back in the shadow the girl pressed her hands to her burning cheeks.

'A strange love – yours,' she said. 'A love that blows hot and cold.'

'Cynthia – that isn't true – I do love you.'

'Please! Please let us – forget.' She stepped into the moonlight, fine, brave, smiling. 'Do we – dance?'

'Cynthia!' he cried unhappily. 'If only you understood.'

'I think I do. The music has stopped. Harrowby has the next dance – he'd hardly think of looking for me here.'

She was gone! Minot stood alone on the balcony. He was dazed, blind, trembling. He had refused the girl without whom life could never be worthwhile! Refused her, to keep the faith!

He entered upon the bright scene inside, slipped unnoticed to the elevator and, still dazed, descended to the lobby. He would walk in the moonlight until his senses were regained. Near the main door of the De la Pax he ran into Henry Trimmer. Mr Trimmer had a newspaper in his hand.

'What's the matter with the women nowadays?' he demanded indignantly. Minot tried in vain to push by him. 'Seen what those London suffragettes have done now?' And Trimmer pointed to a headline.

'What have they done?' asked Minot.

'Done? They put dynamite under the statue of Lord Nelson in Trafalgar Square and blew it sky-high. It fell over into the Strand.'

'Good!' cried Minot wildly. 'Good! I hope to hell it smashed the whole of London!' And brushing aside the startled Trimmer, he went out into the night.

It was nearly twelve o'clock when Mr Minot, somewhat calmer of mind, returned to the De la Pax. As he stepped into the courtyard he was surprised to see a crowd gathered before the hotel. Then he noticed that from a second-floor window poured smoke and flame, and that the town fire department was wildly getting into action.

He stopped – his heart almost ceased beating. That was her window! The window to which he had called her on that night that seemed so far away – last night! Breathlessly he ran forward.

And he ran straight into a group just descended from the ballroom. Of that group Cynthia Meyrick was a member. For a moment they stood gazing at each other. Then the girl turned to her aunt.

'My wedding dress!' she cried. 'I left it lying on my bed. Oh, I can't possibly be married tomorrow if that is burned.'

There was a challenge in that last sentence, and the young man for whom it was intended did not miss it. Mad with the injustice of life, he swooped down on a fireman struggling with a wobbly ladder. Snatching away the ladder, he placed it against the window from which the smoke and flame poured. He ran up it.

'Here!' shouted the chief of the fire department, laying angry hands on the ladder's base. 'Wot you doing? You can't go in there.'

'Why the devil can't I?' bellowed Minot. 'Let go of that ladder!'

He plunged into the room. The smoke filled his nostrils and choked him. His eyes burned. He staggered through the smoky dusk into another room. His hands met the brass bars of a bed

– then closed over something soft and filmy that lay upon it. He seized the something close, and hurried back into the other room.

A fireman at another window sought to turn a stream of water on him. Water – on that gown!

'Cut that out, you fool!' Minot shouted. The fireman, who had suspected himself of saving a human life, looked hurt. Minot regained his window. Disheveled, smoky, but victorious, he half fell, half climbed, to the ground. The fire chief faced him.

'Who were you trying to rescue?' the chief demanded. His eyes grew wise. 'You idiot,' he roared, 'they ain't nobody in that dress.'

'Damn it, I know that,' Minot cried.

He ran across the lawn and stood, a panting, limp, battered, ludicrous figure before Cynthia Meyrick.

'I – I hope it's the right one,' he said, and held out the gown.

She took his offering, and came very close to him.

'I hate you!' she said in a low tone. 'I hate you!'

'I – I was afraid you would,' he muttered.

A shout from the firemen announced that the blaze was under control. To his dismay, Minot saw that an admiring crowd was surrounding him. He broke away and hurried to his room.

Cynthia Meyrick's final words to him rang in his ears. Savagely he tore at his ruined collar.

Was this ridiculous farce never to end? As if in answer, a distant clock struck twelve. He shuddered.

Tomorrow, at high noon!

Chapter XX
Please Kill

Early Tuesday morning, while Mr Minot still slept and merci-
fully forgot, two very wide awake gentlemen sat alone in the
office of the *San Marco Mail*. One was Manuel Gonzale, proprietor of that paper, as immaculate as the morning; the other
was that broad and breezy gentleman known in his present
incarnation as Mr Martin Wall.

'Very neat. Very neat indeed,' said Mr Wall, gazing with
evident approval at an inky smelling sheet that lay before him.
'It ought to do the work. If it does, it will be the first stroke of
luck I've had in San Marco.'

Gonzale smiled, revealing two very white teeth.

'You do not like San Marco?'

Mr Wall snorted angrily.

'Like it? Does a beheaded man like an axe? In a long and
professional career, I've never struck anything like this town
before for hard luck. I'm not in it twenty-four hours when I'm
left alone, my hands tied, with stuff enough to make your eyes
pop out of your head. That's pleasant! Then, after spending
two months and a lot of money trailing Lord Harrowby for the
family jools, I finally cop them. I give the crew of my borrowed
boat orders to steam far, far away, and run to my cabin to gloat.
Do I gloat? Ask me. I do not gloat. I find the famous Chain
Lightning's Collar is a very superior collection of glass, worth
about twenty three cents. I send back the glass, and stick around,
hoping for better days. And the best I get is a call from the owner
of my yacht, with orders to vacate at once. When I first came here
I swore I'd visit that jewelry store again – alone. But – there's
a jinx after me in this town. What's the use? I'm going to get out.'

'But before you go,' smiled Manuel, 'one stroke of luck you
shall have.'

'Maybe. I leave that to you. This kind of thing' – he motioned toward the damp paper – 'is not in my line.' He bent over a picture on the front page. 'That cut came out pretty well, didn't it? Lucky we got the photograph before big brother George arrived.'

'I have always found San Marco lucky,' replied Gonzale. 'Always – with one trifling exception.' He drummed reminiscently on his desk.

'I say – who's this?' Mr Wall pointed to a line just beneath the name of the paper.

'Robert O'Neill, Editor and Proprietor,' he read.

Manuel Gonzale gurgled softly somewhere within, which was his cunning, non-committal way of indicating mirth.

'Ah – my very virtuous managing editor,' he said. 'One of those dogs who dealt so vilely with me – I have told you of that. Manuel Gonzale does not forget.' He leaned closer. 'This morning at two, after O'Neill and Howe had sent today's paper to press as usual, Luypas, my circulation manager, and I stopped the presses, we substituted a new first-page form. O'Neill and Howe – they will not know. Always they sleep until noon. In this balmy climate, it is easy to lie abed.'

Again Manuel Gonzale gurgled.

'May their sleep be dreamless,' he said. 'And should our work of the morning fail, may the name of O'Neill be the first to concern the police.'

Wall laughed.

'A good idea,' he remarked. He looked at his watch. 'Nine-fifteen. The banks ought to be open now.'

Gonzale got to his feet. Carefully he folded the page that had been lying on his desk.

'The moment for action has come,' he said. 'Shall we go down to the street?'

'I'm in strange waters,' responded Martin Wall uneasily. 'The first dip I've ever taken out of my line. Don't believe in it either – a man should have his specialty and stick to it. However, I need the money. Am I letter perfect in my part, I wonder?'

The door of the *Mail* office opened, and a sly little Cuban with an evil face stepped in.

'Ah, Luypas,' Gonzale said, 'you are here at last? Do you understand? Your boys they are to be in the next room – yes? You are to sit near that telephone. At a word from my friend, Mr Martin Wall, today's edition of the *Mail* is to flood the streets – the newsstands. Instantly. Delay might be fatal. Is that clear?'

'I know,' said Luypas.

'Very good,' said Gonzale. He turned to Martin Wall. 'Now is the time,' he added.

The two descended to the street. Opposite the Hotel de la Pax they parted. The sleek little Spaniard went on alone and mounted boldly those pretentious steps. At the desk he informed the clerk on duty that he must see Spencer Meyrick at once.

'But Mr Meyrick is very busy today,' the clerk objected.

'Say this is – life and death,' replied Gonzale and the clerk, wilting, telephoned the millionaire's apartments.

For nearly an hour Gonzale was kept waiting. Nervously he paced the lobby, consuming one cigarette after another, glancing often at his watch. Finally Spencer Meyrick appeared, pompous, red-faced, a hard man to handle as he always had been. The Spaniard noted this, and his slits of eyes grew even narrower.

'Will you come with me?' he asked suavely. 'It is most important.'

He led the way to a summerhouse in a far forgotten corner of the hotel grounds. Protesting, Spencer Meyrick followed. The two sat down.

'I have something to show you,' said Gonzale politely, and removed from his pocket a copy of the *San Marco Mail*, still damp from the presses.

Spencer Meyrick took the paper in his own large capable hands. He glanced casually at the first page, and his face grew somewhat redder than its wont. A huge headline was responsible:

HARROWBY WASN'T TAKING ANY CHANCES.

Underneath, in slightly smaller type, Spencer Meyrick read:

Remarkable foresight of English Fortune Hunter Who Weds Miss Meyrick Today Took Out a Policy for Seventy-five Thousand Pounds With Lloyds Same to be Payable in Case the Beautiful Heiress Suffered a Change of Heart

Prominent on the page was a large photograph which purported to be 'An Exact Facsimile of the Policy'. Mr Meyrick examined it. He glanced through the story, which happened to be commendably brief. He told himself to remain calm, avoid fireworks, think quickly. Laying the paper on his knee, he turned to the little white-garbed man beside him.

'What trick is this?' he asked sharply.

'It is no trick, sir,' said Gonzale pleasantly. 'It is the truth. That is a photograph of the policy.'

Old Meyrick studied the cut again.

'I'll be damned,' he remarked.

'I have no desire to annoy,' Gonzale went on. 'But – there are five thousand copies of today's *Mail* at the office ready to be distributed at a signal from me. Think, sir! Newsboys on the street with that story at the very moment when your daughter becomes Lady Harrowby.'

'I see,' said Meyrick slowly. 'Blackmail.'

Manuel Gonzale shuddered in horror.

'Oh, I beg of you,' he protested. 'That is hardly it. A business proposition, I should call it. It happens that the men back of the Star Publishing Company, which issues the *Mail*, have grown tired of the newspaper game in San Marco. They are desirous of closing out the plant at once – say this morning. It occurs to them that you might be very glad to purchase the *Mail* – before the next edition goes on the street.'

'You're a clever little dog,' said Meyrick, through his teeth.

'You are not exactly complimentary. However – let us say for the argument – you buy the *Mail* at once. I am, by the way, empowered to make the sale. You take charge. You hurry to the office. You destroy all copies of today's issue so far printed. You give orders to the composing room to kill the first-page story – good as it is. Please kill you say. A term with newspaper men.'

'You call yourself a newspaper man?'

'Why not? The story is killed, another is put in its place – say, for example, an elaborate account of your daughter's wedding. And in its changed from the *Mail* – your newspaper – goes on the street.'

'Um – and your price?'

'It is a valuable property.'

'Especially valuable this morning, I take it,' sneered Meyrick.

'Valuable at any time. Our presses cost a thousand. Our linotypes two thousand. And there is that other thing – so hard to estimate definitely – the wide appeal of our paper. The price – well – fifteen thousand dollars. Extremely reasonable. And I will include – the goodwill of the retiring management.'

'You contemptible little –' began Spencer Meyrick.

'My dear sir – control yourself,' pleaded Gonzale. 'Or I may be unable to include the goodwill I spoke of. Would you care to see that story on the streets? You may at any moment. There is but one way out. Buy the newspaper. Buy it now. Here is the plan – you go with me to your bank. You procure fifteen thousand in cash. We go together to the *Mail* office. You pay me the money and I leave you in charge.'

Old Meyrick leaped to his feet.

'Very good,' he cried. 'Come on.'

'One thing more,' continued the crafty Gonzale. 'It may pay you to note – we are watched. Even now. All the way to the bank and thence to the office of the *Mail* – we will be watched. Should any accident, now unforeseen, happen to me, that issue of the *Mail* will go on sale in five minutes all over San Marco.'

Spencer Meyrick stood glaring down at the little man in white. His enthusiasm of a moment ago for the journey vanished. However, the headlines of the *Mail* were staring up at him from the bench. He stooped, pocketed the paper, and growled:

'I understand. Come on!'

There must be some escape. The trap seemed absurdly simple. Across the hotel lawn, down the hot avenue, in the less hot plaza, Meyrick sought a way. A naturally impulsive man, he had difficulty restraining himself. But he thought of his daughter, whose happiness was more than money in his eyes.

No way offered. At the counter of the tiny bank Meyrick stood writing his check, Gonzale at his elbow. Suddenly behind them the screen door slammed, and a wild-eyed man with flaming red hair rushed in.

'What is it you want?' Gonzale screamed.

'Out of my way, Don Quixote,' cried the red-topped one. 'I'm a windmill and my arms breathe death. Are you Mr Meyrick? Well, tear up that check!'

'Gladly,' said Meyrick. 'Only –'

'Notice the catbirds down here?' went on the wild one. 'Noisy little beasts, aren't they? Well, after this take off your hat to 'em. A catbird saved you a lot of money this morning.'

'I'm afraid I don't follow –' said the dazed Spencer Meyrick.

'No? I'll explain. I have been working on this man's paper for the last week. So has a very good friend of mine. We knew he was crooked, but we needed the money and he promised us not to pull off any more blackmail while we stayed. Last night, after we left the office, he arranged this latest. Planned to incriminate me. You little devil –'

Manuel, frightened, leaped away.

'We usually sleep until noon,' went on O'Neill. 'He counted on that. Enter the catbird. Sat on our window sill at ten a.m. and screeched. Woke us up. We felt uneasy. Went to the office, broke down a bolted door, and found what was up.'

'Dog!' foamed Manuel. 'Outcast of the gutter –'

'Save your compliments! Mr Meyrick, my partner is now at the *Mail* office destroying today's issue of the *Mail*. We've already ruined the first-page form, the cut of the policy, and the negative. And we're going north as fast as the Lord'll let us. You can do what you please. Arrest our little lemon-tinted employer, if you want to.'

Spencer Meyrick stood, considering.

'However – I've done you a favor,' O'Neill went on. 'You can do me one. Let Manuel off – on one condition!'

'Name it.'

'That he hands me at once two hundred dollars – one hundred for myself, the other for my partner. It's legitimate salary money due us – we need it. A long walk to New York.'

'I myself –' began Meyrick.

'Don't want your money,' said O'Neill. 'Want Gonzale's.'

'Gonzale's you shall have,' agreed Meyrick. 'You – pay him!'

'Never!' cried the Spaniard.

'Then it's the police –' hinted O'Neill.

Gonzale took two yellow bills from a wallet. He tossed them at O'Neill.

'There, you cur –'

'Careful,' cried O'Neill. 'Or I'll punch you yet –'

He started forward, but Gonzale hastily withdrew. O'Neill and the millionaire followed to the street.

'Just as well,' commented Mcyrick. 'I should not have cared to cause his arrest – it would have meant countrywide publicity!' He laid a hand on the arm of the newspaper man.

'I take it,' he said, 'that your fortunes are not at the highest ebb. You have done me a very great service. I propose to write two checks – one for you, one for your partner – and you may name the amounts.'

But the red-haired one shook his head.

'No,' he replied, 'Nix on the anticlimax to virtue on a rampage. We can't be paid for it. It would sort of dim the glory. We've got the railroad fare at last – and we're going away from here. Yes – away from here. On the choo-choo – riding far – riding north.'

'Well, my boy,' answered Spencer Meyrick, 'if I can ever do anything for you in New York; come and see me.'

'You may have to make good on that,' laughed O'Neill, and they parted.

O'Neill hastened to the *Mail* office. He waved yellow bills before the lanky Howe.

'In the nick of time,' he cried. 'Me, the fair-haired hero. And here's the fare, Harry – the good old railroad fare.'

'Heaven be praised,' said Howe. 'I've finished the job, Bob. Not a trace of this morning's issue left. The fare! North in parlor cars! My tobacco heart sings. Can't you hear the elevated –'

'Music, Harry, music.'

'And the newsboys on Park Row –'

'Caruso can't touch them. Where shall we find a timetable, I wonder?'

Meanwhile, in a corner of the plaza, Manuel Gonzale spoke sad words in the ear of Martin Wall.

'It's the jinx,' moaned Wall with conviction. 'The star player in everything I do down here. I'm going to burn the sand hot-footing it away. But whither, Manuel, whither?'

'In Porto Rico,' replied Gonzale. 'I have not yet plied my trade. I go there.'

'Palm Beach,' sighed Wall, 'has diamonds that can be observed to sparkle as far away as the New York society columns. But alas,

I lack the wherewithal to support me in the style to which my victims are accustomed.'

'Try Porto Rico,' suggested Gonzale. 'The air is mild – so are the police. I will stake you.'

'Thanks. Porto Rico it is. How the devil do we get there?'

Up the main avenue of San Marco Spencer Meyrick walked as a man going to avenge. With every determined step his face grew redder, his eye more dangerous. He looked at his watch.

Eleven.

The eleventh hour! But much might happen between the eleventh hour and high noon!

Chapter XXI
High Words at High Noon

In the Harrowby suite the holder of the title, a handsome and distinguished figure, adorned for his wedding, walked nervously the rather worn carpet. His brother, hastily pressed into service as best man, sat puffing at a cigar with a persistency which indicated a slightly perturbed state of mind on his own part.

'Brace up, Allan,' he urged. 'It'll be over before you realize it. Remember my own wedding – gad, wasn't I frightened? Always that way with a man – no sense to it, but he just can't help it. Never forget that little parlor, with the flower of Marion society all about, and me with my teeth chattering and my knees knocking together.'

'It is a bit of an ordeal,' said Allan weakly. 'Chap feels all sort of – gone – inside –'

The telephone, ringing sharply, interrupted. George Harrowby rose and stepped to it.

'Allan? You wish Allan? Very well. I'll tell him.'

He turned away from the telephone and faced his brother.

'It was old Meyrick, kid. Seemed somewhat hot under the collar. Wants to see you in their suite at once.'

'Wha – what do you imagine he wants?'

'Going to make you a present of Riverside Drive, I fancy. Go ahead, boy. I'll wait for you here.'

Allan Harrowby went out, along the dusky corridor to the Meyrick door. Not without misgivings, he knocked. A voice boomed 'Come!'

He pushed open the door.

He saw Spencer Meyrick sitting purple at a table, and beside him Cynthia Meyrick, in the loveliest gown of all the lovely gowns she had ever worn. The beauty of the girl staggered

Harrowby a bit; never demonstrative, he had a sudden feeling that he should be at her feet.

'You – you sent for me?' he asked, coming into the room. As he moved closer to the girl he was to marry he saw that her face was whiter than her gown, and her brown eyes strained and miserable.

'We did,' said Meyrick, rising. He held out a paper. 'Will you please look at that.'

His lordship took the sheet in unsteady hands. He glanced down. Slowly the meaning of the story that met his gaze filtered through his dazed brain. 'Martin Wall did this,' he thought to himself. He tried to speak, but could not. Dumbly he stared at Spencer Meyrick.

'We want no scene, Harrowby,' said the old man wearily. 'We merely want to know if there in existence a policy such as the one mentioned here?'

The paper slipped from his lordship's lifeless hands. He turned miserably away. Not daring to face either father or daughter, he answered very faintly:

'There is.'

Spencer Meyrick sighed.

'That's all we want to know. There will be no wedding, Harrowby.'

'Wha – what!' His lordship faced about, 'Why sir – the guest must be – downstairs.'

'It *is* – unfortunate. But there will be no wedding.' The old man turned to his daughter. 'Cynthia,' he asked, 'have you nothing to say?'

'Yes.' White, trembling, the girl faced his lordship. 'It seems, Allan, that you have regarded our marriage as a business proposition. You have gambled on the stability of the market. Well, you win. I have changed my mind. This is final. I shall not change it again.'

'Cynthia!' And any who had considered Lord Harrowby unfeeling must have been surprised at the anguish in his voice.

'I have loved you – I love you now. I adore you. What can I say in explanation – of this. We gamble, all of us – it is a passion bred in the family. That is why I took out this absurd policy. My dearest – it doesn't mean that there was no love on my side. There is – there always will be, whatever happens. Can't you understand –'

The girl laid her hand on his arm, and drew him away to the window.

'It's no use, Allan,' she said, for his ears alone. 'Perhaps I could have forgiven – but somehow – I don't care – as I thought I did. It is better, embarrassing as it may be for us both, that there should be no wedding, after all.'

'Cynthia – you can't mean that. You don't believe me. Let me send for my brother – he will tell you that I love you, too –'

He moved toward the telephone.

'No use,' said Cynthia Meyrick, shaking her head. 'It would only prolong a painful scene. Please don't, Allan.'

'I'll send for Minot, too,' Harrowby cried.

'Mr Minot?' The girl's eyes narrowed. 'And what had Mr Minot to do with this?'

'Everything. He came down here as the representative of Lloyds. He came down to make sure that you didn't change your mind. He will tell you that I love you –'

A queer expression hovered about Miss Meyrick's lips. Spencer Meyrick interrupted.

'Nonsense,' he cried. 'There is no need to –'

'One moment,' Cynthia Meyrick's eyes shone strangely, 'Allan. And – for – Mr Minot.'

Harrowby stepped to the telephone. He summoned his forces. A strained unhappy silence ensued. Then the two men entered the room together.

'Minot – George, old boy,' Lord Harrowby said helplessly. 'Miss Meyrick and her father have discovered the existence of a certain insurance policy about which you both know. They have believed that my motive in seeking a marriage was purely mercenary – that my affection for the girl who is – was – to have become my wife can not be sincere. They are wrong – quite wrong. Both of you know that. I've sent for you to help me make them understand – I can not –'

George Harrowby stepped forward, and smiled his kindly smile.

'My dear young lady,' he said. 'I regret that policy very deeply. When I first heard of it I, too, suspected Allan's motives. But after I talked with him – after I saw you – I was convinced that his affection for you was most sincere. I thought back to the gambling schemes for which the family has been noted – I saw it was the old passion cropping out anew in Allan – that he was really not to blame – that beyond any question he was quite devoted to you. Otherwise I'd have done everything in my power to prevent the wedding.'

'Yes?' Miss Meyrick's eyes flashed dangerously. 'And – your other witness, Allan?'

The soul of the other witness squirmed in agony. This was too much – too much!

'You, Minot –' pleaded Harrowby. 'You have understood –'

'I have felt that you were sincerely fond of Miss Meyrick,' Minot replied. 'Otherwise I should not have done – what I have done.'

'Then, Mr Minot,' the girl inquired, 'you think I would be wrong to give up all plans for the wedding?'

'I – I – yes, I do,' writhed Minot.

'And you advise me to marry Lord Harrowby at once?'

Mr Minot passed his handkerchief over his damp forehead. Had the girl no mercy?

'I do,' he answered miserably.

Cynthia Meyrick laughed, harshly, mirthlessly.

'Because that's your business – your mean little business,' she said scornfully. 'I know at last why you came to San Marco.

I understand everything. You had gambled with Lord Harrowby, and you came here to see that you did not lose your money. Well, you've lost! Carry that news back to the concern you work for! In spite of your heroic efforts, you've lost! At the last moment Cynthia Meyrick changed her mind!'

Lost! The word cut Minot to the quick. Lost, indeed! Lost Jephson's stake – lost the girl he loved! He had failed Jephson – failed himself! After all he had done – all he had sacrificed. A double defeat, and therefore doubly bitter.

'Cynthia – surely you don't mean –' Lord Harrowby was pleading.

'I do, Allan,' said the girl more gently, 'it was true – what I told you – there by the window. It is better – father! Will you go down and – say – I'm not to be married, after all?'

Spencer Meyrick nodded, and turned toward the door.

'Cynthia,' cried Harrowby brokenly. There was no reply. Old Meyrick went out.

'I'm sorry,' his lordship said. 'Sorry I made such a mess of it – the more so because I love you, Cynthia – and always shall. Goodbye.'

He held out his hand. She put hers in it.

'It's too bad, Allan,' she said. 'But it wasn't to be. And, even now, you have one consolation – the money that Lloyds must pay you.'

'The money means nothing, Cynthia –'

'Miss Meyrick is mistaken,' Minot interrupted. 'Lord Harrowby has no consolation. Lloyds owes him nothing.'

'Why not?' asked the girl defiantly.

'Up to an hour ago,' said Minot, 'you were determined to marry his lordship?'

'I should hardly put it that way. But – I intended to.'

'Yes. Then you changed your mind. Why?'

'I changed it because I found about this ridiculous, this insulting policy.'

'Then his lordship's taking out of the policy called off the wedding.'

'Y-yes. Why?'

'It may interest you to know – and it may interest Lord Harrowby to recall – that five minutes before he took out this policy he signed an agreement to do everything in his power to bring about the wedding. And he further promised that if the wedding should be called off because of any subsequent act of his, he would forfeit the premium.'

'By gad,' said Lord Harrowby.

'The taking out of the policy was a subsequent act,' continued Minot. 'The premium, I fancy, is forfeited.'

'He's got you, Allan,' said George Harrowby, coming forward, 'and I for one can't say I'm sorry. You're going to tear up that policy now – and go to work for me.'

'I for one am sorry,' cried Miss Meyrick, her flashing eyes on Minot. 'I wanted you to win, Allan. I wanted you to win.'

'Why?' Minot asked innocently.

'You ought to know,' she answered, and turned away.

Lord Harrowby moved toward the door.

'We're not hard losers,' he said blankly. 'But – everything's gone – it's a bit of a smash-up. Goodbye, Cynthia.'

'Goodbye, Allan – and good luck.'

'Thanks.' And Harrowby went out with his brother.

Minot stood for a time, not daring to move. Cynthia Meyrick was at the window; her scornful back was not encouraging. Finally she turned, saw Minot and gave a start of surprise.

'Oh – you're still here?'

'Cynthia, now you understand,' he said. 'You know why I acted as I did. You realize my position. I was in a horrible fix –'

She looked at him coldly.

'Yes,' she said, 'I do understand. You were gambling on me. You came down here to defend your employer's cash. Well, you have succeeded. Is there anything more to be said?'

'Isn't there? On the ramparts of the old fort the other night –'

'Please do not make yourself more ridiculous than is necessary. You have put your employer's money above my happiness. Always. Really, you looked rather cheap today with your sanctimonious advice that I marry Harrowby. Aren't you beginning to realize your own position – the silly childish figure you cut?'

'Then you –'

'Last night when you came staggering across the lawn to me with this foolish gown in your arms – I told you I hated you. Do you imagine I hate you any less now? Well, I don't.' Her voice became tearful. 'I hate you! I hate you!'

'But some day –'

She turned away from him, for she was sobbing outright now.

'I never want to see you again as long as I live,' she cried. 'Never! Never! Never!'

Limp, pitiable, worn by the long fight he had waged, Minot stood staring helplessly at her heaving shoulders.

'Then – I can only say I'm sorry,' he murmured. 'And – goodbye.'

He waited. She did not turn toward him. He stumbled out of the room.

Chapter XXII
Well, Hardly Ever

Minot went below and sent two messages, one to Jephson, the other to Thacker. The lobby of the De la Pax was thronged with brilliantly attired wedding guests who, metaphorically, beat their breasts in perplexity over the tidings that had come even as they craned their necks to catch the first glimpse of that distinguished bridal party. The parlor that was to have been the scene of the ceremony stood tragically deserted. Minot cast one look at it, and hurried again to his own particular cell.

He took a couple of timetables and sat down in a chair facing the window. All over now. Nothing to do but return to the North as fast as the trains would take him. He had won, but he had also lost. He felt listless, weary. He let the timetables fall to the floor, and sat gazing out at that narrow street – thinking – wondering – wishing –

It was late in the afternoon when the clamor of his telephone recalled him to himself. He leaped up, and seized the receiver. Allan Harrowby's voice came over the wire.

'Can you come down to the room, Minot?' he inquired. 'The last call, old boy.'

Minot went. He found both the Harrowbys there, prepared to say goodbye to San Marco forever.

'Going to New York on the *Lady Evelyn*,' said George Harrowby, who was aggressively cheerful. 'From there I'm taking Allan to Chicago. Going to have him reading George Ade and talking our language in a week.'

Lord Harrowby smiled wanly.

'Nothing left but Chicago,' he drawled. 'I wanted to see you before I went, Minot, old chap. Not that I can thank you for all you did – I don't know how. You stood by me like – like a gentleman. And I realize that I have no claim on Lloyds – it was all my fault – if I'd never let Martin Wall have that confounded policy – But what's the use of if-ing? All my fault. And – my thanks, old boy.' He sighed.

'Nonsense,' said Minot. 'Business proposition, solely, from my point of view, there's no thanks coming to me.'

'It seems to me,' said George Harrowby, 'that as the only victor in this affair, you don't exhibit a proper cheerfulness. By the way, we'd be delighted to take you north on our boat. Why not –'

But Minot shook his head.

'Can't spare the time – thank you just the same,' he replied. 'I'd like nothing better –'

Amid expressions of regret, the Harrowbys started for the elevator. Minot walked along the dusky corridor with them.

'We've had a bit of excitement – what?' said Allan. 'If you're ever in London, you're to be my guest. Old George has some sort of berth for me over there –'

'Not a berth, Allan,' objected George, pressing the button for the elevator. 'You're not going to sleep. A job. Might as well begin to talk the Chicago language now. Mr Minot, I, too, want to thank you –'

They stepped into the elevator, the door slammed, the car began to descend. Minot stood gazing through the iron scroll work until the blond head of the helpless Lord Harrowby moved finally out of sight. Then he returned to his room and the timetables, which seemed such dull unhappy reading.

Mr Jack Paddock appeared to invite Minot to take dinner with him. His bags, he remarked, were all packed, and he was booked for the seven o'clock train.

'I've slipped down the mountain of gold,' he said in the course of the dinner. 'But all good things must end, and I certainly had a good thing. Somehow, I'm not so gloomy as I ought to be.'

'Where are you going, Jack?' Minot asked.

Mr Paddock leaned over confidentially.

'Did I say her father was in the plumbing business?' he inquired. 'My error, Dick. He owns a newspaper – out in Grand Rapids. Offered me a job any time I wanted it. Great joke then – pretty serious now. For I'm going out to apply.'

'I am glad of it.'

'So am I, Dick. I was a fool to let her go back like that. Been thinking it all over – and over – one girl in – how many are there in the world, should you say? The other day I had a chill. It occurred to me maybe she'd gone and married the young man with the pale purple necktie who passes the plate in the Methodist Church. So I beat it to the telegraph counter. And –'

'She's heart whole and fancy free?'

'OK in both respects. So it's me for Grand Rapids. And say, Dick, I – er – I want you to know I'd sent that telegram before the accident last night. As a matter of fact, I sent it two days ago.'

'Good boy,' said Minot, 'I knew this game down here didn't satisfy you. May I be the first to wish you joy?'

'You? With a face like a defeated candidate? I say, cheer up! She'll stretch out eager arms in your direction yet.'

'I don't believe it. Jack.'

'Well, while there's life there's still considerable hope lying loose about the landscape. That's why I don't urge you to take the train with me.'

An hour later Mr Paddock spoke further cheering words in his friend's ear, and departed for the North. And in that city of moonlight and romance Minot was left (practically) alone.

He took a little farewell walk through that quaint old town, then retired to his room to read another chapter in the timetable. At four-twenty in the morning, he noted, a small local train would leave for Jacksonville. He decided he would take it. With no parlor cars, no sleepers, he would not be likely to encounter upon it any of the startled wedding party bound north.

The call he left did not materialize, and it was four o'clock when he awoke. Hastily in the chill dawn he bade farewell to town and hotel. In fifteen minutes he had left both behind, and was speeding toward the small yellow station set on the town's edge. He glanced feverishly at his watch. There was need of haste, for this train was made up in San Marco, and had had as yet no chance to be late.

He rushed through the gate just as it was being closed, and caught a dreary little train in the very act of pulling out. Gloomy oil lamps sought vainly to lessen the dour aspect of its two coaches. Panting, he entered the rear coach and threw himself and his bag into a seat.

Five seconds later he glanced across the aisle and discovered in the opposite seat Miss Cynthia Meyrick, accompanied by a very sleepy-eyed family!

'The devil!' said Minot to himself. He knew that she would see in this utter accident nothing save a deliberate act of following. What use to protest his innocence?

He considered moving to another seat. But such a theatric act could only increase the embarrassment. Already his presence had been noted – Aunt Mary had given him a glare, Spencer Meyrick a scowl, the girl a cloudy vague 'where have I seen this person before' glance in passing.

Might as well make the best of it. He settled himself in his seat. Once again, as on another railroad car, he sought to keep his eyes on the landscape without – the dim landscape with the royal palms waving like grim ghosts in the half light. The train sped on.

A most uncomfortable situation! If only it would grow light! It seemed so silly to be forced to find the view out the window entrancing while it was still very dark.

Spencer Meyrick went forward to the smoker. Aunt Mary, weary of life, slid gently down to slumber. Her unlovely snore filled the dim car.

How different this from the first ride together! The faint pink of the sky grew brighter. Now Minot could see the gray moss hanging to the evergreens, and here and there a squalid shade where human beings lived and knew nothing of life. And beside him he heard a sound as of a large body being shaken. Also the guttural protest of Aunt Mary at this inconsiderate treatment.

Aunt Mary triumphed. Her snore rose to shatter the smoky roof. Three times Minot dared to look, and each time wished he hadn't. The whole sky was rosy now. Somewhere off behind the horizon the good old sun was rising to go to work for the passenger department of the coast railroad.

Some sense in looking out now. Minot saw a shack that seemed familiar – then another. Next a station, bearing on its sad shingle the cheery name of 'Sunbeam'. And close to the station, gloomy in the dawn, a desiccated chauffeur beside an aged automobile.

Minot turned quickly, and caught Cynthia Meyrick in the act of peering over his shoulder. She had seen the chauffeur too.

The train had stopped a moment, but was underway again. In those brown eyes Minot saw something wistful, something hurt – saw things that moved him to put everything to a sudden test. He leaped to his feet and pulled madly at the bell cord.

'What – what have you done?' Startled, she stared at him.

'I've stopped the train. I'm going to Jacksonville as I rode to San Marco – ages ago. I'm not going alone.'

'Indeed?'

'Quick. The conductor will be here in a minute. Here's a card and pencil – write a note for Aunt Mary. Say you'll meet them in Jacksonville! Hurry, please!'

'Mr Minot!' With great dignity.

'One last ride together. One last chance for me to – to set things right if I can.'

'If you can.'

'If – I admit it. Won't you give me the chance? I thought you would be game. I dare you!'

For a second they gazed into each other's eyes. The train had come to a stop, and Aunt Mary stirred fretfully in her sleep. With sudden decision Cynthia Meyrick wrote on the card and dropped it on her slumbering relative.

'I know I'll be sorry – but –' she gasped.

'Hurry! This way! The conductor's coming there!'

A moment later they stood together on the platform of the Sunbeam station, while the brief little train disappeared indignantly in the distance.

'You shouldn't have made me do that!' cried the girl in dismay. 'I'm always doing things on the spur of the moment – things I regret afterward –'

'I know. You explained that to me once. But you can also do things that you're glad about all your life. Oh – good morning, Barney Oldfield.'

'Good morning,' replied the chauffeur with gleeful recognition. 'Where's it to this time, mister?'

'Jacksonville. And no hurry at all.' Minot held open the door and the girl stepped into the car.

'The gentleman is quite mistaken,' she said to the chauffeur. 'There is a very great hurry.'

'Ages of time until luncheon,' replied Minot blithely, also getting in. 'If you were thinking of announcing – something – then.'

'I shall have nothing to announce, I'm sure. But I must be in Jacksonville before that train. Father will be furious.'

'Trust me, lady,' said the chauffeur, grinding again at his hooded music box. 'I've been doing stunts with this car since I saw you last. Been over a hundred miles from Sunbeam. Begins to look as though Florida wasn't going to be big enough, after all.'

He leaped to the wheel, and again that ancient automobile carried Cynthia Meyrick and the representative of Lloyds out of the town of Sunbeam. But the exit was not a laughing one. The girl's eyes were serious, cold, and with real concern in his voice Minot spoke:

'Won't you forgive me – can't you? I was only trying to be faithful to the man who sent me down here – faithful through everything – as I should be faithful to you if you gave me the chance. Is it too late – Cynthia –'

'There was a time,' said the girl, her eyes wide, 'when it was not too late. Have you forgotten? That night on the balcony, when I threw myself at your feet, and you turned away. Do you think that was a happy moment for me?'

'Was it happy for me, for that matter?'

'Oh, I was humiliated, ashamed. Then your silly rescue of my gown – your advice to me to marry Harrowby –'

'Would you have had me throw over the men who trusted me –'

'I-I don't know. I only know that I can't forgive what had happened – in a minute –'

'What was that last?'

'Nothing.'

'You said in a minute.'

'Your ears are deceiving you.'

'Cynthia – you are not going to punish me because I was faithful – Don't you suppose I tried to get someone in my place?'

'Did you?'

'The day I first rode in this car with you. And then – I stopped trying –'

'Why?'

'Because I realized that if someone came in my place I'd have to go away and never see you again – and I couldn't do that. I had to be near you, dear girl – don't worry, he can't hear, the motor's too noisy – I had to be where I could see that little curl making a question mark round your ear – where I could hear your voice – I had to be near you even if to do it I must break my heart by marrying you to another man. I loved you. I love you now –'

A terrific crash interrupted. Dolefully the chauffeur descended from the car to make an examination. Dolefully he announced the result.

'Busted right off,' he remarked. 'Say, I'm sorry. I'll have to walk back to the garage at Sunbeam and – and I'm afraid you'll have to jest sit here until I come back.'

He went slowly down the road, and the two sat in that ancient car in the midst of sandy desolation.

'Cynthia,' Minot cried. 'I worship you. Won't you –'

The girl gave a strange little cry.

'I wanted to be cross with you a little longer,' she said almost tearfully. 'But I can't. I wonder why I can't. I cried all night at the thought of never seeing you again. I wonder why I cried. I guess – it's because – for the first time – I'm really – in love.'

'Cynthia!'

'Oh, Dick – don't ever let me change my mind ever again – ever – ever!'

With one accord they turned and looked at that quaint southern chauffeur plodding along through the dust and the sunshine. It did not seem to either of them that there was any danger of his looking back.

And, happily, he didn't.

Biographical note

Earl Derr Biggers was born Ohio in 1884, and attended Harvard University. He began his literary career as a journalist, writing humour columns and theatre reviews. Having being fired from the *Boston Traveler*, he decided to turn his hand to writing instead and his first novel, *Seven Keys to Baldpate*, was published in 1913 – it was so successful it was made into a film five times in the next thirty years. The financial success of his new found career enabled him to marry Eleanor Ladd. In 1914, Biggers wrote *Love Insurance*.

His most famous creation would be the Chinese detective Charlie Chan – in fact its popularity was such that it quickly became virtually impossible for Biggers to write any other form of story – he would write six novels in the series, most of which were made into films.

Biggers died of a heart attack in California in 1933, at the age of just forty-eight.

Under our three imprints, Hesperus Press publishes over 300 books by many of the greatest figures in worldwide literary history, as well as contemporary and debut authors well worth discovering.

Hesperus Classics handpicks the best of worldwide and translated literature, introducing forgotten and neglected books to new generations.

Hesperus Nova showcases quality contemporary fiction and non-fiction designed to entertain and inspire.

Hesperus Minor rediscovers well-loved children's books from the past – these are books which will bring back fond memories for adults, which they will want to share with their children and loved ones.

To find out more visit www.hesperuspress.com
@HesperusPress

SELECTED TITLES FROM HESPERUS PRESS

Author	Title	Foreword writer
Pietro Aretino	*The School of Whoredom*	Paul Bailey
Pietro Aretino	*The Secret Life of Nuns*	
Jane Austen	*Lesley Castle*	Zoë Heller
Jane Austen	*Love and Friendship*	Fay Weldon
Honoré de Balzac	*Colonel Chabert*	A.N. Wilson
Charles Baudelaire	*On Wine and Hashish*	Margaret Drabble
Giovanni Boccaccio	*Life of Dante*	A.N. Wilson
Charlotte Brontë	*The Spell*	
Emily Brontë	*Poems of Solitude*	Helen Dunmore
Mikhail Bulgakov	*Fatal Eggs*	Doris Lessing
Mikhail Bulgakov	*The Heart of a Dog*	A.S. Byatt
Giacomo Casanova	*The Duel*	Tim Parks
Miguel de Cervantes	*The Dialogue of the Dogs*	Ben Okri
Geoffrey Chaucer	*The Parliament of Birds*	
Anton Chekhov	*The Story of a Nobody*	Louis de Bernières
Anton Chekhov	*Three Years*	William Fiennes
Wilkie Collins	*The Frozen Deep*	
Joseph Conrad	*Heart of Darkness*	A.N. Wilson
Joseph Conrad	*The Return*	Colm Tóibín
Gabriele D'Annunzio	*The Book of the Virgins*	Tim Parks
Dante Alighieri	*The Divine Comedy: Inferno*	
Dante Alighieri	*New Life*	Louis de Bernières
Daniel Defoe	*The King of Pirates*	Peter Ackroyd
Marquis de Sade	*Incest*	Janet Street-Porter
Charles Dickens	*The Haunted House*	Peter Ackroyd
Charles Dickens	*A House to Let*	
Fyodor Dostoevsky	The Double	Jeremy Dyson
Fyodor Dostoevsky	Poor People	Charlotte Hobson
Alexandre Dumas	*One Thousand and One Ghosts*	

George Eliot	*Amos Barton*	Matthew Sweet
Henry Fielding	*Jonathan Wild the Great*	Peter Ackroyd
F. Scott Fitzgerald	*The Popular Girl*	Helen Dunmore
Gustave Flaubert	*Memoirs of a Madman*	Germaine Greer
Ugo Foscolo	*Last Letters of Jacopo Ortis*	Valerio Massimo Manfredi
Elizabeth Gaskell	*Lois the Witch*	Jenny Uglow
Théophile Gautier	*The Jinx*	Gilbert Adair
André Gide	*Theseus*	
Johann Wolfgang von Goethe	*The Man of Fifty*	A.S. Byatt
Nikolai Gogol	*The Squabble*	Patrick McCabe
E.T.A. Hoffmann	*Mademoiselle de Scudéri*	Gilbert Adair
Victor Hugo	*The Last Day of a Condemned Man*	Libby Purves
Joris-Karl Huysmans	*With the Flow*	Simon Callow
Henry James	*In the Cage*	Libby Purves
Franz Kafka	*Metamorphosis*	Martin Jarvis
Franz Kafka	*The Trial*	Zadie Smith
John Keats	*Fugitive Poems*	Andrew Motion
Heinrich von Kleist	*The Marquise of O–*	Andrew Miller
Mikhail Lermontov	*A Hero of Our Time*	Doris Lessing
Nikolai Leskov	*Lady Macbeth of Mtsensk*	Gilbert Adair
Carlo Levi	*Words are Stones*	Anita Desai
Xavier de Maistre	*A Journey Around my Room*	Alain de Botton
André Malraux	*The Way of the Kings*	Rachel Seiffert
Katherine Mansfield	*Prelude*	William Boyd
Edgar Lee Masters	*Spoon River Anthology*	Shena Mackay
Guy de Maupassant	*Butterball*	Germaine Greer
Prosper Mérimée	*Carmen*	Philip Pullman
Sir Thomas More	*The History of King Richard III*	Sister Wendy Beckett
Sándor Petőfi	*John the Valiant*	George Szirtes
Francis Petrarch	*My Secret Book*	Germaine Greer